HAMMOND INNES's highly individual and successful novels are the result of travel in outback parts of the world. Many of them follow the central character to strange countries where the forces of nature, as much as people, provide the conflict. He has also written two books of travel and one of history. His international reputation as a story-teller keeps his books in print; they have been translated into over thirty foreign languages.

The killer mine is an abandoned Cornish tin mine, the cleverly contrived base of a gang of up-to-date smugglers engaged in running valuable contraband from the Continent. These old mines, with their adits running out to sea and their shafts honeycombing the cliffs around Cape Cornwall, fascinated Hammond Innes in the years before he took to sailing.

HAMMOND INNES

The Killer Mine

FONTANA/Collins

First published by William Collins Sons & Co. Ltd 1947
First issued in Fontana Paperbacks 1964
Twenty-first impression September 1990

Printed and bound in Great Britain by
William Collins Sons & Co. Ltd, Glasgow

CONTENTS

CHAPTER ONE

The 'Arisaig' Reaches Cornwall

The fo'c'sle was hot with the heat of the engines. Yet I shivered as I set down my glass and reached for the bottle. The glare of the naked light hurt my eyes. I filled my glass again. The liquor spilled fire down my throat as I drank, but it did not warm me. I was cold through to my very spine. Boots rang on the steel deck above our heads. A body stirred in its hammock, snorted, rolled over and then settled itself again. The hammock swayed like a bundle of straw to the roll of the boat. The sour odour of human bodies mingled with the fumes of the cognac and the blue fog of tobacco smoke made my eyes smart.

'What's the time?' I asked. My mouth was dry — a dusty cavity in which my tongue moved like a rubber pad. The words came harsh and unnatural as I put the question.

'You speak me what is the time two minutes ago?'

'Well, I'm asking you again,' I said harshly. Damn all Italians to hell! Why did I have to sit drinking with an Italian? Must Mulligan have Italians in his crew? But the British wouldn't drink with me, blast 'em. The Egg was only drinking with me because he was drunk and would drink with anybody. Or was it because he enjoyed watching the fear that welled up from the chilled hollow of my bowels? He was laughing at me. I could see it in his dark eyes. 'What's the time, damn you?' I shouted at him.

He pulled a large silver watch out of his breast pocket and turned the ornate gilt face towards me. A quarter past three. If Mulligan was right in his reckonings we should be in sight of the English coast. We had passed the Bishop Light well to starboard at dusk.

The Egg put the watch back in his pocket and picked up his glass. He drank with a noisy, sucking sound. His thick lips shone wet in the swinging light. They smiled and his eyes watched me.

What was he thinking? What went on under that bald skull of his? The lips were cruel, the eyes — brown like a dog's, dark like a passionate girl's — were cold. 'God damn it,' I cried. 'What are you smiling at?' I felt anger surge up in my body, drowning the chill of fear so that my body seemed to swell out until the cramped fo'c'sle was too small to hold it. His sallow eyelids flickered and when I looked into his eyes again they were wide so that I could look through to the rotten core of him. He did not speak. He just gazed at me with those wide-open, cruel eyes.

The anger left me and I felt cold again. 'God damn all Italians,' I heard myself mutter. How long had I been drinking? What did it matter? What did anything matter? I was clear of Italy. England lay ahead, out there in the darkness beyond the steel bulkhead.

The man who had stirred in his hammock rolled over on to his back, stretched his arms and then sat up, rubbing the sleep out of his eyes. 'Wot, drinking again, Emilio?' he said to the Italian. 'Gawd! don't yer never stop drinkin'?' He peered down at the bottle. 'Cognac, eh? Where did you get that? Bet yer've ripped open one of them cases.'

The Italian smiled. 'You like a drink, Ruppy?'

'Don't mind if I do,' the bos'n grinned. 'But Gawd 'elp yer if the skipper finds yer bin at the cargo. Mulligan ain't pertic'lar wot 'e does ter blokes that get in 'is 'air. All right. I know you're pretty quick with that knife o' yours. But 'e got a gun, ain't 'e?'

The Italian's bald skull cracked in a grin that showed the white gleam of his perfect teeth. 'Signor Mulligan, he is on deck, yes? He not come down here. The stink, it is too much for him.' And he laughed silently.

'Well, it's your funeral, mate.' Ruppy swung his legs out of the hammock and slid to the floor. He buttoned his jersey into his trousers and pressed both hands into his belly as though thrusting his guts into place. He suffered from hernia — that was why he was called Ruppy. He was thin and scrawny with the face of a turtle and an Adam's apple that moved up and down in his scraggy neck as he swallowed. A two days' growth of sparse, grey stubble grew out of the seamed dirt of chin and neck. He brought out an enamel mug and filled it half full from the bottle. 'Well, 'ere's to the bleedin' perisher wot pays through the nose fer short measure on them cases.' He wiped his mouth on the sleeve of his jersey and looked down at me, swaying gently to the motion of the ship. 'S'ppose you're trying to get up enough courage ter go ashore, eh?' The sneer was unconcealed. 'Why the hell didn't yer stay in Italy? That's where your sort belong. All right. I know why yer shipped a't o' Naples. You had ter, that's why. Soon as there weren't no British Army, the Ities got nasty an' turned on yer. Don't blame 'em, niever. Runnin' away — reckon that's all you ever done.'

Anger surged up in me again, drumming at my temples. I banged my glass down and jumped to my feet. He was such an insignificant, wizened little object. What right had he to sneer at me? I felt my hand clench. With one blow I could smash him against the steel of the bulkhead.

'That's right — go on, 'it me.' His watery eyes peered up at me. 'Go on,' he cried again, ''it me, why don't yer? Ain't yer even got the guts ter do that?' he sneered as I lowered my fist. 'No — afraid of Mulligan. That's what it is. You've always bin afraid o' something, ain't yer?'

'What do you know about what makes men afraid?' I cried.

'As much as most men,' he snapped back. 'I did me time in the Army, didn't I? Three years before the war and then Dunkirk and fru the desert to Alamein. Wasn't my fault, was it, that I got a rupture an' they slung me out?'

'Sure you done your time,' I said.

'Sawd me country through like any decent man, that's wot I done. Rank o' corporal I 'ad when me belly went back on me.'

'All right,' I said, 'So you saw your country through. But look at you now — a rotten little scab running liquor for a crook that got his dough in and out of North African ports whilst you were sweating in the desert.'

'Well, a bloke's got to live, ain't he?' He gulped at the cognac, rinsing it round his mouth like a mouth-wash. His Adam's apple jerked as he swallowed the liquor and breathed out fiercely. 'Ain't that so, Emilio?' he asked, turning to the Egg. 'A bloke's got to live. Wot d'yer fink the ruddy Ministry o' Labour offered me when I got discharged as unfit fer dooty? — a job da'n the mines! An' me wiv a rupture the size of a barn door got in the defence o' me country. Liftin' the barrel of a bleedin' ack-ack gun, that's 'ow I got it. Now I ast yer — do I look like a Bevin boy? I got me rights, same as anybody else. So I sez to meself, Charlie, I sez, you fer a job wot's easy on the belly, and wot pays fer the time yer servin' your country.' He thrust his face suddenly close to mine. 'You comin' the 'igh an' mighty! Blimey, who d'yer fink you are ter be tellin' me I'm a scab and a racketeer? Wot yer goin' ter do when yer get ashore, anyway — you just tell me that?'

'I got a friend in Penzance,' I said, stung by his sneering face. 'Sent me word he could get me a job.'

'An' told yer Tom Mulligan would give yer passage to England, eh?'

'How did you know?'

''Ow did I know? 'Cos yer ain't the first we brought back from It'ly, that's why? If your pal put you in touch wiv the skipper, then the job he got fer yer ain't no better than wot we're doin' on board the *Arisaig*. Gawd strewf, 'ow the 'ell d'yer fink the likes of you live in England? You ain't got no hidentity card, no ration book — in the eyes of the officials yer don't exist. Yer a floatin' population of scum wot lives off the Black Market. An' if yer want my advice, yer'll make straight fer London when we've landed yer. That's the safest place for your sort. Join the spivs and petty twisters wot 'ang ara'nd the race courses and the dawgs. Yer'll be safe wiv them — fer a bit.' He belched and heaved at his stomach.

I sat down again. God, how I hated myself! I felt the tears burning in my eyes and put my head in my hands to hide my sense of loneliness. A hand suddenly rested on my shoulder and

Ruppy's voice with all the habitual harshness gone out of it, said, 'Come on, chum. Don't take no notice o' me. Yer'll feel better when yer seen yer fam'ly.'

I shook my head and wished he'd go back to his sneering. 'I've no family,' I said.

'No fam'ly! Blimey! That's tough. But yer got friends, ain't yer?'

'No,' I told him. 'Only the fellow in Penzance. You see, I left England when I was four. The only thing I can remember about England is when I was on the deck of a ship that took us to Canada. My father pointed the coastline out to me. It was just a grey smudge on the horizon. That and the day my mother went away — those are about my earliest recollections. We lived at a place called Redruth in Cornwall. That's where I was born.'

'But if yer went to Canada when you were four, why the 'ell didn't yer join the Canadian Army?'

'I didn't stay in Canada. After my father died, I went to Australia, to the gold mines. I was twenty then — a miner, like my father. After the war had been going on for some time I got a ship to England. But France fell and Italy came in and we were held up at Port Said — so I joined Wavell's mob. This is the first time I've been to England since I was four years old.' Damn him — why had he started me off like this? Why didn't he go on sneering at me? I could stand that. I began to swear. It was a pointless waste of words, but it forced the tears of self-pity away.

'You oughter've gone back to Canada, chum,' he said. 'There wouldn't 'ave bin no questions ast there.'

'I couldn't get a ship,' I said. I reached out for the bottle and poured myself another drink.

'Yer don't want no more o' that firewater,' he advised, putting a restraining hand on my arm that was like the claw of a bird. 'Yer goin' ashore soon and yer'll need to be sober.'

But I took no heed, filling the glass and draining it at a gulp.

Footsteps sounded on the companion ladder. The door opened. 'Hey, Pryce! The skipper wants you.' It was a dumpy little man they called Shorty.

'Okay,' I said.

He went back up the companion ladder and his feet sounded again on the steel deck as he made his way aft towards the wheelhouse. The unfastened door slatted back and forth to the movement of the ship. I took another drink and then got to my feet. The watch off duty swayed in their hammocks. The steel walls, peeling and greasy with dirt, dipped and rose, dipped and rose. The naked bulb swung dizzily before my eyes. The Italian watched me. His eyes were on my belt and they glittered like live coals. I hitched up my trousers and my fumbling fingers bit into the flesh of my stomach as I felt for and found the outline of the money belt around my waist.

'What are you staring at?' I snarled.

'At-a nothing, *signore*,' he answered, and his eyes reverted to that soft, expressionless brown.

'You're lying,' I said.

He shrugged his shoulders, spreading his arms and drawing down the corners of his mouth, a picture of abject docility and innocence.

I took a step towards him. 'So that's why you're drinking with me, is it? You thought you'd get me stinking. You thought you'd rob me, eh?' He cringed away from me, those brown eyes suddenly mirroring his fear.

'Better go up and see the skipper, mate,' Ruppy said, catching me by the sleeve. But I suddenly wanted to hit the Italian — just one blow to show what I thought of the whole bloody race of 'em. And then I realised it would do no good. It wouldn't change his nature — it wouldn't make him any less avaricious, any less cruel. It wasn't his fault. He was a Neapolitan and it was the dirt and filth and poverty of Naples that had made him what he was.

I shrugged my shoulders and went up into the clean wholesome air of the deck. The night was still and dark with the sails flapping idly like bat's wings spread against the velvet backcloth of the sky that was all studded with stars. There was scarcely a breath of wind. Over the side our navigation lights showed a flat, oily swell. The tall masts of the little schooner swayed back and forth across the Milky Way and her gear creaked and groaned as the sails drew fitfully. I went aft, watching the faint, white blur of our wake as the engines drove us steadily towards the land. Every now and then a beam of light swept across us from a lighthouse on our starboard quarter. Almost astern was another, but below the horizon, so that it was like a faint flicker of the Northern Lights. And over the port bow, yet another blinked with monotonous regularity, hidden behind a mass of land that showed every now and then against the sudden brightening of the night.

The clean smell of tar and sea-wet cordage was strong after the sour fumes of the fo'c'sle. I breathed in great gulps of this fresh, salt air as I made my way towards the little wheelhouse. But a hand seemed clutching at my brain so that I couldn't think clearly. I stumbled over a coiled-down length of rope and fetched up at the rail gazing at the smooth, black surface of the water that I sensed rather than saw. I felt the long, flat swells rolling under our keel and gazed towards that dark line of coast that leapt into being every time the light flashed in our direction. And then I looked again at the smooth, comfortable swelling of the sea. It looked so inviting, so restful. Whilst out there, where the coast showed black, was danger and uncertainty.

I shook myself and felt for the belt around my waist. My eyes were tired. I was exhausted, drained of the will to go on. It was the same feeling that I had had that time up by Cassino when the patrol . . . I shivered and turned quickly towards the wheelhouse.

Inside it was warm and bright. Shorty stood at the wheel, his gaze alternating between the faintly glowing compass and the black night outside with the feebly slating sails. Mulligan was bending over a chart, a pair of dividers in his hand. He looked up as I entered. He was a thin, meagre little man with a craggy face, sharp blue eyes and a hare-lip that gave him the look of a stoat. He wasn't the sort of man you'd expect to find in command of anything, let alone a ship. But a devil looked out of those bright blue eyes and he had a tongue on him that was worth two full-sized men when it came to driving others. That tongue, sharp and rasping as the rough edge of a steel file, could get men moving faster than a pair of outsize fists. Men were afraid of that tongue and of those sharp little ferret eyes. He'd talk to a man, quiet and soft as a kitten, till he'd discovered his weakness, and then that tongue of his would get to work so that the man hated and feared him.

I held on to the edge of the chart table as the ship swayed and dipped. Mulligan watched me. He didn't speak, but just stood there gazing up at me, a sarcastic little smile on his deformed mouth. 'Well, what do you want me for?' I asked. I couldn't stand him staring at me. 'Are we nearly there?'

He nodded. 'There's our position.' He pointed to the chart. 'That's the Longships Light way to starb'd noo. We'll drop ye off at Whitesands Bay, just north o' Sennen.' His voice, with its queer Scots accent, droned on, giving me directions and pointing out landmarks on shore for my guidance. But I didn't listen. How can anyone listen to a voice purring out of a half Scots, half French parentage when the cognac is mounting to his head and making the blood hammer through his veins? The voice suddenly changed and the new rasp in it penetrated my mind. 'What about yer fare?' The question was repeated in a sharp, staccato bark.

'I paid it to you when I came aboard at Naples,' I reminded him. What was he getting at? My brain struggled to focus on what he was saying. 'I paid you fifty pounds in English notes. And it was twice what I ought to have paid.'

'That's as may be,' he answered, and his eyes never left my face. 'You paid me for a passage to England. But ye didn't pay me for putting ye ashore at dead o' night on a desairted stretch o' the coast. Smuggling a man into England is agin the law. It's dangerous, man, and Ah'm no willing ter take the risk wi'oot Ah get something oot of it.'

'See here, Mulligan,' I said angrily. 'You agreed to take me to England for fifty pounds. You knew what risk you ran when you took my fifty quid. Now you keep your side of the bargain.'

He peered up at me with that crooked, twisted smile of his. 'If that's the way ye want it, man, all reecht. We'll take ye on to Cardiff where we're bound and put ye ashore there. But Ah'm warnin' ye — they're awfu' strict at the docks there and unless ye ken yer way aboot —'

'Come off it, Mulligan,' I said and stretched out my hand to grip him by the collar and shake some sense into him. But he backed away from me, showing his discoloured teeth as he stretched his hare-lip to a grin. His right hand was in his pocket. I forced myself to relax. No good quarrelling with the man on whom my safety depended. 'What's your price?' I said. 'I'll give you an extra ten pounds.'

He shook his head and laughed. 'Ye'll be landed at Cardiff or ye'll pay my price,' he said.

'And what's your price?' I asked him.

'One hundred and thirty pounds,' he answered.

'A hundred and thirty quid!' I gasped. 'But that's —' I broke off.

He was laughing. I could see it in his eyes. 'That leaves ye wi' exactly twenty pounds.'

'How did you know how much I'd got on me?'

'Ye told me yersel' the other nicht. Ye were drunk and boasting of what a man could do wi' that much money, despite all the restrictions and identity cards and ration books. Well, it seems a shame that the police shouldna be given a chance.' Then his voice was suddenly hard and flat. 'A hundred and thirty quid — that's my price for a boat to pull ye to the shore. Ye can take it or leave it.'

The blood roared in my head. I felt my muscles swell. He had the chart table between us. I kicked it over with my boot. But as I went for him he backed away with a snarl and his right hand came out of his pocket with a gun. It stopped me for a second. And then suddenly I didn't care. He could plug me if he liked. I threw back my head and roared with laughter. It was the drink that had got in me. I knew that. But I didn't care. I just stood and laughed at him, crouched so puny and twisted in the corner of his own wheelhouse with that ridiculous little gun in his hand. I saw fear leap in his eyes and then I went for him. If he'd fired I don't think I'd have felt it, so elated was I with the sense of the power of my body. But he didn't fire. He hesitated. And in that second I had swept the pistol out of his hand and had seized him by the neck. The fingers and thumbs of my two hands overlapped as I closed my grip, lifting him from the ground and shaking him like a rat. 'Now what about my boat to the shore, eh?' I cried, and I heard myself let out another bellow of laughter.

I raised him so that his eyes were level with mine. I looked into them. They were so close it was like looking in through windows. And I saw he was afraid. I was glad of that and shook him so that his bones rattled. I shifted the grip of my right hand to the belt of his trousers and raised him to throw him through the window of the wheelhouse.

And then something hit me. A great explosion of pain burst at the foot of my skull. For an instant I saw the wheelhouse clear through the splitting agony of my eyeballs. My arms sagged beneath Mulligan's weight and his face came close to mine. Then my legs seemed to melt under me and everything was as black as hell as I crumpled up.

Next thing I knew was there was water on my face. It was cold and salt. I was going under again. There was a swimming blackness all about me. I struggled, thrusting upwards with my arms and legs. Again the sting of water on my face and the cold of the night air. I breathed in a great gulp that hurt my lungs. The darkness was shot with flame and then I was sinking again. This time I didn't struggle. I let the suffocating blackness steal over me. It was such a restful way to go. The water was cool and still as I sank. But the urge to live rose in me and I began to struggle upward again. My hands reached out, clutched and broke their nails against something solid. I grasped hold of it and fought my way back to consciousness. It was wood — a wooden board. It lifted slightly and then clamped down, pinching my fingers.

"E's comin' r'and, skipper.' The voice was right above me. It was Shorty.

'He's a skull on him like a rhinoceros,' Mulligan's voice replied. 'Ye hit him hard enough to split it open, yet he's no bin oot more'n fifteen minutes.'

I opened my eyes. It was dark, but I could see the darker outline of a pair of knees hunched against the stars. Then I closed my eyes again. The pain was unbearable. It was as though a great lump of lead had got loose inside my skull and was being pitched around by the movement of the sea. But it didn't hurt me to listen and my ears told me all I wanted to know. Waves were slopping at the gunnels of the boat and there was a steady creak of the rowlocks as the oars swung in and out. I was being rowed to the shore. The bow pitched violently and smacked into a small wave that slopped water over on to my face. I struggled up to my elbow.

'Ye'd best lie still,' said Mulligan in his phoney Scots. 'If ye don't Ah'll gi' ye anither crack on the head wi' the butt end o' me pistol.' His face was so close to me as he bent down that I could smell the reek of cognac on his breath.

'Okay, I'll keep still,' I breathed. My voice sounded faint and far away. I relaxed against the gunnel, the nerves of my whole body racked and wearied by the hammering pain in my head. A slight wind had got up, and over Shorty's rhythmically swinging shoulders the lights of the *Arisaig* danced in the ruffled water. The little schooner was hove to under mains' and stays'l. She was about three hundred yards astern of us, a graceful shadow in the faint light of the stars and the swinging beam of the Longships.

I twisted my head round and caught the gleam of Mulligan's

eyes watching me. Pain stabbed at my eye sockets as I turned my neck muscles. I shifted the weight of my body to my right elbow, so that I could look for'ard without turning my head. Mulligan made a threatening movement with the pistol, which he held by the barrel. Then he relaxed as I lay still. The shore was a black shadow reared up against the night sky. With each sweep of the oars it came closer and blacker. Soon it towered above us, blotting out half the sky with its rugged, granite cliffs, and through the still night came the steady thud and suck of waves breaking.

'Where are you landing me, Mulligan?' I asked.

'Just where I said I would,' he replied. 'Northern end at Whitesands Bay. You'll be aboot two miles from Sennen. Or, if ye climb straight up from the beach and strike inland, ye'll reach the main road an' that'll take ye into Penzance.'

I didn't say anything. The black line of the coast was very near now. I thought I could see the faint white of the waves breaking. I strained my eyes into the darkness. But it made them ache so that I had to close them.

So that was England, and only a few miles from where I was born. My father had talked so much about the Cornish coast that I seemed almost to recognise it, even in the dark. But it was a queer way to be coming back — to be landed alone from a boat at dead of night with no friend and —

A sudden fear seized me. I forgot the pain in my head for a second as my fingers fumbled for the belt. I could feel it there against my skin. I searched for the pocket. Yes, it was still solid and packed with notes. Or was it less packed? Had they fooled me? Fifteen minutes they said I'd been out. Time enough for them to take the money.

I glanced up at Mulligan. His eyes were fixed on me.

Was it a trick of the dark or was there a sardonic gleam in them?

'What about the boat fare, Mulligan?' I asked. 'How much have you taken?'

'Lie still,' he hissed, and he held out the butt of his pistol ready.

The great granite cliffs were very near now. They seemed reared up, high, high into the night. A line of white seethed at their foot.

I slipped my hand under my jersey, beneath my vest, till I felt the leather of the belt lying against my skin. I found the pocket. It bulged. But when I got my fingers inside it the crispness of the notes had changed to paper, as though the pouch were stuffed with worthless Italian lire. I looked at Mulligan. 'How much did you take?' I asked him.

His face was so close to mine I could see the hare-lip stretch as he grinned. 'What Ah said Ah'd take, plus fifteen quid for the inconvenience ye caused me. Ye've got five quid, me bonnie boy, and that's five quid more'n ye deserve.'

'Five quid!' And I'd had two hundred when I hailed him at Port Santa Lucia in Naples Bay. 'Why didn't you take the five quid as well?' I asked.

He laughed. It was a hard, grating sound, like the creak of the oars in the rowlocks. 'Because Ah'm no wanting inquiries made about the *Arisaig*. Five pounds'll last ye quite a bit. The will to stay free is awfu' strong in a man. Ah could've filled ye full of lead and thrown ye overboard wi' some old iron in yer boots. But I dinna trust me crew when it comes to murdering a man. Though it's what ye deserve.'

'How do you know what I deserve?' The anger boiled up in me, stronger than the pain in my head. 'What were you doing sailing in and out of the North African ports when Rommel held the coast? I'll bet you weren't talking your phoney Scots then.'

He laughed again. '*Mais non, mon vieux — je parlais toujours le francais quand j'etais en Afrique.*'

'Or German,' I added. Who was he to tell me what I deserved, this rotten, crooked little bastard of a Scots father and a French mother.

A wave broke and the white of its crest licked along the gunnel, wetting my sleeve and slopping water into my face. We were very near the beach now. I could see it — a faint smudge of steeply rising sand that ended in a granite wall. Damn them! Why should I let them get away with my money like that?

'Do you know how long it took me to make that two hundred pounds?' I asked.

'No — and Ah dinna care,' was the reply.

'Two years,' I answered. 'Two years up in the lignite mines near Florence. Nearly a half a million lire. I had to pay through the nose for sterling.'

'More fool you,' Mulligan snapped back. 'Ye could've made it in a single trip wi' one of the gangs operating the Black Market in the Naples area.'

'Well, I made it the honest way,' I answered him. I looked up at him out of the corner of my eyes. He was watching me intently, the pistol grasped by the barrel. He must have seen me watching him, for his hand tightened on the weapon. I shifted my arm so that my hand was almost touching his boot. I glanced at the waves seeping against the steep sandy shore. The stern of the boat lifted. We were almost in the break now. The suck of the backwash was quite loud. I shifted my weight so that I could use my arms. One heave and he'd be in the water and then we'd see who'd have the money. I felt my fingers touch the wet rubber of his sea boots. I braced my back against the gunnel. And at that moment the stern lifted again and Mulligan said, 'Reecht, boys — run her in.' He looked down at me and said, '*Mais avec toi, mon petit, je ne cours pas des chances*.' The butt of the pistol rose and fell. My head seemed to crack like a broken eggshell and everything went black.

When I came to I thought I was in my bunk with a hangover. It was so comfortable and my head throbbed with pain. I felt chilly and moved my hands to pull the bedclothes up. But there were no bedclothes. A slight breeze was ruffling through my hair and my feet were wet. My head throbbed and the waves flopped and seethed to the hammer of the pain. I rolled over on my back and opened my eyes.

Above me the stars were dimming with the pale light of morning. I moved my hands under me and encountered sand. The sound of a wave scattered pain through my head and water swilled up to my buttocks. I sat up with a groan and gazed about me through pain-dimmed eyes. I was sitting on a beach of yellow sand, my feet stretched over the tide mark. A wave rose up out of the half light, broke white and flooded up the beach, wetting me to the waist.

I scrambled back out of reach of the advancing tide. I fingered my scalp gently. Through matted hair my fingers encountered an ugly bump just above the left ear and another right at the back of the skull. When I looked at my hand there was half-congealed blood mixed with sand. For a moment I sat there with my head in my hands, trying to collect my thoughts. This must be England — the Cornish coast, right by Land's End. And — yes — that was it — I had just five pounds. Five pounds and no background. It wasn't much of an introduction to my native land. In a sudden frenzy of fear I thrust my fingers into the zip-fastened pocket of my money belt. I brought out the wad of paper that had replaced my hundred and fifty one pound notes. Toilet paper. With trembling hands I shredded it through, searching for the five pounds that swine Mulligan had said he'd left me. Piece by piece I separated those sheets of toilet paper and let them drift away in the wind. Then I ran through the pockets of my jacket. Nothing. But in the right hand pocket of my trousers I found it. It was a mean little wisp of folded notes, wet and stained. But, oh God, how glad I was of it. In my fear that I had been left nothing, those five sodden notes seemed suddenly gigantic wealth.

I put them in the pocket of my belt and struggled to my feet. I felt faint and slightly sick. The cliffs reeled and toppled. I stumbled to the edge of the sea and doused my head with water till my scalp wound tingled with the salt. Then I turned and began to struggle along the sands towards the inward curve of the bay.

The dawn came reluctantly, cold and grey, showing me the

sweep of the bay. The farther tip of it was thrust out into the sea and ended in a tumble of jagged rocks. The village of Sennen Cove huddled beneath the headland. The wind had freshened from the sou-west and the sea was already flecked with little white-caps. Before I was halfway across the bay, the sun had risen above the hills inland − an angry red disc that barely penetrated the mist of low cloud that had trailed with the dawn across the sky. A few minutes later the sun disappeared. An autumnal chill was in the air. I stopped and looked back. The black granite cliffs which I had left were capped with a veil of cloud. Even as I watched the mist thickened and swept down, blotting out the northern limit of the bay entirely. Within a few minutes the mist had closed down and I was walking through a thin grey void, my world reduced to sand and the surf of breaking waves. The chill of the moist blanket of the mist seeped through my damp jersey and ate into my very bones. So this was England! I thought of the sunshine and the blue skies of Italy. Forgotten in that moment was all the dirt and flies and squalor, the vindictive sneers of the Italians, the loneliness. I wished I had not come.

CHAPTER TWO

At the Ding Dong Mine

I have set down in detail the manner of my return to my native Cornwall because, like the prelude to an opera, it was all of a part with the strange events that followed. As an outcast myself, it was inevitable that I should be thrown into company with men who themselves lived outside the law. At the time, I admit, I felt that I was the subject of a series of most fatal coincidences. But now that I look back on the whole affair, I feel that it was less a series of coincidences than a natural sequence, one thing leading inevitably to another. From the moment that I decided to take Dave Tanner's advice and reurn to England on the *Arisaig* I was set upon a course that led me with terrible directness to Cripples' Ease.

It may sound fantastic. But then is anything more fantastic than life itself? I have so often been angered by people who damn books from the comfortable security of their armchairs for being too fantastic. I have read everything I have ever been able to lay my hands on, from the *Just So Stories* to *War and Peace* — that's the way I got myself educated — and I have yet to read any book that was more fantastic than the stories I've heard in the mining camps of the Rockies or down under in the Coolgardie gold district of Western Australia. And yet, I will say this, that if I had been told as I strode over the mist-shrouded road to Penzance, that I was walking straight into a terrible mine disaster — not only that, but into a pitiful story of madness and greed that involved my own family history — then I just should not have believed it.

For one thing I was far too absorbed in my own wretchedness. I had dreamed so often of this homecoming. All Cornishmen do. Their dream is of a lucky strike and then back to Cornwall to swagger their wealth in the mining towns with big talk of the things they've done and the places they've been. And here was I, back in Cornwall, an outcast — alone and penniless. I doubt whether there was any one more depressed, more completely dispirited by his own sense of loneliness — yes, and his sense of fear — than I was. And all round me was the deep, soundlessness of the mist in place of the blazing blue of the Italian skies.

There was no traffic on the road. Everything was dead and cold and wet. Old tales of the tinners — old superstitions that I'd heard by the camp fires — came to my mind. I'd thought them stupid tales at the time. Piskies, the Giants, the Knockers, the Black Dogs, the Dead Hand and a host of other half-remembered beliefs — they all seemed real enough up there in the mist on the road to Penzance. There were times when I could have sworn somebody was following me. But it was just my imagination. That and the fact that I'd have been scared of my own shadow if the sun had suddenly broken through the mist.

The trouble was that I hadn't understood what it would be like coming back to an organised society. I hadn't realised quite how much of an outcast I should feel. Four years in Italy is apt to give you the idea that the organisation of the masses is such an impossible task that any individual can discreetly lose himself in the crowd.

But in Sennen Cove, after breakfasting at the inn under the curious gaze of the waiter, I had gone into the little general stores to get a map of the district. The shop was warm and friendly, full of seaside things with a stand of postcards crudely illustrating old seaside jokes. It reminded me of little places near Perth. A girl was talking to a man with a little brushed-up, sandy moustache — obviously an officer on leave. 'You wouldn't think it possible, more than three years after the end of the war,' she was saying, 'Nearly fifteen thousand, it says. Listen to this — *"You'll find them on the race tracks, in the Black Market, running restaurants, selling bad liquor, organising prostitution, gambling and vice, dealing in second hand cars, phoney antiques, stolen clothing — they're mixed up in every rotten racket in the country."* Parasites — that's what this paper calls them. And that's what they are.' She threw the paper down on the counter. It lay open at the page she had been looking at. The headline ran — FIFTEEN THOUSAND DESERTERS. 'I know what I'd do with them if I were the Government,' the girl added. 'Round them up and send them to the coal mines for three years. That'd teach them.'

I had bought my map and hurried out of the shop, scared that the girl would notice me. Unseen eyes seemed watching me from the blind windows of the cottages as I hastened up the damp street and footsteps seemed to follow me as I climbed the hill to the main road. A little knot of people waiting for the bus at the school watched me curiously as I hurried by. I felt like a leper, so raw were my nerves and so much did I hate myself.

I reached Penzance shortly after noon, having been given a lift over the last three miles of the road by a lorry loaded with china clay. It was market day in Penzance. I strolled down to the waterfront. There were men dressed much the same as myself in seamen's jerseys and a jacket. Nobody took any notice of me. I felt suddenly at ease for the first time since I had landed in England.

Drifters and single-funnelled coasters lay alongside the piers and the rattle of cranes and donkey engines kept the gulls wheeling over the oily harbour scum. The mist had lifted and thinned to a golden veil. The streets were already beginning to dry. Across the Albert Pier, St. Michael's Mount gleamed like a fairy castle in a shaft of sunlight.

I lit a cigarette and, leaning against the iron railing by the car park, fished in my wallet for Dave Tanner's address. As I unfolded the crumpled sheet of notepaper the sun came through and the rain-washed faces of the houses smiled down at me from the low hill on which the town is built. I felt warm and relaxed as I read through Tanner's letter: —

2 Harbour Terrace
Penzance, Cornwall
29th May.

Dear Jim,

I hear things are not what they were in Italy now that the Army's moved north and the peace treaty has been signed. If you're getting tired of the Ities and would like a change of air, I can fix you up with a job in England — no questions asked! The bearer of this note — name of Shorty — can fix passage for you in the *Arisaig* which will be taking on cargo in Livorno.

Is Maria the same dark-eyed little bitch I knew or has she retired to raise a brood of American bambini? If she is still at the Pappagallo, give her my love, will you? England is all controls and restrictions, but those who know their way about do all right, same as we do in Italy. But I miss the sun and the signorinas.

Hope you take this opportunity to come over — it's a mining job and right up your street.

Your old chum,
Dave.

I folded the note and put it back in my wallet. Shorty had come out to the lignite mine with it himself. That had been in August with the sun beating fiercely down, the earth baked brown and the dust rising in choking clouds. How different, I thought, to this clean, sparkling air with the sun shimmering on the wet pavements. In that moment I held my fate in my hands. I didn't know it then, of course, but I had only to forget all about Dave Tanner and seek a job on my own and the thread that was leading me to Cripples' Ease would be broken. And I came so very near to breaking it. I thought of the *Arisaig* and how Mulligan had cheated me. If those were the sort of men Dave mixed with . . . and the job he had for me — *no questions asked*, that was what he had written. That could only mean one thing — a racket of some sort. I recalled the man himself. Neat, dapper, quick-witted — a Welshman. He wasn't the sort to live strictly within the law. Even as a corporal in charge of a Water Transport coastal schooner, he'd had his own little rackets — shipping personal consignments of silk stockings, wrist watches and liquor from Livorno to Civitavecehia and Napoli, and on the north-bound trips, olive oil, sweets and nuts. I put my hands in my pockets and immediately encountered the remains of my meagre five pounds.

I turned then and went along the quay. In that moment the fatal decision was made. Harbour Terrace was behind the gas works, a narrow street running up from the harbour. Number Two was next to a corn merchants, the end house of a long line, all exactly alike. There were torn lace curtains in the window and that air of faded respectability that belongs to the boarding house throughout the English-speaking world.

A girl answered my ring. She was about twenty-eight and wore a yellow jumper and green corduroy slacks. She smiled at me brightly, but with the lips only. Her grey eyes were hard and watchful.

'Is Mr Tanner in?' I asked.

Her lips froze to a thin line. Her eyes narrowed. 'Who did you say?' she asked. Her voice was thin and unmusical.

'Tanner,' I repeated. 'Mr Dave Tanner.'

'There's nobody of that name living here,' she said sharply and started to close the door as though to shut out something she feared.

'He's an old friend of mine,' I said hurriedly, leaning my bulk against the door. 'I've come a long way to see him. At his request,' I added.

'There's no Mr Tanner living here,' she repeated woodenly.

'But —' I pulled the letter out of my wallet. 'This is Number Two, Harbour Terrace, isn't it?' I asked.

She nodded her head guardedly, as though not trusting herself to admit even that.

'Well, here's a letter I received from him,' I showed her the signature and the address. 'He's a Welshman,' I said. 'Dark hair and eyes and a bit of a limp. I've come all the way from Italy to see him.'

She seemed to relax. But there was a puzzled frown on her face as she said, 'It's Mr Jones you're wanting. His name's David and he has a bit of a limp like you said. But he's away to the fishing now.' And then the guarded look was back in her eyes as though she'd said too much.

'When will he be back?' I asked. There was an uneasy emptiness in my stomach, for he must have had a reason for changing his name, and I didn't like the frightened look in the girl's eyes.

'He left on Monday,' she said. 'And this is Wednesday. He can't possibly be back till tomorrow. Might even be Friday. It depends on what the weather's like.'

'I'll come back this evening,' I told her.

'It won't be any use,' she said. 'He can't be back till tomorrow.'

'I'll come back this evening,' I repeated. 'What's the name of his boat?'

'No good coming this evening. He won't be here. Come to-morrow.' She gave me a bright, uncertain smile and closed the door on me.

I lunched on fish and chips and then went down to the South Pier to make a few inquiries. From an old salt I learned that David Jones was skipper of the *Isle of Mull*, a fifty-five ton ketch used for fishing. He confirmed that the *Isle of Mull* was unlikely to be back for at least another day. But when I asked him where the *Isle of Mull* did her fishing, his blue eyes regarded me curiously and I had that same sense of withdrawal, almost of suspicion, that I had had when talking to the girl at Harbour Terrace. 'Over to Brettagny mebbe, or out to the Scillies,' he told me. 'T'edn't like 'erring, 'ee knaw. 'Tis mackerel and pilchard 'e be after, an' it depends where 'e do find'n.' And he stared at me out of his amazingly blue eyes as though daring me to ask any more questions.

After that I went back into the town. It was just after three. The sun had gone out of the sky and the mist was coming down in a light drizzle. Penzance looked wet and withdrawn. Until shortly before eight o'clock, when I walked back through the gathering dusk to Harbour Terrace, I was still free to make my own decision. For the space of a few hours I could have broken that thread of destiny and with luck I'd have eventually got passage in a ship to Canada, and so would never have discovered what happened to my mother.

But fear and loneliness combined is a thing few men can fight. Tanner was the only soul I knew in a strange country. He was my one contact with the future. What did it matter if he were mixed up in some shady business? I was a deserter. And since that put me outside the law so long as I remained at liberty, it was outside the law that I should have to earn my living. To that extent I faced up to the reality of my situation. What I could not face up to was the uncertainty and difficulties of the unknown if I tried to fend for myself. I took the easy way, comforting myself that if I didn't like Tanner's proposition, I could decide against it later.

And so as a clock down by the harbour struck eight I turned up by the gas works into Harbour Terrace. The single street light showed the rain dancing on the roadway and water swirling down the gutters of the steep little street. It was an older woman who answered the door this time. 'Is Mr David Jones back yet?' I asked her.

Her face paled and she glanced quickly over her shoulder at the stairs which ascended in a rigid line to the unlighted interior of the house. 'Sylvia! Sylvia!' she called out in a hoarse, agitated voice.

A door at the top of the stairs opened and the girl I had seen before stood framed in the flood of light. 'What is it, Auntie?'

'There's a gentleman inquiring for Mr Jones.'

The door was instantly closed, shutting out the light, and the girl came down the stairs. She was still dressed in her yellow jumper and green corduroys. But her face was pale and drawn as she faced me in the doorway. 'What do you want?' she asked. And then almost in the same breath: 'He's not back yet. I told you he won't be back till tomorrow. Why've you come again — now?' Her voice dropped uncertainly on the last word.

'I'd said I'd come back this evening,' I reminded her. Then my eyes fell to her hand. There was blood on it, and more on her slacks. And there was an impersonal, familiar smell about her. A surgical smell. Iodine!

She saw the direction of my gaze. 'One of our lodgers,' she muttered. 'He's cut himself on a glass. Excuse me, I must go up and finish bandaging his arm.' As soon as she'd said the word 'arm' her eyes widened. For a second she stared straight at me, quite still. Then panic leapt into her fear-struck eyes and she flung herself at the door.

But I brushed her and the door back and stepped inside. 'He's back, isn't he?' I said, closing the door. 'He's back and he's hurt.'

She leapt to the stairs and stood there, panting, barring my way like a tigress defending her young. 'What do you want with him?' she breathed. 'Why have you come? All that about coming from Italy at his request — that was all lies, wasn't it? You were asking questions about him down at the harbour this afternoon. That's what I was told. Why?'

I said, 'Look, I don't mean any harm. It's true what I said this morning.' I fished the letter out of my wallet again. 'There, if you don't believe me, read that letter. That's his handwriting, isn't it?'

She nodded, But she didn't read it immediately. She stood there with her eyes fixed on mine as though I were a wild beast and she was afraid to release me from her gaze. 'Read it,' I said. 'Then perhaps you'll believe what I say.'

Reluctantly she lowered her eyes. She read through. Then she folded it carefully and handed it back. Her face had lost the strained look. But the wide eyes looked tired and drained. 'Was Maria — his girl?' she asked. Her voice was soft, yet somehow harsh.

'Oh, God!' I said. 'She was nobody. Just a girl in a trattoria.'

The door at the top of the stairs opened and Dave Tanner's voice called down sharply, 'What the devil are you doing, girl? Come and fix this arm before I lose any more blood.' His figure was black against the light from the room behind. The wide shaft of light showed the grey cupids on the peeling wall-paper. Across it sprawled his shadow. He was in his shirt sleeves and held a bloodstained towel to his left arm. His hair was damp with the rain, or maybe it was sweat. 'Who the hell was it anyway?'

'It's all right, Dave,' she answered. 'It's a friend of yours. I'll come and fix that arm now.'

'A friend of mine?' he echoed.

'Yes,' I called up to him. 'It's me — Jim Pryce.'

'Jim Pryce!' He peered down into the unlighted hallway. His face caught the light. It was drained of all colour, the bones standing out like a caricature in marble. 'A helluva moment you've chosen to come visiting,' he said. Then impatiently: 'Well, come on up, man. Don't stand there gaping at me as though I were Jesus Christ.'

The girl suddenly came to life and hurried up the stairs. I followed her. We went into the bedroom and she shut the door and started to work on his arm. 'What happened?' I asked.

'Oh, just a spot of trouble,' he said vaguely and his face contracted with pain as the girl dabbed iodine into what was obviously a bullet wound.

'Who was Maria?' the girl suddenly asked.

'That's a pretty nasty wound,' I said quickly.

'It's nothing — nothing whatever. A flesh wound, that's all. What did you say, Syl?'

'I asked who was Maria?' the girl said and dabbed iodine into the wound so that the sweat stood out in beads on his forehead.

'Just a girl,' he snapped. He looked across at me. His black eyes gleamed in his taut face. 'What've you been telling her?'

'Nothing,' I said. 'I had to show her your letter. She wouldn't let me in.'

'Oh,' Then to the girl in a curt voice: 'That's enough of the iodine. Now bandage it. No, he can do that. Get me some dry clothes. And when you've done that we'll need some food to take with us.' As she opened the wardrobe, he said to me. 'We'll cut up by Hea Moor and Madron. You'll not be minding a night march, will you now?'

'Yes, but what's happened, Dave?' I asked.

'Nothing,' he said and held out his arm for me to bandage. With his other hand he took a gold case from his hip pocket and lit a cigarette. The lighter was gold too. A diamond ring flashed on his finger. The girl put a pile of clothes on the chair at the foot of the bed. 'Now get the food,' he said. He spoke with the cigarette clinging to his underlip. 'It's time we were going. And see if you can find another raincoat.' The girl's face was sullen and her eyes flickered up at me with fierce hatred. She wanted to be going with him. She went out and I began to bandage his arm. 'Hey, not too tight, bach,' he said. 'Yes, that's better.' He grunted as I pressed against the arm muscles to tie the bandage. 'Was it Mulligan you came over with?' he asked as he began to change his wet clothes.

'Yes,' I said. 'And the dirty bastard robbed me when he brought me ashore.'

'Did he now?'

'You don't seem very surprised,' I said.

'Why should I be surprised? The man's as crooked as an eel.' He turned suddenly. 'Look you now, don't be blaming me, man. The *Arisaig* is the only vessel we have on the Italian run. It was the best I could do. It's not every skipper who will take the chance of smuggling a deserter into the country.' A flicker of a smile creased the corners of his eyes. 'It wouldn't surprise me, you know, if you were to meet Mulligan again.'

'How's that?' I asked. His back was turned towards me and he was struggling into a dry pair of workman's corduroys. He did not answer. 'Look, Dave,' I said, 'what's this job you've got for me? Is it still available?'

'Yes, I think so,' he said. He pulled on a seaman's jersey. As his head emerged from the neck, his mouth was twisted in pain and the sweat ran down his face. He put his cigarette back between his lips and drew in a great lungful of smoke. 'It's a good job, you know — mining, did I tell you?'

'Yes,' I said. 'You told me that in your letter.'

He nodded and forced his injured arm into his jacket. 'Come on now,' he said. 'Your way is the same as mine. I'll tell you about it as we go.' He stuffed some cigarettes into his pocket and transferred his case and lighter and a thick wallet from his sodden jacket to the one he had put on. His quick eyes glanced round the room. Then he opened the door. He seemed in a great hurry to be gone.

I followed him down the stairs. In the dark hallway he leaned over the banisters and shouted down into the basement for the girl. 'Just coming, Dave,' she answered. The tip of the cigarette glowed red as we waited. He was puffing at it nervously. The gloom of the little hall was lessened by the light from the street that entered by a dirty fanlight above the front door.

The girl's feet sounded hollow on the bare stairboards. I could hear her quick, frightened breathing as she emerged from the basement. 'There's sandwiches and an old raincoat of father's,' she said, her voice breathless.

'Listen, Syl.' Dave's voice was a harsh whisper. 'Those clothes upstairs — burn them. Clean up everything. Leave nothing whatever to show that I returned — you understand? And when they come around asking questions, tell them I never came back. See that the old woman doesn't jabber.'

He turned to leave then, but the girl clung to him. 'Where can I get in touch with you?' she asked quickly.

'You can't.'

'You'll come back, won't you?' This in a fierce whisper.

'Yes, indeed I will,' he assured her. 'I'll send a message. But understand — I never came back here. And don't let on to them where I've gone.'

'How can I when I don't know?'

'Indeed you can't — that's why I didn't tell you.' He turned to me. I could see his eyes in the dim light. 'Open the door and see if there's any one about.'

I pulled the door open. The street was deserted. The rain came down in a steady stream. In the light of the street lamp it slanted in thin steel rods to dance on the roadway and run gurgling down the gutters. I looked back into the hallway. The girl was clinging to Dave, her body pressed to his in a primitive declaration of passion that stripped her bare. Dave was looking past her to the open doorway, the cigarette still in his mouth.

When he saw me nod he detached himself from the girl and came towards me. The girl started to follow him. He turned to her. 'See that you get those things burned,' he said. Then he kissed her quickly and we left Number Two, Harbour Terrace. As I shut the door I saw the girl standing alone at the bottom of the stairs. She was staring straight at me, but she didn't see me. The skin was tight and drawn on her face and I had the impression that she was crying, though there were no tears in her eyes.

It's a strange thing but it never seemed to occur to me to leave Dave to fend for himself. I didn't know what had happened. But a man doesn't get a bullet wound in his arm for nothing. Nor does he abandon his girl and his lodgings, with instructions for his blood-stained clothes to be burned, unless he's been mixed up in something pretty shady. For all I knew he might be involved in murder. But I was swept up in the thing now and, as I say, it never occurred to me to leave him. Probably it was the company and the fact that he was an outcast, like myself. There is nothing to my mind so terrible as loneliness — not the loneliness that comes to a man in a town when he is afraid of his fellow creatures.

We kept to mean, badly lit streets as we threaded our way out of Penzance. We didn't talk. Yet I found immeasurable comfort in the presence of that small figure limping along beside me.

We came out at last on to a main road and as we climbed a short hill through the rain we left the lights of Penzance behind us. At the top I paused and looked back. The town was just a ragged huddle of lights, faintly visible through the driving rain.

'Come on, man,' Dave said impatiently. And I knew he was afraid of those lights.

'How far are we going?' I asked.

'Eight or nine miles,' he answered. We trudged on. 'We'll separate at Lanyon,' he added.

'Where are you going?' I asked.

'A farm. I'll be hiding up for a bit.'

'Another girl?' I asked.

His teeth showed in the darkness as he grinned up at me. 'Is it Casanova you think I am?' My remark had flattered his vanity. He was one of those men who for no apparent reason is attractive to women, and he enjoyed the sense of power it gave him.

'What about me?' I asked. 'Where am I going?'

'Botallack,' he replied. 'There's a message I'll be wanting you to carry too.'

'Good God!' I said. 'My father worked at Botallack.'

'Indeed. Then you'd better change your name, you know. Let me see — Canada wasn't it? Any Irish in Canada?'

'Fair number,' I told him.

'In the mining districts?'

'Some.'

'Well then — what do you say to O'Donnel? That's a good Irish name, indeed it is. And it's very suitable for a big man, look you. From now on you're Jim O'Donnel. Okay?'

'Sure,' I said. 'What's in a name?'

He laughed sardonically. 'A hell of a lot sometimes, you know.' He was silent for a moment. I knew he was looking up at me, and I knew what he was thinking. 'Did you have to ask for me by my real name?' he said at length.

'How was I to know you had changed it?' I said.

He grunted. 'She didn't know Jones wasn't my real name.

35

Damn it, man, you might have thought of that. And showing her the letter. It's pretty mad, she was. She's nothing particular in the way of looks and she knows it.'

After that we walked in silence, mile after weary mile, through the driving rain. We went on through Hea Moor and Madron and then up the long hill flanked by cedar woods and rhododendrons to the moors. We met no one. Only two cars passed us and each time my companion drew me out of the line of the headlights. He was taking no chances of being seen. On the long hill out of Madron his pace became slower and slower, so that I had to keep on waiting for him. His breathing was heavy and his limp more pronounced. Out on the moors at the top we came into the wind and the rain slanted across our faces from the sou'-west. It was pitch dark, and silent save for the steady swish of the rain.

I was soon wet to the skin. The raincoat was an old one and though made for a man much bigger than Dave, it was too short for me and did not meet across the chest. I could feel the water coursing down my body underneath my clothes. It began at the neck, where two little pools formed in my collar bones and trickled icily down my sides, running together at my loins and then down the insides of my legs and so into my squelching shoes.

Dave's feet began to drag. He was stumbling along. Soon I was supporting him with one hand under his arm. It was clear he couldn't go much farther. His breath was coming in hard, rasping sobs and he limped heavily. I stopped him. 'Let's look at that arm,' I said.

It's nothing,' he answered fiercely. 'Come on now. We need to be clear of the moors by daybreak.'

But I got out my matches and, after breaking two, managed to keep one alight for a second. His left hand was sodden with blood, which mingled with the rain to form pale red drops on his fingertips. 'That arm's got to be bound up,' I said. 'Where can we get some shelter — a barn or something?'

He hesitated. Then he said, 'All right. There's a turning a little way on to the right. It leads down to Ding Dong. It's an old mine working, and there's the remains of a blowing house that's more like a cave than anything else. We'll be safe enough there.'

We kept to the right of the road and about a quarter of a mile farther on came to a dirt road leading away into the moors. It was half an hour's walk to that mine at the pace we were going and before we got there I was practically carrying Dave. He hadn't much strength left in him. The road deteriorated to a stone-strewn moorland track. It led to a grassy mound and, dimly visible through the black soundlessness of the night, loomed the blacker shape of one of those granite engine houses that will stand to the end of time. A little farther on we came upon a huddle of mine-workings, vague mound shapes of broken rock. We scrambled in amongst these and after a bit of searching Dave found what he wanted, a low stone archway. This was the 'Castle' of the old blowing house.

We stumbled through and found ourselves miraculously out of the rain and wind.

Gorse and furze grew in abundance and in a short while we were squatting naked before a sizzling blaze, our clothes hung over branches to dry. I fixed Dave's arm with a tourniquet and then we started in on the sandwiches. I had pulled whole bushes up by the roots and these, with some old baulks of timber I had found, gave us plenty of fuel. The smoke from the blaze was whipped out of the doorway by the wind. If anybody had seen us squatting there completely nude before the fierce blaze of the fire, our shadows dancing on the broken rock of the walls, they would have thought it a trick of time and gone away believing they had been piskey-led back into the days of the ancient Britons. But there was no one to see us. We were on a wild stretch of the moors and outside it was teeming with rain and blowing half a gale.

With water from a pool in the doorway I washed the blood off Dave's arm. Then I renewed the bandage. The wound no longer bled, even when I took the tourniquet off. The bullet had passed through the fleshy part of the upper arm. It did not seem to have damaged the muscles for he could still flex his fingers and move his wrist and elbows. I put on a fresh bandage of strips torn from the tails of our shirts. As I worked I began asking questions. He lit a cigarette and didn't answer. 'I suppose you were running liquor?' I suggested finally.

His gaze met mine. I could see the flames of the fire dancing in his dark eyes. He had the look of an animal that's been cornered. His silence exasperated me. I wanted to knock the cigarette out of his mouth and shake the truth out of him. 'What happened?' I asked again. 'Did a revenue cutter board you? What happened to the *Isle of Mull*? There was shooting. Did you shoot back?'

His eyes narrowed. The small dark features were immobile, the cigarette dangling from his bloodless lips. His stony silence chilled me. Suddenly I had to know. Ever since we had left the house in Harbour Terrace my energies had been concentrated on leaving Penzance behind us. But now as I knelt naked by the blazing fire that scorched my buttocks, I had time to think. Racketeer he undoubtedly was. The skipper of a fishing boat doesn't have gold cigarette cases and diamonds. I didn't mind that. But a killer was different.

'Dave,' I said, 'for God's sake tell me — did you shoot back? Was anybody else — hurt?'

His eyes didn't leave my face. They were cold and hard. They were like the eyes of a panther I had once seen looking down at me from a branch of a tree as it lay crouched to spring. I suddenly caught hold of him and shook him, 'What happened?' I cried, and my voice sounded strange.

The thin line of his lips curled. The expression of his eyes changed so that he was looking through me. He was seeing a scene that was indelibly planted in his mind. And he was enjoying it. He began to hum a tune, crooning it to himself in an ecstasy of reminiscence. 'They insisted on taking the hatches off. I warned them not to. But they insisted.' He suddenly looked at me. He was still smiling secretly. 'What could I do, man? It was their own fault, wasn't it? I jumped for the other boat. That's when I got this bullet through the arm. And then they opened the hatches. It was a lot of noise she made and then she sank, just as though she'd hit a mine. Just lovely, it was. But it's sorry I am about the old boat. Fond I was of her — fonder than I've ever been of a boat.'

'How many were killed?' I asked.

His eyes went dead and the muscles of his face hardened. 'It's nothing to do with you, man. Their own fault, wasn't it now?' He put his hand on my arm. 'Don't be asking any more questions, Jim,' he said. 'It's shooting my mouth off, I've been. Forget what I've said. I'm feverish, that's all.' He stared into the fire. His face relaxed so that he looked little more than a kid.

I squatted back on my haunches. I felt cold and wretched in the blaze of the fire that burned my neck. I thought of the stories I'd heard of the wreckers that had operated along these rugged coasts before the lighthouses were built, and how the fiends had knifed the survivors that struggled in through the break of the waves. Here was something just as horrible. And I was mixed up in it. A few hours ago I had been a deserter — nothing more. Now I was mixed up in murder. I shivered. 'What about this job?' I asked huskily. 'Is it anything to do — to do with your activities?'

His lips remained set and his eyes hard. Yet somehow I knew he was smiling to himself. 'It's scared you are,' he said.

'Of course I'm scared,' I said, suddenly finding my voice. 'There's men been killed tonight and I'm involved. I've only done one thing wrong in my life. I ran when I should've gone on and got killed like any decent fellow. I ran because my nerves were shot in ribbons with three consecutive nights' patrolling through mines and booby traps in that hell of Cassino. I couldn't take it. But that's all I've done. And now here I am hiding on a desolate stretch of moors with — with a murderer.'

His eyes leapt to mine. They were like hard, glittering coals. His right hand slid across towards his clothes. I watched him — not afraid, but fascinated. He felt in the pocket of his jacket.

Then his eyelids drooped and he relaxed. His hand shifted to the breast pocket of his jacket and he brought out his cigarette case. He shivered as he lit a cigarette and when he'd put the case back, he moved nearer the fire. He huddled over it, watching me out of the corners of his eyes. He was nervous and uncertain. He sat there for a while, so close to the blaze that his thin white body glowed red. He stared into the flames and every now and then he shivered. It was as though he saw in the heart of the flaming wood, his future. I realised that he was scared.

The silence became oppressive. I remembered how he had slid his hand to the side pocket of his jacket. Suppose he became scared that I'd give him away? There was no forecasting his reactions. 'Forget about it and get some sleep, why don't you?' I said.

He raised his head and looked at me slowly. 'I never killed anybody before, you know,' he murmured. Then he turned back and continued to gaze into the flames. 'All through the war I never killed a soul — never even saw a dead body. The R.A.S.C. company I was with kept pretty well in the rear. And then, because I'd been in coal ships out from Swansea, I was transferred to a Water Transport Company. It wasn't me, you know, that thought up that idea of booby-trapping the hatches. The Captain, it was — damn his eyes. How was I to know the whole bloody vessel would go up in a sheet of flame? I thought it would just scuttle her. How was I to know — tell me that, man?' His eyes were excited and his whole body moved with the widespread disavowal of guilt made by his hands. 'Why is it you sit there so silent? You think it's damned I am? What right have you to judge? Didn't you walk out on your pals — a deserter? There's nothing rottener. Isn't it true that a man who deserts is — is —' He opened his arms again, unable to find the word. 'I didn't desert, did I? I jumped to save my skin. Any one would have done the same.' He leaned forward on his elbow and peered up at me. 'I'm not a murderer, I tell you.' It was a cry of desperation. Then he muttered. 'By God, if that's what you think —' In a single lithe movement he had risen and was feeling in the pocket of his jacket.

I braced myself. My tongue felt dry. 'For God's sake, sit down,' I said. 'I'm in no position to do you any harm.'

He hesitated. Then he seemed to relax. 'That's right,' he said. 'You're not, are you?' he smiled. It wasn't a real smile. It was no more than a drawing back of the lips to show the flash of his even white teeth. He looked like some devil, his body all red with the firelight and his teeth bared. Behind him his distorted shadow sprawled menacingly over wall and roof.

I passed my tongue across my lips. It rasped like a piece of adhesive tape. 'Sit down,' I said again. 'You're all hepped up. I can't do you any harm. Besides, I need your help.'

He didn't say anything. He stood there, looking at me for the moment, his dark head thrust forward like a snake considering whether to strike. Then he shivered and went into the corner of the cave and relieved himself. Away from the fire his body was white again. He was watching me all the time. I could see his eyes like two red coals in the gloom. Then he came back to the fire and stood right over it with his legs apart so that the warmth of it seeped up his body. He was shivering so that I wondered whether he wasn't a bit feverish.

After a moment he crouched down and began staring into the flames again. 'Funny what your childhood's days do to you,' he said softly. 'We lived in the Rhondda. My father was a miner. Two pounds ten a week, that's what he got, and my mother to keep the six of us. Three sisters I had and me the eldest of the children. I was at work in the pits when I was twelve and by the time I was sixteen it's a man's job I was trying to do, and me so weak I could hardly walk home after the end of each shift. It's not much food there is when there's six mouths to feed, and the pits closing all along the valley. By the time I was eighteen I was drawing dole. So I went down to Cardiff, you know, and worked as stevedore. It wasn't long before I was handling stuff brought in by the sailors. Why should a man starve himself when there's crooks earning thousands of pounds that have the law on their side?' He gave a sudden harsh laugh. 'I've been back to the Rhondda once or twice. Shall I tell you something? There's boys that used to play in the Valley with me that are old men now. No wonder the country's in a bad way for coal. And it's nobody but themselves they've got to blame.' He wriggled closer to the fire. 'They've sucked the life blood out of a great race of people for years. Why shouldn't I do a little bloodsucking? If I murdered a thousand of them I'd be justified, wouldn't I?' He picked a flaming brand out of the fire and held it aloft. 'Them and their bloody laws − I don't care that much for them.' He flung the blazing log out through the door. The flame of it died and vanished in a sizzle of steam as the rain swept over it. 'See what I mean?' His eyes blazed at me across the fire. 'What are laws? They're not made by the men who starve. They're made to protect the moneyed class. They're my enemies, aren't they? Well, aren't they?' His voice died suddenly and he turned his gaze back into the fire. 'But I didn't know the old boat would go up like that.'

I was beginning to feel chilly. My clothes were dry now and I got up and put them on. Dave watched me for a while, then he did the same. When he was fully dressed, he went to the entrance and looked out at the weather. Then he came back to the fire. 'No use whatever going out in that. We'd best kip down here for the night.'

'What about your farm?' I said. 'You said you wanted me there by daybreak.'

He rounded on me. 'Who said I was going to a farm?' he snarled.

'You did,' I reminded him.

He crossed over to me, dragging his left foot. 'Understand this,' he said, 'I never told you I was going to a farm. I never told you anything. You never met me. You never came to see me. You don't know me. Understand?'

I nodded.

He searched my face. Finally he seemed satisfied and went back to the other side of the fire. 'We'll go on tomorrow,' he said. Then he wrapped himself up in his raincoat and curled up close to the smouldering heap of timber. His eyes closed for a second. But I noticed that he slept with his right hand in his jacket pocket. His face, with the eyes closed, looked old and drawn. There was no trace of the boy in him that I'd seen earlier.

I was dead tired, but though I lay down with my raincoat round me, I could not get to sleep. Through long hours I lay huddled close to the fire, thinking over the events of the day and listening to my companion's regular breathing. Outside the rain streamed down, the monotonous sound of it being relieved only when a gust of wind lashed at the mouth of the cave. Strange shadows flickered across the broken rock of wall and roof and occasionally a piece of timber moved in the fire sending up a shower of sparks. God, I kept on thinking, what a mess I've got myself into! How much easier would it have been if I had kept right on at Cassino, and got myself killed like the rest of the platoon. Or would I have still lived on, crippled and disfigured, a relic of human idiocy in some home for wrecks that they dare not show to the public? At least I was alive and intact.

I suppose I must have dozed off, for a little later it seemed I opened my eyes to find the fire nearly out and a wan light creeping furtively through the entrance-way. It was very cold. I got up and went out. The rain was still sheeting down out of a leaden sky. All about me was a scene of bleak confusion. The walls of the mine buildings had collapsed and mingled with the dumps of rock to form desolate mounts of sharp-edged stone. I got furze and more timber and built up the fire again. Dave's eyes were open and he lay watching me. His face was very white so that his eyes looked like two black sloes. His right hand was still in the pocket of his jacket.

As I moved about the cave I was uncomfortably aware of his watchfulness. The damp of the morning had chilled me to the marrow. It made me nervous and every time my back was turned towards him I felt an almost uncontrollable urge to glance quickly back over my shoulder. At last he got to his feet. His hand was still in his pocket and he was watching me. I tried to understand the expression in his eyes. But I couldn't. They were the eyes of a monkey — mischievous, cruel and without reason. At last I could stand it no longer.

'Why do you stare at me like that?' I asked.

He gave a little shrug and his lips stretched to a thin smile. He lit a cigarette. I watched the deliberate movements of his hands. They had long, slender fingers and small wrists — the hands of an artist or a man who lives on his nerves and drink. 'I was just trying to decide whether I could trust you,' he said at last. Again the smile. 'You see, I don't know very much about you, do I? We drank together at the Pappagallo, that's all.'

'I might say the same about you,' I answered, my eyes on his hand, which he had put back in the pocket of his jacket.

'Yes, but I don't carry your life in my hands.' He nodded towards the fire. 'Suppose you sit down and tell me about yourself,' he suggested.

I hesitated. The hair was prickling along my scalp as I looked into the utter blankness of his eyes. I suddenly felt an overwhelming desire to get that gun — to get it before he used it. 'Sit down.' It was softly spoken, but there was a harshness in his voice that made me obey without further hesitation. 'Now let's have your story.' He had seated himself across the fire from me. He was puffing nervously at his cigarette. In the bleak light that came in through the entrance his face looked wretchedly drawn, the lines etched deeply into the white skin.

I began to tell him how I had left England when I was four, moved to Tin Valley in the Canadian Rockies, had started washing dishes in one of the local saloons when I was ten, became a miner when I was twelve. But he interrupted me. 'I don't want data. I want your background. Why did your father leave England and go to Canada?'

'My mother left him.' I sat staring into the fire, thinking back down the lane of my life. 'If you want my background,' I said, 'my father was a drunk. He drank to forget. My mother was very lonely. I found a photograph of her amongst my father's things after his death.' I pulled out my wallet and took from it my mother's photograph. Across the bottom was written in a round, childish hand — 'To Bob, from his love — Ruth Nearne.' I passed it across to Dave. 'My father talked of nothing but Cornwall. He was desperately sick for home. But he never made a fortune and he wouldn't come back to be mocked. That's what he used to tell me. He was afraid of being mocked for having lost his wife. She went with a miner from Penzance. My father hated her and loved her all in the same breath.'

I had forgotten why I was saying all this. I'd never spoken about it to any one. But suddenly, up on those bleak moors in the derelict waste of that old tin mine, it seemed right that I should be talking about it.

'I don't know about Welshmen,' I went on, 'but Cornish miners go all over the world. There's not many mines that haven't got Cornishmen working in them. And they cling together. Up there in the Rockies my father found plenty of Cornishmen. He'd bring them back to our hut and they'd talk mining by the hour over bottles of bad rye, feeding pinewood into the stove until the iron casing became red hot. And when there wasn't any company he'd tell me about our own country and the mines along the tin coast. Botallack and Levant — he'd worked in them both, and even now I reckon I could find my way around in those mines from the memory of what he told me of them. He was a thin, wiry little man with sad eyes and a hell of a thirst. That and silicosis killed him at the age of forty-two.'

'Did you ever hear from your mother?'

I looked up. I had almost forgotten that Dave was there, so absorbed had I become in my memories. 'No,' I said. 'Never. And I was never allowed to refer to her. The only clue I ever got as to her whereabouts was when he was raving drunk one night and mouthed curses upon a place called Cripples' Ease.

There's a village of that name near St. Ives. I found it on the map. But I shall never go there. He was dead drunk for a week then. I think he must have heard something. He died when I was sixteen. I think I would have asked him about her when he was dying, but he had a stroke and never regained consciousness.'

'Oh — that's terrible!'

I looked up to find Dave with a look of genuine sadness in his eyes.

'And you never found out what happened to her?' he asked.

'No,' I said.

'But now that you are in Cornwall?'

I shook my head. 'No,' I told him. 'Let the past lie buried. He wouldn't have wanted me to try to find out. He may have been a drunk, but I loved him.'

That secret smile was back on Dave's lips. But this time it was different. It was as though he was really amused at something. 'Maybe the past will not lie buried.'

'What do you mean?' I asked.

He shrugged his shoulders and handed back the faded print.

After that we sat in silence for a long while. Outside the rain swept across the waste of mine workings in a leaden curtain and the grey light glistened on the piled-up mounds of slag. At length Dave got up and sniffed at the weather. 'It'll clear up after midday,' he said. 'You'll be able to start out then. Our ways part from here.'

'Where do I go?' I asked.

'Botallack,' he replied. 'Ask for Captain Manack. And give him this.' He tossed his gold cigarette lighter across to me. 'That'll prove that I sent you to him. Now I'm going to get some sleep and I suggest you do the same.'

'What about your arm?' I asked.

'Indeed it's all right,' he said and curled himself up in his raincoat in front of the hot embers.

For some time I sat staring out into the black curtain of the rain. At length I grew sleepy and dozed off.

When I woke the sun was shining and I was alone in the cave. I went outside. The moors looked warm and friendly and the rubble of the old mine workings steamed gently in the warmth of the sun. The gold of the gorse shimmered in the heat and birds were singing.

I called. But no one answered. Dave had gone.

CHAPTER THREE

Cripples' Ease

The sun was westering as I climbed Carn Kenidjack. The great granite blocks of the carn were black against the flaming sky and the heather of the hillside was dark in shadow. But when I reached the top and stood on the huge, flat-topped slabs, I felt the faint warmth of the sun, and the heather on the farther slope glowed a warm purple. The moors spilled away from under my feet to a coastline that was torn and broken by old mine workings. It was as though one of the giants of Cornish legend had rootled along this rugged coast in search of boulders to hurl at some neighbouring Titan. The sea beyond was like a tray of burnished copper. A line of storm clouds lay black along the horizon, their ragged edges crimsoned by the red disc of the autumn sun. The wind blew strong and salt in my face.

So this was the Cornish tin coast. There was a lump in my throat. Since I was old enough to understand, my father had talked to me of little else but this strip of Cornwall where he had lived and worked until he married. And I was actually standing on Carn Kenidjack — the Hooting Carn. This was where the two tinners were supposed to have watched the Devil's wrestling match.

Below me three tracks sprouted from the heather and thrust dirty-brown fingers down to the stone-tilted roofs of the miners' cottages on the coast road. I got my bearings from my map. That was St. Just, away to the left there, and Botallack, and Boscaswell where my father had been born, and Trewellard. Yes, and there was Pendeen — I could just see the white pimple of the lighthouse peeping above the rim of the coast. A little to the left the two shafts of Wheal Geevor showed black scaffolds against the copper sea. And that waste of broken rock down by the cliff edge, that was Levant.

I knew the line of the coast by heart as though I had spent my boyhood exploring it. I needed no map to tell me which was Cape Cornwall and Kenidjack Castle. I had felt a sudden excitement as I found Botallack Head and recognised, in the scored cliff-top behind it, the surface workings of the Botallack mine. I could even pick out the various shafts, getting my bearings from the broken ruins of the old engine houses that were the only ordered things in that chaos of tumbled stone. The mine was derelict now, but in my father's day it had been a great copper producer. He had taken me through it gallery by gallery, describing each level in the minutest detail, so that looking down on it from Carn Kenidjack I could almost see the outline of the underground workings just as my father had so often traced it for me on the dusty floor of our hut.

I thought of Kalgoorlie and the seething mine valleys of the Rockies and the big new concrete buildings that housed their plants. And they seemed so recent and characterless beside this little strip of torn-up coast where tin had been streamed by men who had left traces of their rude hut circles and megalithic burial chambers up here on these desolate moors. These were the mines that had given the Ancient Britons the ore to barter with for ornaments and silks with Greek merchants from Marseilles way back in the Bronze Age . . . And only fifty years ago the whole area had seethed with activity, as thousands of men worked beneath the rugged cliffs and even out under the sea. And now it was all derelict. Just that one mine — Wheal Geevor — still working.

The ruddy glow of the sun began to fade out of the heather. The great red ball was sinking behind the gathering storm clouds. I watched until the last red slice of it disappeared. And when I looked down the slope of the hillside to the coast again, the sea had become a dark abyss and the worked cliff-tops and broken hillside were gloomy and unfriendly. The heather was like burnt stubble now and the rocks took on weird shapes in the gathering dusk. The country seemed to shiver in the cold wind and withdraw into its dark past.

I went on again then, making for the nearest of the tracks that led down into Botallack. But I went slowly, almost reluctantly. Now that I was face to face with the future I felt ill at ease again. I tried to pretend that if I didn't like the job I could go elsewhere. But back of my mind there lurked a fear that I should not be allowed to do that. All sense of excitement at returning to my father's own country was drained out of me. Perhaps it was because all warmth had left the country with the setting of the sun. It was bleak and bare — and depressing. Or perhaps I had a sense of premonition.

By the time I had reached the coast road that runs from St. Ives to the Land's End it was almost dark. The clouds that had fringed the horizon when the sun set were now a black mass piled up half across the sky. Distant lightning forked in jagged streaks, providing the only indication where cloud ended and sea began. After each flash, the far-off roll of thunder sounded above the dull roar of the sea and the moan of the wind in the telegraph wires. To the north, the revolving light of Pendeen Watch swung in a white glare through the dark of the gathering storm.

Many of the cottages must have disappeared since my father's day, for Botallack was now little more than an inn and a few farm buildings. There was not a soul on the road. But from the lighted doorway of the inn came the sound of an accordion and men's voices. They were singing 'The Old Grey Duck.' I hadn't heard that old song since my father had died. It had been a great favourite with him when he was drunk. I hesitated. I did not want to face the curious gaze of the inhabitants of this tiny village. Yet I had to find out where Captain Manack lived and I needed a drink to steady myself. I needed time to think too.

There were about half a dozen men seated in the bar when I went in. Two were playing Cornish skittles; the rest were grouped around the accordion player. He was a big, burly man with short, grizzled hair and he sang with an old clay pipe clamped between toothless gums. The singing was punctuated by the clatter of the wooden pins as the ball on its string swung through their ranks. A big fire blazed in the grate and the place looked warm and cheerful. I crossed over to the bar and ordered a pint of beer, very conscious of the fact that the singing had almost ceased as they watched me. Samples of ore stood among the bottles and glasses that twinkled at their reflections in the mirror that backed the shelves. There was a leaden chunk of mother tin and a big lump of iron pyrites that glittered brighter than gold in the strong light. The landlord was friendly enough, and I began talking to him about the mining industry. He was short and wide in the shoulders. Every now and then he gave a little rasping cough and his skin had the grey pallor of silicosis.

I suddenly realised that the accordion had stopped playing. The singing had ceased, so had the click of the skittles. I turned quickly. No one was talking. They were all looking at me. I was seized with a panic desire to run. But my feet seemed to be rooted to the floor. I took a grip on myself. They couldn't tell just by the look of me. 'Why do you all stare at me?' I heard myself ask.

It was the accordion player who answered. 'We bin trying to make 'ee out from yer talk. Thee's a furriner sure, an' yet 'ee's a fitty way of speaking.'

'I'm Canadian,' I said.

'Iss, iss, but thee's got Cornish blood in 'ee,' the old man insisted.

I felt relieved. But I wondered how he could tell. I suppose it was the fact that I'd been brought up to Cornish dialect. I could drop into it quite easily and did now. 'Iss,' I said. 'Me father was a tinner over to Redruth afore we went to Canada. Born at Boscaswell, he was, an' worked cores down in Botallack till they knacked the bal.'

The old man nodded approvingly. 'A' thort so,' he said. The whole room was smiling at me. 'The way 'ee were talking,' the old man went on, 'puts me in mind of the old days in Camborne and Redruth. I mind the time when the bals were working full blast and the kiddiwinks was full o' Cornishmen tarkin' all sorts of strange, outlandish tongues. They'd packed their traps when things were bad — that were in the Nineties. Iss, an' there weren't a corner o' the world they hadn't been to, 'ee knaw; Chile, Peru, the silver mines at Lima where old Dick Trevithick went, Kimberley, Jo'burg, the States — they'd been most everywheres there'd been a mine working. They came home soon's the bals began to open up again. Strange clo's they wore an' strange 'abits they had, but they hadn't forgot their native Cornish way o' speakin', no more'm 'ee have, boay.' He shook his head sadly. 'There was money about in them days, 'ee knaw. Not laike it is now. Why me father would tell me o' the days when there was nigh on fifty bals working in this part o' the country alone. Now there's only the one.' He took his pipe out of his mouth and spat. 'Navvies' work, that's what it is now. Mind 'ee, they was rough lads that came back in the old days. Whilst 'ee got 'eesel' eddicated.' He peered across at me. 'Thee's not looking for work, is 'ee boay?' I didn't say anything and he didn't seem to expect a reply.

'Thee wouldn't find much mining work in these parts now. Edn't I right, Garge?' he asked the landlord.

'Thas right, Bill.' The landlord turned to me. 'Thee'll hear people say that the bals in Cornwall is worked out,' he said. ''Taint so. But 'ee's got to go deep, deeper'n they'll go these days for all their modern equipment. Started some o' the mines up, the Government did during this last war. Thee can see one of'n in the cove down beyond Cape Cornwall. That was when Malay was took by the Japs. Spent a mint o' money they did in the valley there. But it were the same as it were with the adventurers. No sooner'n they were gettin' near the tin than they knacked 'er — found they could get tin from Bolivia or some sich place. When I was a boay, copper were 'bout all anybody thort on around here. An' when the copper was worked out, the mine closed down. But under the copper there's tin — and plenty of it. Thee can ask any of the boays who've worked deep. They'll tell 'ee the same. There's tin under the copper. I seen it meself. But it would cost a heap of money to get at it, for the mines is all full o' water now, full right up to the adits.'

52

'What about the eyebits?' I asked. 'There must be some rich patches left above water. Isn't anybody working them?'

'Ar, there's one or two little groups gettin' an uneasy living out of'n,' replied the landlord. 'But there edn't no future in it.'

'An' there's others wastin' their money fiddlin' about just below the adit level,' put in the old man. 'There's one of'n right here in Botallack. Got control of the old Wheal Garth, 'e 'as. Installed a pump and cleared to about the hundred an' twenty fathom level. Just wastin' 'is money, that's what 'e's doin'. Yet she's a rich mine, the old Wheal Garth. They knacked 'er after the adventurers had had a row — that was back in the depression, in '31 or mebbe 'twas '32. Some o' the adventurers got cold feet. Thort they were spendin' too much on development. They didn't knaw the difference atween prills and dradge most of 'em when the mine was workin' copper. All they knawed was the price copper fetched in the market and the amount of copper that was being brought to the surface. When it came to developing down through bad country for the tin what lay deeper — well, they knacked 'er an' near on two 'undred men were out o' work.'

But I wasn't listening any more. My eyes had been attracted by a headline in the paper that lay on the bar. It read: 'MYSTERY OF ABANDONED REVENUE CUTTER — Crew of four disappear.'

I glanced quickly round the bar. They were all intent upon their argument on the future of Cornish mining. Half fearful that my interest in the story would be noticed, I furtively pulled the paper towards me. The first line produced a sudden leaden sensation in my stomach and I read on, absorbed to the exclusion of all other sounds:

A revenue cutter, which had been sent out to intercept a vessel suspected of smuggling, was found abandoned this morning on a lonely stretch of beach near Marazion. No trace has so far been discovered of the four officials who formed the crew of the cutter and the Customs office at Penzance state that they have received no information regarding the missing men.

Percy Redcliff, a fisherman, of 4 Hillside, Marazion, discovered the vessel beached on the sand at 6 a.m. He immediately reported to the police. Police and Customs officials have examined the boat. They state that the wheelhouse and starboard side of the hull are damaged as though by a very heavy sea.

The cutter was seen by several ships during the previous afternoon. The last to sight her was a Naval corvette. The Captain of this vessel reported the cutter about five miles off Newlyn heading south at about six knots through calm seas. Inquiries are now being made concerning the *Isle of Mull*, a fifty-five ton ketch owned by Mr David Jones. It is believed that this vessel may have sighted the cutter later than the corvette. Until this vessel is located officials are unwilling to make any statement.

It is possible that the cutter came into collision with another vessel last night and was abandoned by her crew. Mr Redcliff, however, pointed out in an interview that when he found the cutter she was quite seaworthy. His opinion was that the crew would have had no justification in abandoning her. Further, he stated that the damage was not, in his opinion, the result of any collision.

The names of the missing men are Frank Riley . . .

I stopped reading then and looked up. Something said by one of the men in the bar had thrust itself into my mind. The landlord was speaking. 'Ar,' he said. 'Reckon 'e knaws summat.' And then I understood why my interest had been aroused. 'Who – Manack?' asked the old accordion player. 'He's just daft, that's all.'

'Ar, 'e's daft right enough,' put in one of the skittle players, 'Bin queer in the 'ead ever since his wife was killed, poor soul.'

'An' then there was that 'ooman who went mad down there,' put in another.

'Iss,' the landlord said to me, 'walked over the cliff, she did.'

54

'Tedn't a place I'd go near at night, anyway,' said the skittle player.

'Nor me,' agreed the old man with the accordion. 'I'd be scared o' seeing the death fetch o' one o' they women.' And he chuckled softly to himself.

'I don't care what 'ee say,' put in the landlord, 'I reckon 'ee knaws summat. One way and another 'ee's got control of the whole mine. Bought the other adventurers out for next to nothing, I'm thinking.'

'Then why was he one of the ones that wanted to knack her?' asked the skittle player.

The landlord shook his head. 'Dunno,' he said. 'Mebbe it was so as he could get control of the mine.'

In the short silence that followed I leaned across to the landlord and asked, 'Is it Captain Manack you're talking about?'

He gave me a quick glance. 'No. The old man. Captain Manack is his son. Why? Do you know'n?'

'Mebbe,' I said. 'Where's he live?'

And then I got the second surprise that evening, for the landlord turned to me and said, 'Just down the road, at Cripples' Ease.'

'Cripples' Ease,' I echoed.

He laughed. 'Yes,' he said. 'Queer sort o' name, eh? Used to be a pub. That was before my time when everybody round here worked at the Botallack. Then it came into Manack's possession and the licence was allowed to lapse.'

'When was that?' I asked.

'Oh, let me see. Just after the first war it would be. There was some tale that he got it from the woman who kept house for him, the same that went mad an' walked over the cliff. But then, 'cos 'e's reck'ned a bit daft, there's all sorts of stories about him. Can't believe 'alf o' what you're toald in a village laike this.' He grinned. 'Leastways, 'e's the one man that believes there's tin down in Wheal Garth and tryin' to get it. He and 'is son — though what 'is son knows about mining I don't know. They employs a couple o' men down there — furriners, they are, an' we don't see much o' them. Seems they're more like quarry men than miners. About all they do is cut granite slabs for kerb stones and things. Lorries come down from Bristol, sometimes Lunnon even, about once a week.' He shook his head. 'Old Manack'll never do no good with that mine, I'm thinking.'

'Whereabouts is Cripples' Ease?' I asked.

He looked at me sharply. 'Just down the road,' he said vaguely. 'Why?'

I hesitated. Then I said, 'I've come here to see Captain Manack.' I had the feeling he was eyeing me closely.

'Thee don't want to be going down to Cripples' Ease,' put in the old man with the accordion. 'Leastways not this time o' night. T'edn't a very friendly place.' He smiled, showing his gums. He did it without removing the clay pipe. 'It's the old man. Daft, that's what I say 'e is. 'E were all right until his wife had that assident.'

'What happened?' I asked.

'Fell down a mine shaft, she did, poor 'ooman,' he told me. ''Tain't difficult. The cliffs is littered with old shafts. They found her at the bottom. Her head was stove in and she had her dog layin' aside of 'er. They say as 'ow she went down after the dog. But there's others thinks different,' he added darkly.

'What was her name?' I asked.

'Er name? What was 'er name, Garge?' he asked the landlord.

'Harriet, if I remember rightly.'

'Ar, that were it — Harriet Manack. She was a widow woman from Penzance. They say it was she brought 'im 'is interest in Wheal Garth.'

'When did this happen?' I asked.

'It'd be nine or ten years ago,' he replied.

'Was he married before?'

The old man shook his head. 'Not to my recollection.' I felt relieved. I didn't want to go digging up the past.

I finished my beer. 'Which road do I take for Manack's place?' I asked the landlord.

'Turn right outside here,' he said. 'About fifty yards on, the road bends sharp right. That's where 'ee turns off to the left. Thee'll find a track. That'll take ee' down to Botallack. Cripples' Ease is by the mine workings. Thee'll not mistake it — 'edn't nothing else down there, 'cept ruins.'

Outside thick darkness shut in the village and thrust back the light that stole out through the open doorway of the inn. The wind had risen and the roar of it swallowed the sound of my footsteps on the roadway. A fork of lightning ripped open the under-belly of the clouds that hung above the coast. In the flash of it the drab stone of the cottages that edged the roadway stood out sharp and black, as in a woodcut. The thunder cracked, heavy and close, like a giant whip slashed across the heavens, and then died away in a grumbling murmur over the sea.

I found the track without difficulty. It ran west towards the sea and the great streaks of forked lightning were reflected in the tumbled waters. The roar of the waves beating against the cliffs grew louder as I walked on and soon the flickering light showed me the surf boiling at the foot of Kenidjack Castle. The thunder rolled round the heavens in an almost unbroken orchestra of sound. Tumbled, broken heaps that had once been mine buildings loomed up out of the night, the stone almost white in the dazzle of the lightning. A fine mist of sea spray drove against my face, salting my lips. Old engine houses stood like dilapidated keeps along the clifftop and, between them, were piled broken heaps of crushed stone, tier on tier, like terraces. It was a devil's mockery of the hanging gardens of Babylon where not even thistle and chickweed would grow.

Then, black against a flash of lightning, I saw a building that was whole and intact. It was a gaunt, ugly building standing four-square to the winds that roared across the top of the cliffs. It was there for an instant, outlined against luminous clouds and still more luminous sea. Then it was gone, swallowed up in the inky blackness that followed each flash. I saw the house next against a crackle of lightning far off along the horizon. It was nearer and seemed to crouch like some animal bunched to withstand the impact of the storm. Then suddenly a great flare of lightning split the sky right over my head. The jagged rent of crackling light sizzling in a single streak to stab the hills inland. The thunder was instantaneous. The clouds seemed to split with light and sound at one and the same time. And in that vivid flash I saw the windows of the building shine, cold and dead, like a blind man's eyes. The face of the house was black with a weather coating of pitch. Beside it was the remains of a garden, a poor broken thing of hydrangeas and foxgloves all choked with thistles. There were several little fruit trees, too – gaunt, wasted things whose branches flared away from the wind as though in mad flight for shelter.

With that splitting crash of thunder, the heavens seemed ripped open. The rain swept down in a solid, sodden curtain, driven in flurries by the wind, which now blew in heavy gusts. I ran, stumbling, to the door of the building and beat upon it. A flash of lightning showed me two lines of writing above the lintel. Several coats of more recent paint had flaked away to reveal the old lettering. In the next flash I was able to read it, 'James Nearne, licensed to sell wines, spirits and tobacco.'

Nearne. James Nearne. It was a strange coincidence. Nearne wasn't such a common name. Nor, for that matter, was Cripples' Ease. A gust of wind blew a chilling sheet of rain against me. I lifted the latch and threw myself against the door. It was locked. There was no knocker so I beat upon it with my fists. But the sound of my knocking must have been lost in the roar of the storm for nobody came. The water was pouring off the slates on to my neck in a steady stream. I flattened myself against the door, rattling at the latch. The rain was seeping through to my underclothes. I felt damp and chilled. In the incessant flicker of the lightning the rain showed like a dull tin-plate curtain. Violent gusts drove it across the broken mine workings and beat it into the sodden ground.

I turned the collar of my jacket up and splashed my way round the walls of the house. At the back a chink of light glimmered from a curtained window. I sloshed through more puddles and grasped the sill. The rain beat against the window, washing in solid water down the panes. Through the chink I looked in upon a small, low-ceilinged room lit by lamplight. The walls were of a brown, glossy paint and that had peeled away in places to show a gay powder-blue underneath, or had disintegrated so completely with age and neglect to reveal the mouldering white of old plaster. A cheerful fire blazed in a cheap Victorian grate.

It was not the room that attracted my attention but the man seated behind a big desk near the fire. He was broad in the shoulders and powerfully built. His head was small and rather square, the skin dark and lined with little wrinkles at the corners of his eyes, and he had a moustache. Above a rather high, lined forehead his short hair stood up almost straight. This and his high cheek bones gave him the appearance of a character from Grimm. He was talking to somebody I could not see and at the same time counting notes from a thick wad on the desk. At his elbow was a bottle and a glass full of some yellowish liquor. Beside the desk, against the wall, stood a big safe. The door of the safe was open.

Had I known who the other occupant of the room was I should not have tapped on that window. I should have stepped back into the deluging blackness and tried to find my way back to the inn. One glimpse of the other occupant of that room would have told me the sort of set-up I was getting mixed up with. That would have been enough for me. I'd have cleared out.

But I could only see the one man. I could see he was talking to someone. But I couldn't see who. And because I was wet through and cold and this was the place Dave had told me to come to, I tapped on the window. The man at the desk looked up. His eyes had narrowed and his head was cocked a little on one side. He had stopped talking and was staring straight at the window. I tapped again with the tips of my nails.

The effect was instantaneous. The man jumped to his feet,

swept the bundle of notes into the safe, whisked the bottle in as well and closed the door. He said something to the person I could not see, at the same time throwing the contents of his glass into the fire which blazed violently. Then he stepped across to the window and pulled back the curtain. Our faces were about a foot apart with the streaming glass of the window panes between us. His eyes were excited, almost wild-looking. 'Who are you? What do you want?' His voice was faint.

'I want to speak to Captain Manack,' I shouted back.

'I'm Captain Manack. What do you want?' he sounded suspicious.

'Dave Tanner sent me,' I said.

I saw him start. The man seemed strung up. Or was it that he had been drinking?

'Can you let me in?' I shouted. 'It's wet out here.'

He hesitated. I fished in the pocket of my jacket and produced Dave's lighter, holding it up for him to see. 'Dave told me to give you this,' I called.

He peered at it with a quick, bird-like glance. Then he nodded. 'Go round the back and I'll let you in,' he said and dropped the curtain.

After staring into that lamplit room, the sudden darkness was indescribably black. As I turned from the window a gust of rain lashed my face. It seemed to beat upon my bare body, so sodden had my clothes become. I shivered and stood still, for it was too dark for me to move. Then a blinding sheet of lightning showed me a line of outbuildings jutting from the house. As I made for them a door opened and Manack stood there with a lamp in his hand.

He shut the door behind me. I was in a stone-flagged scullery, and though it was cold, I felt the instant relief from the fury of the wind and rain outside. He held the lamp higher and peered at me. He was quite a short man. His size accentuated the breadth of his powerful shoulders. His eyes glittered in the uncertain light. 'You're not one of the crew of the *Isle of Mull* are you?' he said.

I shook my head.

'I thought not.' And then: 'Why did Dave send you? And how is it you know his real name?' His voice was sharp, almost a bark. It expressed nervousness and excitement, and the habit of command.

'He said you had a job for me,' I explained. 'I'm a miner. He said it was a mining job.'

'Oh,' He nodded as though that explained everything. 'You're from Italy. A deserter. Yes, he told me about you.' He said it quite matter-of-factly as though being a deserter were a profession. 'Just arrived, have you?'

'Yes,' I said. 'Got in yesterday.'

'Who brought you over — Mulligan?'

I nodded, too surprised to speak.

'Give me the lighter, will you,' he said. I handed it to him and then he said, 'Better come into my office. There's somebody there who can check your identity.' He smiled to himself and led the way through into a big stone-flagged kitchen where iron pots simmered on a glowing range. Copper glinted warmly from the walls and a collie sheep dog lay stretched before the fire. A girl looked up from her ironing as we entered. She was big and strong looking and her face was flushed with the heat of the fire. 'Kitty — there'll be one extra for dinner,' he told the girl. 'And he'll be staying the night, so get a room for him.'

She gave me a quick glance. It was intended to be casual, I'm certain of that. But when she saw me, her eyes widened and a puzzled expression crossed her face. She stared at me as she said in a low voice, 'There's only the attic room.'

'Well, get that fixed up for him,' Manack said.

Her gaze was still fixed on me. I felt embarrassed. I don't know why. Girls often stare at me. I suppose it's because I'm more than usually big. That seems to attract them. It had caused me a lot of trouble in Italy. But somehow this was different. It was as though she couldn't believe her eyes.

Almost reluctantly it seemed she turned to my companion. 'You know what your father said — I mean about the attic room not being used.'

'I don't care what he said,' Manack snapped. 'If it's the only room, use it.'

I was conscious of the girl's gaze as I followed Captain Manack out into a damp-chilled corridor. Our footsteps sounded loud on the stone floor. Manack set the lamp down on a table and opened a door. I followed him into the room I had looked into from the window.

And then I stopped. Standing by the fire, a drink in his hand, was Mulligan. Our eyes met at the same moment and he stiffened suddenly with his drink halfway to his lips and his mouth slightly open. Then his hand slid to his hip pocket. He held it there, his body tensed.

Manack went straight over to the desk. 'This the man you brought over from Italy?' he asked Mulligan.

'Yes.' Mulligan's eyes never left my face.

Without looking round Captain Manack sat down in his chair and began unscrewing the lighter. I remained standing by the door. Two thoughts were chasing themselves through my mind. The first was that I didn't want to be mixed up with anything that Mulligan was mixed up in. The second was that I wanted to get back the money he had stolen from me. Between the desire to beat it and the desire to get my money back, I stood like a dummy. 'This fellow's joining us,' Manack said. 'He's a miner.' He had the base of the lighter unscrewed now and was fishing inside it with a pin. Beside him lay a copy of the evening paper. It was folded so that the story of the abandoned revenue cutter was uppermost. I could read the headlines from where I stood. He extracted a screw of paper from the lighter and smoothed it out on the desk.

I suddenly decided that I didn't want anything to do with this set-up. Manack was mixed up with Dave and the death of the revenue men. And Mulligan was in his employ. Hadn't I seen him paying out money to the man? And Mulligan was a crook — a liquor-running French bastard. But, by God, before I left I'd have my money back. He wouldn't get away with that. With a hundred and fifty quid I'd be all right. I'd get myself a passage to Canada.

I glanced at Mulligan. He still had his hand on his hip pocket. But he was looking at Manack. His mind was on the note that Manack was reading. In two quick strides I had him. I caught him by the arms, twisting them back and at the same time lifting him clear off the ground. The hare-lip bared his blackened teeth in pain. 'Now Mulligan,' I said. 'Hand over that money you stole from me.'

I heard the scrape of Manack's chair as he rose. I backed away, still holding Mulligan off the ground and twisting his arms back so that he uttered a wild cry of pain. Then he kicked me — kicked me right in the crutch. The blinding pain of it bent me double. I heard Mulligan's body hit the floor. When I had eased myself sufficiently to look up, he had scrambled to his feet and was backing to the window, a little black Beretta in his hand.

'Put that gun up, Mulligan. What the hell's the matter with you two?' Manack's voice was sharp, authoritative. Then I doubled up with pain again, cursing Mulligan through gritted teeth. Hands gripped me by the shoulder and pushed me gently into the armchair by the fire. A hand at the back of my neck kept me bent right down. The pain gradually eased and I stopped cursing. I wanted to straighten up, but that hand held me down. It was very strong. 'Why did you go for Mulligan like that?' Manack's voice was soft, almost gentle. But the ring of command was still there.

I told him as I stared down through tear-dimmed eyes at the worn leather of the chair. The hand released my neck and I looked up. Mulligan was still standing by the window. He had put his gun away, but his eyes were watchful and angry. 'Is that correct?' Manack asked him.

Mulligan shifted uneasily at the peremptory query. 'How the

divil was I to know he was going to work for ye, Captain?' he said. His manner was half injured, half apologetic. 'I charge 'em fifty for the trip. But that doesna include putting 'em ashore. That's dangerous work, and I take what I can get for it. This man's a trouble maker.'

'We'll see about that,' replied Manack.

'I don't wish to make any trouble,' I said. The pain had eased and I stood up. 'Just give me the money and I'll go.'

'You don't have to go,' Manack said. Then to Mulligan: 'Give me that money.' Mulligan counted the amount out from a wad of treasury notes which he took from his pocket.

'I want to go,' I told Manack.

At that he swung round. 'Oh, so you want to go?' His eyes were grey and hard and his teeth showed in a smile beneath his moustache. He went over to the desk and counted out the notes. 'How much did you say?' he asked as he finished counting.

'One hundred and forty-five,' I told him.

He nodded. 'That's the lot then.' He put the notes into an envelope, stuck it down and then placed the envelope in the safe. 'There's your money,' he said to me as he closed the safe door. 'You can have it just as soon as you've finished the job you were sent here to do.'

'But —'

He stopped me. 'Listen, you,' he said, and his voice was harsh now. 'You're a deserter. What's more, you're implicated in the disappearance of four Customs officials.' He laid a significant stress on the word 'disappearance.' His accusation took my breath away. For a moment I was too surprised to speak. I just stood there and stared into his hard, smiling face. Then I found my voice. 'That's a damned lie,' I said. 'The first I knew about it was when I met Dave with a bullet wound in his arm.'

He laughed. It was a quick, barking sound. 'So you know all about it, eh? Well, you go to the police and see if they believe your story. The English police are rather conservative. There's no amnesty for deserters in this country and the police don't like them. I use 'em because it's convenient, not because I enjoy their company. You walk out of here and see what happens. How did you get into the country? You'll say Mulligan here, skipper of the *Arisaig*, brought you over. But did he?' he turned to Mulligan.

Mulligan grinned. 'Never set eyes on the man before in my life. Ah'm no in the habit of carrying desairters in the *Arisaig*.'

Manack turned back to me. He was smiling with his eyes, but not with his lips. 'Dave Tanner will go to Italy in the *Arisaig*. But before he goes he'll leave with me a written confession. The names of the crew will include yours, together with a description. You're too big a man to slip through a police net.' He suddenly smiled, and his smile was friendly. 'Sorry to have to show you that I'm quite ruthless, but it's best for you to know where you stand right away. The job is not a long one. When you've finished it you can go or stay as you please. The pay is good and will be added to the rest of your money. You'll collect the total when the job's done. Now, if you go back into the kitchen, the girl will show you where you feed and introduce you to the others.'

I hesitated. What the hell was I to do? There were two of them. They stood watching me. My limbs were stiff with the pain. I suddenly felt weak and humiliated. It was as though I had walked into a net carefully spread for me and it had tightened about me, so that I was helpless.

'Well?' Manack snapped.

'Okay,' I mumbled. I looked across at Mulligan. 'If I ever meet you again,' I said, 'watch out for yourself.'

'Okay,' he replied. '*Mais pour ça, je ne passerai pas des nuits blanches*.' And he laughed.

I turned then and left the room.

CHAPTER FOUR

The Room of the Past

I shut the door behind me and stood undecided for a moment in the passage. Manack was talking. But his voice came to me as an unintelligible drone through the thick oak. The passage was a pool of lamplight fading into dark shadows. The chill of it struck through me, reminding me of my wet clothes. I shivered. What the hell was I going to do now? I could, of course, walk right out of the house. There was nothing to stop me — nothing at all — except that I was a deserter. I felt bitter and angry and helpless. Manack was dangerous; far more dangerous than Mulligan. That talk about implicating me with the affair of the revenue cutter — he'd meant that. Those eyes of his and the wild look he'd had. That was nerves. He was the sort of man who lived on his nerves. He was like a man walking a tight-rope. That was it — a man walking a criminal tight-rope. That sort would take any risk.

Through the oak door I heard Mulligan's voice on a higher note. Then Manack's voice cut in, sharp and peremptory. I was shivering and my teeth chattered. I couldn't hear what they were saying. Irresolutely I set off down the passage to the kitchen. I'd feel better with dry clothes and some food inside me. The thought of food brought the juices up under my tongue. I hadn't eaten all day. Time enough when I'd eaten to decide what I was going to do.

When I opened the kitchen door the girl was still at her ironing. She looked up and smiled. It was a slow, friendly smile. I went over to the fire. The smell from the pots was good. 'What time do you feed?' I asked.

She glanced at the alarm clock on the mantelpiece. It was just after eight-thirty. 'About nine,' she said. 'We're late tonight. I'll show you your room afterwards. It's being got ready now. Have you any things?'

'No,' I said. I had got myself right in front of the fire and my clothes were beginning to steam.

'Well, I'm afraid you won't be able to borrow any pyjamas,' She was looking straight at me. 'You're a bit larger than any of the men in this house except Mr Manack, and he wears a nightshirt.' Then she noticed the steam rising from my clothes. 'You'd better get your clothes dried.' She stripped the blanket off the ironing board. 'Here you are,' she said, and tossed it over. 'Take them off and wrap that round you.' And when I hesitated, she said, 'Don't worry about me. I'm used to half-naked men around. Wheal Garth's a pretty wet mine.'

As I stripped off my things and hung them on the clothes horse, I saw her looking at me several times curiously. I felt flattered. It was good to have a girl around again. But then she said, 'There's something strangely familiar about you.'

'How do you mean?' I asked, wrapping the blanket round me and slipping out of my wet trousers.

'I don't know,' she answered, with a puzzled frown. 'Almost as though I'd seen you before.'

'Ever been out of England?' I asked.

She shook her head and smiled. 'Never been out of Cornwall,' she said.

'Then you can't have seen me before,' I told her, 'This is the first time I've been back in England since I was four.'

'Oh.' But the puzzled frown was still on her face. 'What's your name?' she asked.

'Jim,' I said. 'Jim Pr —' I just stopped myself in time. 'Jim O'Donnel. I'm a Canadian.'

She smiled. 'You're a deserter, aren't you?'

That startled me. I started to deny it. But I stopped and said, 'How did you know?'

'You have to be a deserter or a jailbird to get a job here.' There was a trace of bitterness in her voice, and she bent over her ironing.

'What's the racket?' I asked.

She looked up then, her face stony and sullen. 'Ask Captain Manack,' she said.

I didn't say anything then. I turned and let the glow of the fire warm my belly through the blanket. A chair was set beside me and two hands took hold of my shoulders and pressed me into it. Her hands were still touching me as I sat down and her face was close to mine. It was a nice face, flushed with the heat of the fire and the lips slightly parted to show the gleam of white, even teeth. The lips had no make-up on, but they were red. I suddenly wanted to kiss them. God, it was ages since I had had a woman.

I think she sensed my urge for she drew quickly back, but her eyes sparkled and I knew she wasn't angry. She was a big girl, but well proportioned with firm breasts that thrust at the cotton of her blouse, so that I could see the outline of her nipples.

I looked quickly down into the hot glow of the fire. I heard her go back to her ironing. 'You've got fine shoulders,' she said softly. 'You're not a miner, are you?'

'Yes,' I said.

'You said this was the first time you'd been back in England since you were four,' she said. 'What were you doing over here at the age of four?'

'Getting myself born,' I told her.

'Getting born? You mean you were born over here? Where?' There was a note of excitement in her voice.

'Redruth,' I said.

'Then you're Cornish?'

'I suppose so — by birth,' I added cautiously. 'My father was, anyway.'

'Your father was a Cornishman?' She seemed unusually interested. 'What about your mother?'

'She was Cornish too.'

'Is your mother still in Canada?'

'No,' I replied. And then for some reason I added. 'I don't know where she is. She ran off with somebody else. That's why we went to Canada.'

I suddenly realised that she had stopped ironing. I looked round quickly to find her leaning on the iron, staring at me with her eyes wide and that puzzled expression on her face. 'What's your name?' she asked.

'I told you,' I said. 'O'Donnel.'

'No, no,' she said impatiently. 'Your real name?'

At that moment the door opened and Manack came in. He glanced quickly from me to the girl and then back to me again. 'I see you've made yourself at home,' he said, and I thought there was a trace of sarcasm in his tone.

'I'm getting myself dried,' I explained.

'The men here have their own quarters,' he said.

'The stove's not lit in there,' the girl put in. 'They haven't come in yet, and it's not worth lighting it now. They'll go straight to bed if they're to get up at the time you want them in the morning.'

Manack nodded. 'Come into my office,' he said to me. 'Mulligan's gone. I want to talk to you about the job I want done. Don't bother to put any clothes on. If Kitty can put up with you half-undressed, no doubt I can.'

I followed him along the passage to his office. He shut the door. 'Better get near the fire,' he advised and poured me out a stiff drink. 'Take it you don't mind Italian cognac?'

'I'm pretty used to it,' I said.

His eyes watched me as I raised my glass and drank. They were steel grey and their movements were quick as though he found it a strain to look at anything for more than a few seconds. His hands were long and slender, and when his fingers weren't drumming on the arm of his chair or running through his thick, wiry hair, they hung loosely from the wrist. Sitting there with only a blanket and a pair of pants on I felt at a disadvantage. He knocked back his drink and poured himself another. 'Rotgut,' he said. 'Still, it's better than nothing. If that revenue cutter hadn't butted in we'd have been drinking French brandy or champagne. Damn 'em.' He filled my glass. The liquor was warming. 'What's your name?' The question came abruptly.

'O'Donnel,' I said. 'Jim O'Donnel.'

His eyes met mine with a glint of amusement. 'Irish, eh?' He smiled. 'Funny thing. You fellows always pick on Irish names. You seem to think it fits this sort of job. There's a boy working for me here now — O'Grady he calls himself. Cockney right through to his backside.' He shrugged his shoulders. 'What experience have you had of mining?'

'Pretty fair,' I told him. 'Started working underground in the Canadian Rockies when I was sixteen. I'm thirty-two now and, with the exception of four years in the army, I've been working in mines all the time — various goldmines in the Coolgardie district of Australia, a short spell in Malaya on tin, and finally in lignite mines in North Italy.'

'Know anything about blasting?'

'I ought to,' I said. 'You can't help knowing about it after twelve years of mining.'

He nodded as though satisfied by my reply. His fingers were drumming on the chair arm again. 'You understand the nature of the business we're engaged on?' It was more a statement than a question and he looked at me sharply.

I raised my glass. 'I guess so,' I said. 'Liquor running.'

He nodded and pulled a sheet of paper towards him across the desk.

'Suppose I tell you I don't want anything to do with it?' I said.

He swung round on me then. 'You've no alternative,' he barked. 'Get that clear right from the start. I wasn't joking when you were in here with Mulligan. You're here and you'll do the job I want doing before you leave.'

'That's not the way to get good work out of a man,' I told him. He didn't reply for a moment. He just sat there staring at me. Those eyes of his — they worried me. Most people, when you look them in the eye — you feel in touch with them, you can see their mood even if you can't see what they're thinking. But not with Manack. His eyes told me nothing. I've seen it in animals, particularly dogs. Often as not when you can't trust

70

a dog his eyes have a wild look, they shut you out — you can't see what he's feeling. That's the way Manack's eyes looked.

'Listen,' he said suddenly. 'You come here without a friend in the world. You're broke and the world's against you. Do this job and you get your hundred and forty-five quid back plus a further fifty. Not only that, but I'll fix you a passage anywhere you want to go.'

'And if I say No?'

He nodded to the phone on the desk. 'Then I'll ring the police.'

'Isn't that a bit risky for you?' I asked.

But it's no use trying to scare a man like Manack. 'I don't think so,' he said. 'I'm pretty well known around this end of Cornwall. I've made it my business to be. At worst I'd have to lay off a shipment or two. But you stand a chance of hanging with the evidence that would pile up against you.'

'You mean I'd be accused of having a hand in the revenue cutter business?' I felt a surge of anger at the injustice of it. But it was swamped by my sense of helplessness. What could I do about it? What the hell could I do?

He nodded his head slowly like a doctor agreeing with his patient's worst fears. 'Well, O'Donnel, what do you say?' I thought I detected a derisive emphasis on the name of O'Donnel.

I shrugged my shoulders. Damn it, why wasn't I dressed? Perhaps if I'd been dressed I'd have had the guts to call his bluff and walk out of the place. But one glance at his face told me it wasn't bluff. It wasn't that his features looked fierce or cruel, it was just that it was a tense, reckless face. The man would do what he said. 'How long will the job take?' I asked.

'Not being a miner I wouldn't know,' he replied. 'It might take a week, maybe two. My offer is twenty pounds a week and a fifty-pound bonus on completion of the job. And all free of income tax.' He smiled. It would have been a friendly, pleasant smile but for those eyes.

'Okay,' I said. My voice sounded hoarse. 'What's the job?'

'That's more like it,' he said, and seemed to relax. His gaze wandered to the bottle. 'Another drink?' I finished mine at a gulp and held out my glass. I needed that drink. 'That's another thing,' he said as he poured it out, 'there's no shortage of liquor in the place. But I only serve it out after dark. That's just so as nobody goes up to the village drunk.' He picked up the sheet of paper from his desk. 'Now then, what I want you to do is to blow a hole in the sea bed.'

'Blow a hole in the sea bed?' I stared at him in astonishment.

But he was quite serious. 'Yes,' he said. And then added after a moment's thought, 'No point in my not telling you why, since as soon as you see the layout you'll be able to figure it out for yourself. At the moment we bring the stuff in by boat to the main adit of Wheal Garth. The adit empties into a big cave and we've got a large, flat-bottomed barge in there. Well, that method is too dangerous. We've got coastguards' look-out as close as Cape Cornwall, which is the next headland but one to the south. Not only that, it means fine weather runs only. Sometimes our boats have to lie off for several days pretending to fish until the sea's calm enough for the operation to be carried out.'

He handed me the sheet of paper. 'There's a plan of Wheal Garth at the hundred and twenty fathom level — that's fifty feet below sea level. We've de-watered the mine down to this level which is the first of the undersea levels. Now then, see that long gallery running out under the sea?' He pointed it out to me on the plan — a finger of ink stretching almost straight out from the coast. Beside it was the name *Mermaid*. 'That gallery is half a mile long. I've had two men working on it for nearly a year — deserters, same as you. One of them is a stone mason, the other a quarry man. We've straightened it out, squared it off and built up a neat ledge along both sides. On these ledges a carriage drawn by a hawser can run — even when the gallery is full of sea water. No metal rails to rust, you see. What I want you to do is —'

He stopped then, for the door had opened. I looked round. An elderly man had entered. He was tall and blond with a short, pointed beard and small, round eyes that looked at me from beneath shaggy eyebrows. 'I didn't know you'd anybody here, Henry,' he said to Manack and made as though to go. His voice was soft and, but for the trace of a Cornish accent, I would have said he was a Norseman, so fine a figure did he make as he stood there with the firelight glowing on his rugged, bearded features.

'Just a minute, Father,' Manack said. 'This is Jim O'Donnel. He's going to work here for a bit. He's a miner.'

The old man's eyebrows lifted and there was a glitter of something like excitement in his eyes. 'A miner, is he?' He smiled. It was a nice smile, the sort of smile that seemed to warm the room. 'Well, my boy,' he said to me, 'it's good to know there'll be a miner working here at last. I've been trying to persuade my son to take on miners here ever since he came back. But there've always been − ah − difficulties,' he added vaguely. He turned to Manack. His eyes were shining. 'This is kind of you, Henry.' He shook his head sadly. 'Pity you didn't grow up to be a miner. You'd have understood the possibilities of Wheal Garth then. However, one's a help − a very definite help. At least we can make a start now.'

'O'Donnel is working for me.' Manack's voice was sharp. The old man's eyebrows went up again. It was a trick he had. He was all tricks, but I didn't know it then.

'Working for you?' he said. 'And what, may I ask, can you be wanting a miner for? You know nothing about mining. He must work for me. If he's a good miner, then I'll prove to the world that the Cornish mining industry isn't dead.'

'Well, you may as well know about it now as later,' Manack said. 'I'm letting the sea into the Mermaid gallery.'

'Letting the sea in!' The old man's beard shot up. 'You're mad. You can't do it. I won't allow it.'

'I'm afraid that's what I'm going to do.' Manack spoke flatly as though it were all settled.

The old man strode across to the desk. His eyes were wild

73

and he was quivering with anger. 'Do you realise that Wheal Garth belongs to me?'

'Yes, but I provide the money,' replied his son calmly. 'When I came back the mine was full of water right up to the adits. It's only because I've provided the money that you've got it clear of water to the hundred and twenty fathom level. And if there's going to be any more money I've got to let the sea into the Mermaid.'

'I tell you I won't allow it,' thundered the old man, crashing his fist down on the desk.

'You've no alternative,' was the reply. Manack turned to me. 'Leave us, will you?' he said. He had to repeat his request before I moved, so fascinated was I by the astonishing altercation.

As I left the room Manack senior was saying in a voice that quavered. 'For twenty years and more, Henry, I've lived and dreamed of nothing but this mine. I knew it was rich. I knew it. I thought it was only rich at depth. But I found the seam. I found it. I showed it to you the other day. My God, if you'd only gone into the mines as I wanted you to you'd understand what that seam is. There's a fortune in it.'

As I slowly closed the door I heard his son reply in a hard, almost sneering voice, 'Yes, but unfortunately not a tax-free one.'

I went back to the kitchen. The girl was serving food with a stocky little man at her elbow wisecracking in an accent that brought back memories of Kalgoorlie. He had a round cherubic face and the crown of his head was bald. He was like a diminutive monk with his pot belly and round, rosy cheeks. 'Blimey,' he said as he caught sight of me, 'the horiginal wild man from Borneo. Goin' for a swim, mate?' He grinned. It was the widest grin I'd seen in years. It seemed to split his chubby face open and it revealed two red lines of gums propped open by half a dozen decaying teeth. 'You stayin' or just passing through?' he asked.

'He's going to work here,' the girl said. She was half-laughing. 'He's a miner.'

'Thank Gawd!' he said. ''Bout ruddy fed up I am o' never bein' sure when the roof's goin' ter come in on us.'

'My name's O'Donnel,' I told him. 'Jim O'Donnel.'

'The devil it is. It's Oirish I am meself. Me name's O'Grady.' He held out his hand. 'It's grand tales we'll be afther telling each other, man, of those happy days back in Oireland.' The girl laughed. It was a pleasant sound.

'I thought you were Australian,' I said, 'by the way you were talking just now.'

'Australian! Gor' blimey, that's a good one, that is,' he said, falling back into his original accent. 'The nearest I ever got to Australia was coaling a P. and O. boat at Southampton. That was back in thirty-one when the only work I could get was stevedoring. Come on, mate,' he added, 'you'd better get some cloves on if you're goin' to 'ave grub wiv us. You can put 'em on in the men's dining hall.'

He picked up two dishes from the table. I got my clothes and followed him. The girl watched us silently. I stole a quick glance at her as I left the kitchen. She was watching us, a hint of laughter in her eyes. But as she met my gaze the laughter was over-shadowed by something else, and she frowned as though she were still puzzled about something.

We went through the cold scullery and through some old stables. The floor was cobbled here, and there were stalls for horses and curved iron mangers. 'You been here long, O'Grady?' I asked.

'Better call me Friar,' he said. 'Everybody does. O'Grady's sort of a nom de gare — same as your moniker is. You ain't no more Irish than wot I am. Yes, I bin 'ere aba't a year nah. Gettin' quite like 'ome.' He pushed open a door and led the way into a small, bare room with canvas chairs set round a plain, scrubbed table. It was lit by a single oil lamp. An anthracite stove in the corner looked dead and cold, but an oil stove speckled the ceiling with its round ventilation holes. The walls were thinner here and they shook under the full force of the wind. The rain beat against the single curtained window. In one of the canvas chairs a long, cadaverous-featured man sat playing with

75

a knife. His hands were rough and grey as though ingrained with dust. He inspected me slowly out of dark eyes. 'New bloke,' said Friar by way of introduction. 'A miner. Says 'is name's Jim O'Donnel. This 'ere's Slim Matthews.'

Slim Matthews nodded. 'What's the grub?' he asked Friar. He had a bitter, discontented voice.

'Stoo and two veg.' Friar dumped the dishes on the table. 'There y'are, mate.'

I got close to the stove and slipped into my clothes. The two of them began to feed silently. 'Who's the girl in the kitchen?' I asked.

Friar looked up, his mouth full of food. 'Kitty Trevorn,' he said. 'She's the daughter of old man Manack's second wife by her first marriage.'

'He means she's the old man's stepdaughter,' Slim explained.

'That's wot I bin tellin' 'im, ain't it?' Friar answered heatedly. 'Just because yer bin to a Public School. That's a larf nah, ain't it? Slim was at 'Arrer. An' wot's 'e do? Finishes up a ruddy stone mason. If that's all eddication can do for a man, reck'n I'm just as well orf without it.'

Slim Matthews said nothing. He just sat slumped in his chair concentrating on his food and looking down his long nose. He reminded me of some unhappy cur kicked around in the dust of an Arab village street. 'Then you're the quarry man?' I said to Friar to change the subject.

'That's right,' he replied. 'An' there ain't many blokes can swing a biddle like I can. But I'm aba't bra'ned off wiv working da'n there under the sea. It ain't nat'ral, that's wot I say. It ain't the way a man's supposed to work. Fair gives a bloke the creeps. An' wet as a latrine. The Capting says there's thirty feet of rock between us and the sea. But it don't feel like that, I tell yer. The water streams da'n the walls an' most of the time we works wiv the water swurling ra'nd our ankles. Still —' He sighed and scooped up another mouthful of stew in his spoon. 'Mustn't grumble, I s'pose. The pay's good an' nobody don't ask no questions. An' the grub's all right too. They got their own farm.'

That stew seemed about the best food I'd ever tasted. I helped myself to more and asked what the idea was in letting the sea into the Mermaid gallery. He looked at me narrowly out of his small, bright eyes. 'Well, if the Capting ain't told yer, mate, mebbe I'd better keep me ma'f shut. But you mark my words, it's a ruddy good idea he's got. But then 'e's clever as a monkey. Kitty said you come from Italy. Was that where you met the Capting?'

'No,' I said. 'A friend of mine sent me to him.'

'Oh.' He removed a bit of meat from a back tooth with his nail. 'Wonder yer didn't hear of 'im a't there though. Seems 'e was quite a lad. Mulligan — do you know Mulligan?'

'Yes,' I said. 'I come over with him in the *Arisaig*.'

'Well, Mulligan told me 'e was one of the most reckless officers in the 'ole of the Eighth Army.'

'How the hell would Mulligan know?' I said.

He shrugged his shoulders, 'I dunno. Mulligan ain't been anywhere near any fightin'. I know that. Razor slashing, that's the nearest 'e ever bin to any fighting. I 'spect 'e was talkin' of wot 'e 'eard. The Capting was up in the mountains most of the time organising the partisans. Seems 'e was always getting behind Jerry's lines. Looting, I wouldn't wonder. Mulligan says 'e's got a mint of money locked up in Italy.'

'Then why didn't he stay out there?' I suggested.

'Cor luv ol' iron, you're as full of ruddy questions as a sieve is 'oles,' he answered, grinning. ''Ow should I know? If it comes to that, why did you leave Italy? Reck'n it got too 'ot to 'old ye. Same wiv the Capting. Or mebbe 'e thort Wheal Garth an excitin' toy to play wiv. Always after excitement, that's the Capting. Lives on 'is nerves and liquor. If 'e wasn't doin' something wrong, 'e'd die of boredom. It's 'is sort wot war was made for, not the likes of you and me. A soldier of fortune — blimey, if 'e'd lived in the ol' days 'e'd bin a ruddy general.'

'What about the old man?' I asked. 'How does he react to havin' his mine opened up for liquor running? He got pretty mad at his son this evening when he told him he was going to let the sea into the Mermaid gallery.'

'Oh, you don't want ter take no notice of the old man,' Friar answered. 'He's ab't as daft as a coot. Only 'e doesn't look daft. Reck'n 'e oughter be shut up in the loony-bin. Spends all 'is time da'n in the mine, jabberin' away to 'isself. An' yet 'e's a fine-looking ol' cove. Bet 'e played 'avoc wiv the ladies when 'e was a young man. 'E's bin married twice, yer know. The Capting's 'is son by 'is first wife.'

'An' the girl's his daughter by the second?'

'No. She ain't nuffink to do wiv 'im, as yer might say. She's 'is stepdaughter. I told yer that afore. 'Is second wife was 'er muvver. Then there was some sort of 'ousekeeper 'e 'ad 'ere. She went and walked over Botallack 'ead. There's some wot say as 'ow she did it because 'e didn't love 'er any more. An' there's others wot say she was driven to it by her conscience — there's a story that she killed 'is second wife — that's Kitty's muvver — on account of 'er 'aving stolen the ol' man's haffections. I dunno wot truth there is in it. Usually there ain't no smoke wivout there 'aving bin a bit o' fire. But don't go talking to Kitty aba't it. The poor kid's muvver was fa'nd at the bottom o' one of the shafts up the 'ead. Anyway, 'e certainly knocked 'em da'n the ol' Kent Road. But now 'e's reckoned to be a bit daft. Yer see 'e ain't interested in nothing but the one thing — Wheal Garth. 'E's got a bee in 'is bonnet that this is the mine wot'll put the Cornish mining industry on its feet again. Terrible ra's 'im an' the Capting 'as. They were at it only last night. You wouldn't fink by the way they carry on that they was father and son.'

'What's it about?' I asked.

'The mine. Always the ruddy mine.' Friar had finished his stew and sat picking his teeth with a matchstick. 'W'en I come 'ere first — it was all on account o' my being the Capting's batman when 'e was in England. Cor, the larks 'e used to get up to! I remember when 'e started an illicit still. 'E was making gin in one o' the baths in the officers' mess with yeast and juniper berries an' I don't know wot else. The Colonel was a teetotal — that didn't hexactly 'elp when 'e got to know aba't it. Reck'n that's wot got the Capting sent overseas so quick. Not that 'e cared. Anyway, when I comes 'ere first, the mine was all flooded up to the sea level, ol' man Manack was broke an' the 'ouse was a shambles. Well, the Capting gets in touch wiv me and we start blasting a't the main adit till it's wide enuff ter take our barge, and then 'e starts runnin' cargoes. An' as soon as there's some brass comin' in, there's the ol' man wantin' the Capting to open up the mine. "Not bloody likely," 'e says. I 'eard 'im say it meself. Couldn't 'elp it seein' 'as 'ow 'e shouted it at the top of 'is voice da'n in the adit there. Ain't no respecter of persons, the Capting — not even 'is own father.'

'Suppose you stop talking for a moment and get O'Donnel a drink,' Slim Matthews suggested.

'If ye're gettin' firsty why don't yer git it yourself?'

'Oh, all right.' Slim uncoiled his long body from his chair and went out. Friar got up and switched on the radio in the corner. 'See wot was I talkin' aba't?' he said, sitting down beside me again. 'Oh, I remember — the Capting an' the ol' man. Well, a'ter a few runs, the Capting 'as 'is bright idea, see. So 'e gets a pump installed an' starts de-watering the mine da'n aba't fifty foot below sea level.' The radio came on with an announcer reading the news. 'The ol' man's all for goin' deeper. But the Capting 'as 'is own ideas. That's when the ra's begin. Well, one day las' week the ol' man, whose bin ferreting ara'nd da'n in the Mermaid, 'e comes rushin' along the gallery all wide-eyed an' shoutin' blue murder fer the Capting. An' there's 'ell ter pay. The ol' gent's yellin' an screamin' an' the Capting sharp and cool like. I thought the ol' man was goin' right off his —' He suddenly stopped. The announcer's voice had mentioned a name that brought me up with a jolt. The *Isle of Mull*.

'*— out all day searching for the missing ship. The police are also making inquiries about David Jones, captain and owner* *of the Isle of Mull. So far no report has been received of any ship having sighted the Isle of Mull after the time at which it is believed the revenue cutter may have intercepted her.*

Penzance police and Customs officials have reason to believe that the Isle of Mull was engaged in running cargoes of wines and spirits into the country. The revenue cutter was sent out on Wednesday to intercept the Isle of Mull. Since then no trace of the crew of four has been found, though the cutter itself was discovered abandoned on a lonely stretch of beach not far from Penzance this morning. Scotland Yard admitted, in an interview, that considerable quantities of liquor were being smuggled into this country and they have reason to believe that it may be coming in through Cornwall and other areas of the south-west.'

'Cor, chase me up a gum tree!' muttered Friar.

'Is the *Isle of Mull* one of Captain Manack's ships?' I asked, more to see what he'd say than anything else.

He glanced at me sharply. His face, drained of all blood, looked grey and his fat little cheeks seemed to have fallen. He no longer looked genial. There was a mean look in his eyes as though he were scared.

He didn't say anything and when Slim came back with a bottle of cognac, he sat drinking in silence. 'What's upset our chum?' Slim asked me. When I told him about the *Isle of Mull* he smiled sardonically. But he didn't say anything. He seemed withdrawn into his own thoughts. Shortly afterwards Friar and Slim went out. They took the bottle with them.

Left to myself I realised I was very tired. I got up and went through into the kitchen. An old women was sitting by the fire. I asked her to show me my room. She led the way out into the corridor. At the foot of the stairs she stopped and stood aside. 'The master,' she whispered. The old man was coming down the stairs, a lamp in his hand. It shone on his beard and his eyes glittered in his ruddy face.

'Ah, O'Donnel,' he said. 'Just the man I wanted to see. Come into my study a minute, will you?'

I hesitated. He went straight on along the corridor, oblivious of my hesitation. I followed him. He was waiting for me at a door at the end of the passage. With a strangely old-world courtesy, he stood aside to let me go in. I found myself in a small and incredibly untidy room, furnished largely in mahogany. There were microscopes and scales and other laboratory equipment all mixed up with a litter of books, papers and drawings.

He sat down in a worn leather-covered horse-hair chair by the fire. 'I've something I want to show you,' he said. He had a mysterious air and the gleam of his eyes was even more noticeable, so that I thought he had been drinking. He went over to a cupboard and brought out a chunk of dull-grey rock. 'My son tells me you're an experienced tinner, my boy,' he said, coming towards me with the lump of rock in his hand. 'Tell me what you think of this.' He placed the rock in my hand.

It was about the size of a man's head and incredibly heavy. I saw at once that it wasn't rock at all. It was ore. Practically solid ore. 'Well?' he asked, and there was excitement and impatience in his voice.

'It's tin,' I said. 'From a mother lode. By the look of it.'

He nodded and smiled a secretive little smile that crinkled the corners of his mouth where his beard was grey. 'Yes,' he said. 'Mother tin. And what would you say if I told you there was a seam of it in Wheal Garth extending from the hundred and twenty level straight down to the sixteen hundred level?'

'I'd say you were a very rich man,' I said.

'Yes.' He nodded his head several times murmuring, 'Yes' each time. 'I'm a rich man. I'm a very rich man.' He took the lump of ore and held it in his hands as though it was his very heart he held beating there against his roughened palms. 'I'm fabulously rich. I've hit a scovan lode, a mother lode — about the richest in the history of Cornish mining.' Then he suddenly jerked his body erect and flung the lump of ore crashing to the floorboards. 'And my son — damn his eyes — my son doesn't see it; he can't understand.'

He put both his hands up to his head and beat his skull with his clenched fists. 'How can I make him see it?' he asked, swinging suddenly round on me. 'Listen, my boy — all my life I've worked for this. For nearly thirty years nothing else mattered. I worked in Wheal Garth when I was a boy. I saw that ore. I saw it with my own eyes. And no one else saw it. They all missed it. I became a shareholder. I got more shares. They closed the mine. I bought 'em out. Wheal Garth belongs to me. All that tin! And now my son doesn't understand. He's going to let the sea into the Mermaid. And he's got you here to do it. You're the man who's going to wreck my whole life.'

He suddenly took me by the shoulders. His face was so near to mine that his beard touched my chin. 'You can't do it. Do you understand? You mustn't do it, I'll — I'll —' He took his hands quickly from my shoulders. He was trembling all over. He picked up the ore, and fondled it as though it were a child.

I felt sorry for him. I could understand his rage and frustration. Suppose I had struck lucky out there in the Coolgardie and then been unable to get capital to develop. But he could get capital surely. He could float a company. Anybody would back a mine that yielded tin like that. I suggested this, but he rounded on me. 'No,' he cried. 'No, never. Wheal Garth belongs to me. I'll develop it myself or I'll leave it to rot down there under the sea.'

Perhaps he wasn't sure of himself? 'Are you sure it goes right down?' I asked.

'No,' he said. 'Of course I'm not sure. How can any one be sure in mining? All I know is that I saw this lode when I was a boy down at the sixteen level. And only a week ago I found a similar lode at a hundred and twenty fathoms. That proves nothing. But here, look at this.' He threw the lump of ore on to a chair and seized hold of a big diagram. 'When they opened up the Botallack mine they found as many as ten floors of tin, each floor separated by floors of country little more than three foot thick. They were horizontal, beginning with the Bunny. Now, then, look at this. It's a geological map.' He spread the diagram out on the arm of my chair. 'There's Botallack. There's Wheal Garth almost next door. And Come Lucky. See how the strata goes along the coast. It's horizontal. But look at it out here under the sea. It suddenly folds up — from being horizontal it dips at an angle of nearly fifty degrees. When I first met that lode at the sixteen level I was in a gallery that ran a mile out under the sea. The Mermaid is only half a mile out. I can't be sure — but it seems reasonable to suppose that the lode in the Mermaid is the upper end of the lode at the sixteen level.'

'This diagram's accurate, I suppose?' I said.

He nodded. 'It was the result of information pooled by the mine captains of Botallack, Wheal Garth and Come Lucky in 1910 — that's when all three mines were working and making money.' He sighed and rolled up the diagram. 'I'm glad you understand. I've nobody to discuss it with here. If only you were my son.' He fell to pacing the room, combing his beard with his fingers. 'I must stop him letting the sea into the Mermaid. If he does that it will cost so much more to work that lode.' He suddenly turned to me. 'I suppose he has some sort of hold on you. He has on most men who come here. But you could leave this country, couldn't you? How much would you take to leave the country? I'll let you have fifty pounds more than he's going to give you. How much will you take?' His voice was eager. It was incredible how childish was his trust.

I said, 'He would only get another miner.'

'No,' he said. 'No, it's not so easy as that. He's been wanting one for a year, but he couldn't find anyone — er — suitable. And soon he'll get bored with this business of running liquor. It's excitement, not money he likes. Then he'll go away and leave me in peace to develop the Mermaid. Look — I'll give you fifty pounds more than he's giving you and then, when I start work, you shall come back and I'll make you bal captain. We'll start in a small way at first, and we'll gradually build up. The lode will pay for development as we go. We'll start from nothing and build the greatest mine in Cornish history.' His eyes had a far-away look. He was in a dream world of his own. This, I thought, was the real Cornish adventurer — the men my father had talked about, who'd start from small beginnings and build and build and build. Almost he fired my imagination — I who had seen the great mines of the Rockies and Malaya.

'Well,' he asked. 'What do you say, boay?' The Cornish accent had become more pronounced in his excitement.

I said, 'I'll let you know tomorrow, sir.' I was thinking that this was my way out. With money in my pocket I could surely be out of the country before Manack could get the police on my track. I didn't trust Captain Manack. I didn't trust the set-up. The police were on the track of this racket. It would only be a question of time before they raided the place. 'Could you give me cash?' I asked.

He nodded. 'I have a little money put by. How much?'

'He owes me a hundred and forty-five of my own which Mulligan stole from me. And for the work he offered me twenty quid a week and a fifty pound bonus when I'd completed the job. Call it two-fifty.'

'Very well.' He held out his hand. 'That's kind of you, my boy. And I shall not forget. Let me know where you go finally. When I start developing, then I'll let you know, and if you want the job you can come over. That's a promise.'

I left him then. He was standing by the fire, the lump of ore in his hands, and his fine bearded head bent in thought. It was as though all his existence were in that great lump of tin. I remembered the fierce light in his eyes as he told me how he had worked to gain control of the mine. He was a terrible and pathetic figure.

I went along the cold, damp corridor to the kitchen. The girl was there, sitting by the fire, her chin resting on her hands. Her bare arms were red with the glow of the fire. She looked up, startled, as I entered. The old woman was making porridge. The girl stared at me for a second, her lips parted. Then she got to her feet and hurried out into the scullery as though intent on some household task. I called out to her. She stopped, looking at me nervously as though held there by something about me that fascinated her.

'Will you show me to my room, please?' I said.

'No.' Her voice sounded abrupt and harsh. Then, as though to cover her abruptness, she added, 'I — I must see about the milk. It may turn sour in this storm.' She turned to the old woman, who had stopped stirring the porridge. 'Mrs Brynd, show Mr O'Donnel to the — attic-room.' That slight hesitation — I don't know why, but it worried me.

The old woman's face wrinkled up in a leathery smile. 'Do it yourself,' she said. Then she glanced up at me and I saw a flicker of some expression in her eyes. I can't describe it. All I know is that it was hostile.

The girl hesitated. I couldn't see it, but I knew she was trembling — like a horse that is afraid to take a jump. 'All right,' she said, heavily. 'I'll show you.' She picked up the lamp and led the way out into the corridor, leaving the old woman stirring her porridge.

She mounted the stairs slowly, almost reluctantly. The lamplight threw her shadow grotesquely on the walls of the old staircase. The wind beat against the window at the top of the stairs. We went down a narrow landing with peeling walls and then up a narrow, uncarpeted staircase. There was a door at the top with a queer little hatch cut in it. She hesitated, half turned and looked down at me as though to say something. She raised the lamp slightly. It seemed to me that she raised it in order to see me better. Then she turned quickly and opened the door.

The room was bare and close under the roof. The rain beat on the stone tiles above our heads and the wind howled in the chimney. The dormer window was uncurtained. It was fitted with stout iron bars. She lit a candle on the wash-stand. 'I'll leave you now,' she said. But halfway to the door, she stopped. Again I was aware that she was trembling. She seemed to be trying to say something. Her eyes looked frightened and unhappy in the hot light of the lamp. Suddenly it burst from her, startling and abrupt. 'Your name's Pryce — Jim Pryce. Isn't it?'

The way she said it: I can't describe how it jarred on me. It wasn't only that her voice was brittle and harsh. It had fear and hatred and — oh, it was just horrible.

'Your father's name is Robert Pryce?'

I nodded.

'Is he — alive?' she asked.

'No,' I said.

She seemed to shiver. Then she turned quickly and without shutting the door behind her ran down the steep staircase. I heard her footsteps hurrying away into the silent depths of the house as though she feared to look over her shoulder.

I went slowly to bed, wondering how she knew my name. For a time the peculiar behaviour of the girl excluded every other thought from my mind. But then I began to notice the room. I don't know what there was about the room. I know now of course. But I didn't then. It was such a bare, miserable little place. And there were the iron bars across the window and that strange little hatch in the door. It was somehow the way I imagine a prison cell looks.

I lay in bed and, tired though I was, it was some time before I put the candle out. Even then I could not sleep. I lay there in the dark, listening to the sounds of the storm and thinking over the strange events of the day. Sometimes the wind would be no more than a whimper in the eaves. Then it would come roaring against the house, beating at the walls till they shook to their foundations. It would come like a wall of water flung at the tiny barred window. It would ramp and whine and the rain would beat at the glass like a shower of gravel. Then it would die away to a whimper again so that I could hear the solid sound of the breakers thundering against the granite cliffs. And every now and then a flicker of distant lightning would show me the room, and in the sudden darkness that followed, I'd hear the grumble of the thunder away towards the Scillies.

I must have gone to sleep at last. Perhaps I had only just dozed off. Perhaps I had been asleep for hours. I don't know. All I know is that I was suddenly wide awake and instantly conscious of the room. God, how that room wanted to talk to me! I was trembling and sweating. Then in a flicker of lightning I saw the door opening. It was the click of the latch that had awakened me. My body tensed, expecting God knows what. 'Who's that?' I asked. My voice sounded hoarse and unnatural.

'It's me,' a voice whispered back.

A match flared in the dark and was instantly extinguished as a gust of wind crashed against the window. Another match was struck and a candle flame wavered uncertainly.

It was Kitty. She stood there for an instant, the candle trembling in her hand. She had a dark dressing-gown over her nightie and her feet were bare. Her eyes had a wild look and she clutched an envelope to her breast. She didn't say anything. She just stood there looking down at me. It was as though she didn't trust herself to speak.

I sat up leaning on one elbow. 'Why have you come?' I asked.

She found her voice then, but it was strange and husky. 'Because I promised,' was what she said.

'Because you promised? Promised who?' I asked.

'Your mother.' Her voice sounded small and sad in that strange room. 'I didn't want to,' she added quickly. 'But — I'd promised.' She moved forward. It was a timid movement. 'There,' she said. 'Take it.' She thrust the envelope into my hand. Then with sudden relief in her voice: 'I've done what I said I would. I'll go now.' She turned towards the door.

But I caught her dressing-gown. 'Don't go,' I said. 'What was my mother doing here? You knew her. What happened?'

'No.' Her voice trembled. 'Don't ask me anything. Let me go — please. You have the letter now. That's all I promised to do. Let me go, I tell you.' Her voice was frightened now. She struggled, but I had her by the wrist. 'Sit down,' I said. I was determined not to let her go. There were so many questions

I needed answered. 'How did you know who I was?'

'It — it was the way you held your head when you asked a question. That and your eyes. You've got her eyes.'

'You knew her then?'

She nodded. 'Now let me go.' Her voice trembled again.

'No,' I said. 'What was my mother doing here?' She suddenly fought to free her wrist from my grasp.

'What was my mother doing here?' I repeated, and she cried out at the pressure of my hand on her wrist. For a moment she fought to free herself then suddenly she relaxed and sat limply down on the edge of the bed. I felt her trembling all over. She was all wrought up. The candle was spilling hot grease on to her fingers. She reached out and set it down on the table by the bed.

'Now,' I said, 'will you please tell me what my mother was doing here?'

She gave a sob. I looked up at her. She was staring at the little hatch cut in the door. She wasn't crying — she was fighting for breath. I waited. At last she said in a strangled voice, 'She was — she was Mr Manack's housekeeper.'

The housekeeper. In a flash Friar's words came back to me — and the words of the landlord up at the inn at Botallack. And the name of the licensee above the door at Cripples' Ease. I looked down at the envelope in my hand. It was addressed to 'Robert Pryce, or his son, Jim Pryce.' The ink was faded and the writing shaky as though it had been written by someone very old — or someone labouring under great emotion. 'When did she give you this?' I asked.

'A long time ago.' Her voice was little more than a whisper. 'Before the war. Nine years ago it must be. It was just before —' She hesitated. 'Just before her death,' she whispered.

'How did she die?' I asked.

I felt her body stiffen. She did not answer.

I gripped her wrist angrily. 'How did she die?' I repeated.

'She — she went over the cliffs.' Her voice was flat. She spoke like a person in a trance.

I felt suddenly as though all the breath had been knocked out of me. And yet this wasn't half the horror of it. 'Why?' I asked.

She looked down at me then. Her eyes were wide and staring. So might Macbeth have looked on Banquo's ghost. All sorts of terrible thoughts ran through my mind.

'Why?' I cried out. 'Why did she do it?'

'Read the letter,' she said. She was panting for breath. 'Read the letter. Then let me go. I came to give you the letter. That was all. That was what I had to do. Don't you understand? I don't want to answer your questions. I don't want to think about it.'

'How long before her death did she give you this letter?' I asked.

'I don't know. I can't remember. An hour — maybe two or three. I don't remember.'

'My God!' I breathed. 'Then it *was* suicide?'

She nodded slowly.

I ripped open the envelope then. Inside was a single sheet of the same spidery writing. It trembled in my hand as I leaned forward to read it in the dim flicker of the candle. It was headed: 'In my room — 29th October, 1939.' In my room! Not Cripples' Ease, Botallack, Cornwall. Just 'in my room.' As though that were all her world.

Kitty leaned forward and picked up the candle, holding it over the letter for me. It guttered in the draught from the window and the grease spilled across her fingers and dripped on to the bedclothes. I had let go of her wrist and it was only afterwards that I realised that she could have left the room then. Why she didn't, I don't quite know. Curiosity perhaps. The letter had been in her possession all those years. But I'd rather say it was her sympathy — her sense of my need of her company as I read the last thoughts of a woman going out to kill herself on the rocks of Botallack Head, a woman who had once gone through the labour of bringing me into the world.

I have the letter on the desk beside me as I write. That, and the old, faded photograph and a brooch she gave to Kitty —

they're all I possess of my mother. I'll not attempt to describe my feelings as I read that letter. Here it is — read it and judge for yourself how I felt:

MY DARLING BOB,

Yes, you are still that. All these years the memory of you has been like a light shining in the darkness of my life. Pray God you found happiness. I found none. The thought of you and Jim and all the kindness and the love I left — it has been very bitter. They say I am not responsible for my actions now. But please believe me, Bob — at this moment my mind is very clear. I love you, and I have never loved anyone else.

They have shut me away in this room. The windows are barred. It is more than a year I think since I walked on the headland. I cannot even see my little garden from here. But today — today he has forgotten to lock the door. My mind is made up. I am going up to the headland for the last time. I shall give this letter to Kitty, together with the little brooch you bought me in Penzance that day we went over to the Mount by boat. It is all that I have left of you. Poor child. I grew very fond of her. But she is afraid of me now since her mother died.

Tell Jim I love him. He will not remember his mother, but tell him she never forgot him. Oh, Bob, I have paid dearly for my folly. Please, please do not think too hardly of me. I am going now. If this letter ever reaches you, do not fret at my passing. All I ask of you is that you will remember only that I love you both.

Your unhappy,

Ruth.

I sat for a long time staring down at the faded writing whilst the candle guttered in Kitty's hand. So much was hinted at. So much was left unanswered. I felt dazed and there was a lump in my throat. At last I looked up and in a flicker of lightning saw the bars of the window etched black against the storm. 'This was my mother's room, wasn't it?'

She nodded.

I looked down at the letter again. I must have sat staring at it for quite a time. I came out of my daze to find the girl tugging to pull her wrist free of my hand. She was shivering violently. The palm of my hand was moist on her flesh, and my body was bathed in a cold sweat. 'I must go,' she whispered frantically.

'No,' I said. And then I added quickly, 'I can't sleep here. Not in my mother's room.'

'You must,' she said. 'It'd look queer if you didn't.'

'I can't.' The way I said it sounded like a groan. I was afraid she'd go away and leave me. I didn't want to be left alone. 'She was fond of you, wasn't she?' I said.

'I don't know,' she replied. 'I thought so. But I was frightened. She looked at me so queerly sometimes. But she was kind to me — before.'

'Before what?' I asked.

She hesitated. Then she said, 'Before my mother was killed.'

I thrust the letter at her. 'Read it,' I said.

'No,' she answered quickly. 'No, I don't want to.'

'Read it,' I repeated.

But she stood up, wrenching at her arm. 'No,' she said. Her breasts were heaving in agitation. How perverse are a man's reactions. In that moment of all moments my mind could wander to admiration of her breasts as she stooped to free her wrist from my grip. The candle fell to the floor, flared for an instant and then extinguished itself. In the darkness I heard the skin of her bare feet on the floorboards. Then the door opened and closed and I was left alone in the darkness of that room. A flicker of far-off lightning showed me the sloping ceiling and the washstand like a lone sentinel against the crude flower pattern of the wallpaper. The bars of the window leapt into sight with the lightning. Then darkness again and I lay there, cold and numb, with my mother's letter in my hand.

CHAPTER FIVE

The Mermaid Gallery

When I woke it was light. I got out of bed and went over to the window. A grey mist was swirling up from the sea, blotting out everything but the tumbled ruin of the mine buildings that stood like wraiths amid the debris of the mine. It was on this scene of desolation that my mother had looked for a whole year. The bars and the mist — no wonder she had been driven to suicide. I shuddered and, turning to get my clothes, saw her letter crumpled among the blankets of the bed. I picked it up and hurried into my clothes. I wanted to get out of that room. I wanted to get away from Cripples' Ease. And yet there were so many questions to be answered. Why had she been shut away up here? *They say I am not responsible for my actions now.* Was she really mad? It was a horrible thought — as horrible as the girl's dread of saying anything. What was it that Friar had said? My mind shied from the thought of it and I went down the bare staircase into the silent house.

It was a quarter past eight by the grandfather clock in the hall. The girl was not in the kitchen. The old woman looked up at me curiously over a plate of porridge. I went through the scullery and the stables to the men's quarters. The room was empty and cold. I looked through the door beyond. It contained two Army pattern iron beds. The bed clothes were flung back. There was nobody there. I went out into the yard. The mist blanketed everything, deadening the sound of my boots on the cobbles. It was dank and chill.

I went round to the front of the house. To do this I found myself crossing that little waste of choked hydrangeas and foxgloves, and I stood still for a moment surveying the wreckage of the garden my mother had created. I glanced up quickly at the grey, watchful house and then remembered that she had not been able to see her garden. Her window was round the front. It caught my eye as soon as I turned the corner as though it had been waiting for me to appear. It was a little dormer window high up in the slope of the roof. Its dim eye was disfigured by the iron bars. I could picture my mother's white, forlorn face peering down hour after hour, day after day.

The mist swirled, lifted and showed me the black granite of Botallack head across the mine workings. Then it closed down again in a damp veil. I went on, past the front door. Then I stopped and went back to gaze up at the faded lettering that showed through the flaking paint above the lintel. Nearne. That had been her maiden name. James Nearne might be her father. She might have named me after her father.

The old lettering fascinated me. But at length I was interrupted by the sound of voices. They were muffled and distant, yet when I turned I could see the short, round figure of Friar already emerging from the mist and quite close to me. He was coming up the track from the mine workings and he was followed by the taller figure of Slim Matthews.

'You have been working already?' I asked.

'Yep,' Friar replied. 'Since ruddy 'alf past five. An' a fat lot o' good it done us. The bleeding trucks ain't turned up.'

'What trucks?' I asked.

'Never you mind,' he answered. 'But the bastards shoulda bin 'ere at six.' His face looked tired and was filmed with a grey dust.

We had breakfast then. Nobody spoke during the meal. Friar and Slim seemed lost in their own thoughts. At length I said, 'When will I be able to have a look at the mine?'

'Dunno,' Friar replied. 'The Capting's gorn ter Penzance ter see aba't the trucks.'

'It won't do any good,' Slim said quietly. 'They've got scared.'

'An' wot aba't us?' Friar snapped. 'Do they fink we're goin' ter sit on the ruddy stuff till it's all blown over. I'm for dumpin' it into the sea.'

'You tell that to the Captain,' Slim said with a hard laugh.

'Well, I reckon it's aba't time we packed it in. We're runnin' our bleedin' necks into a noose.'

Slim peered at him down his nose and there was a look of contempt in his eyes. 'Maybe,' he said. 'But suppose we do pack it in? Then we're on the run again. Stay and the whole thing may blow over.'

'That's all right for you,' Friar answered. 'You only got a two year stretch ahead o' you if you're caught. I ain't only a deserter. I got about three other charges against me, includin' resistin' arrest an' woundin' a copper. I don't want ter get caught.' His voice was almost a whine. 'I'd get five years at least. Five years is a hell of a long time.'

'You'd better talk to Manack about it.'

'Not ruddy likely. If I clear a't it'll be quiet like an' in my own time. An' don't you tell the Capting wot I bin sayin'. He'd be sore as hell if 'e thort I were runnin' a't on 'im.'

'Yes,' Slim smiled. 'He's not the sort who takes kindly to rats'

Friar was on his feet in an instant, his red cheeks mottled with anger. ''Ere, 'oo you callin' a rat?'

'All right, all right.' A car roared into the yard.

'Here's Manack now,' Slim said. 'Maybe he'll have news.'

'Well, I bet it ain't good news.' Through the window I saw a big, old-fashioned Bentley tourer draw up close to the back of the house. Captain Manack, in riding breeches with a yellow polo-necked sweater under his brown sports coat, got out and came straight over to the outbuildings. He had a newspaper in his hand. A moment later he walked into the room. His thick, wiry hair stood up on end and his eyes looked quickly from one to the other of us as he shut the door. 'The trucks aren't coming,' he said.

'Scared?' asked Slim.

Manack nodded. 'And that's not all,' he added. 'You may as well know the worst whilst you are about it.' And he flung the newspaper down amongst the breakfast things. Staring at me from the centre of the front page was a picture of Dave Tanner.

It was headed — WANTED FOR MURDER. Underneath in black type was the caption:

> *David Jones, owner and skipper of the ketch,* Isle of Mull, *whose real name is Dave Tanner, is wanted by the police in connection with the disappearance of the crew of the revenue cutter found abandoned near Penzance yesterday morning. The four revenue officials who manned the cutter are now thought to have been murdered. One of Tanner's girl friends, Sylvia Coran, of 2 Harbour Terrace, Penzance, has told the police that Tanner returned at about eight p.m. on Wednesday. He had a bullet wound in the arm. He left almost immediately with Jim Pryce, a friend who had just arrived from Italy.* (Full Story, page 4).

I looked up. Manack was pacing backwards and forwards, running his long fingers through his hair. He suddenly rounded on the three of us. 'Damn all Welshmen and their vanity,' he said savagely. 'If he'd been content with just one woman it would have been all right. But the girl was in love with him and when the police proved to her that he'd been keeping one of those artist women over at Lamorna Cove, she told them what she knew. Pray God he never mentioned Cripples' Ease to her. They're on to you too,' he said to me. 'There's a full description of you on the inside page. Pretty accurate, too. Anybody see you in the village last night?'

'Yes,' I said. 'I went into the pub up there for a drink.'

'You didn't tell 'em you were coming down here, did you?'

He noticed my hesitation immediately. 'Oh, my God!' he said. 'And I suppose you told them your real name?'

'No,' I said. 'I asked where Cripples' Ease was. I — I said I wanted to see you.'

'That's a pretty hot trail you've laid.' His voice was grim. 'Who was there? Any visitors?'

'No,' I told him. 'They all looked like locals.'

'Well, we'll just have to hope they don't bother much about the papers. They're pretty slow about putting two and two together in this village. But George Wetheral, the landlord — he's got his wits about him. He'll remember you. Damn and blast!'

'What are you going to do?' asked Slim. He lingered over the words as though enjoying the situation.

'Do?' There was an excited gleam in Manack's eyes. 'This is what we're going to do. We'll wall the *Arisaig*'s cargo up for a start. By tonight there'll not be a trace of our activities in the whole of Wheal Garth. Pryce, you'll get right ahead with breaching the Mermaid gallery. And you'll live underground. We'll fix you with a bed in a dug-out down the mine. It's quite dry there. It's our bolt hole — concealed entrance and everything. Before you leave I want the Mermaid operating as an underwater passageway to connect up with shipping.'

'What aba't the *Ardmore*?' Friar asked. 'She's doo in on Sunday or Monday.'

'I'll look after that,' Manack answered. 'In the meantime we run no more cargoes until the undersea route is open. You're working on kerb stones, if anyone asks you — understand? Both of you. And if the police come around and ask for your identity cards and ration books tell 'em I've got them. You needn't worry. They can't touch you.'

'Wot aba't the ol' man?' Friar asked. 'Suppose the police start questioning 'im?'

'He'll not talk about anything but the mine. He never does.' He looked at Slim and Friar. 'You two get to work walling up that cargo. The sooner that's done, the safer it'll be if the police come round with a search warrant.' Then he turned to me. 'You get shaved now, Pryce. As soon as you're ready I'll take you down to the Mermaid gallery.'

'And when I've done the job?' I asked.

'You'll leave for Italy on the *Arisaig*. I'll hold her until you've finished.'

'But I don't want to go back to Italy,' I said.

96

'You'll go where you're sent.' His voice was brisk and confident. 'You ought to be grateful to me for getting you out of this mess.' Damn him! He knew I had no choice.

'What aba't Dave?' Friar asked.

'He goes on the *Arisaig* too.'

'An' good riddance, that's wot I says.' Friar suddenly looked up. 'Blimey, there's that load o' stuff for the *Arisaig* coming in today or tomorrow. What aba't that?'

'It's not coming. Any more questions? All right then — Get that cargo stowed.'

'Okay.' Friar got slowly to his feet. 'But I don't like it — I tell yer straight I don't,' he grumbled. Then he suddenly asked, 'Wot 'appened to the rest of the *Isle o' Mull*'s crew — Mason, Fergis and Pentlin?'

'You don't need to worry about them,' Manack said. 'They were all on board the *Isle of Mull* when she blew up.'

Friar scowled. 'Did yer 'ave ter kill the 'ole bleedin' lot?'

Manack glared at him.

'Come on, Slim — we'll get that cargo stowed,' Friar said hurriedly.

They went out, leaving me alone with Manack. He was pacing up and down. I sat there trying to make up my mind what to do. Every instinct told me to get out of the place. The sooner I was away from Cripples' Ease the safer I'd be. But something stronger tugged at me — the bars on that window, the name James Nearne over the door, the letter in my pocket.

Manack suddenly stopped his pacing and faced me. 'Well?'

I looked at him. But I didn't say anything. I hadn't made up my mind. He picked up the paper and opened it at an inside page. 'Read that,' he said.

I looked down at the type. It was a description of myself: *A very powerfully built man, broad shoulders, height about 6 ft. 2 ins., slouching walk, dark complexion, blue eyes, thick brown hair starting low on the forehead. When last seen, Pryce was wearing seaman's clothes, dark blue serge jacket and trousers, dark blue jersey. He had no hat and may be carrying a light khaki raincoat several sizes too small for him.* The girl had certainly given them a pretty accurate description.

'Still not want to go to Italy?' Manack's voice was sarcastic. I looked up. 'I don't need to tell you,' he added, 'that on that description you'd be picked up in no time — if you left here.' He suddenly sat down in the chair opposite me. 'Listen, Pryce — I run these cargoes into the mine at the moment in a barge propelled by an electric motor. It's a sort of submarine barge and lies submerged when not in use. We bring it to the surface with compressed air before going out to pick up a cargo. I'll show you when we go down. It's not a bad device. But it's too dangerous. It means my boats have to lie off for good weather. And now that this has happened I daren't risk it any more. The Mermaid gallery runs out just on half a mile. I plan to blow the end of it so that cargoes can be lowered on buoyed guide wires down into the gallery. They'll come into the mine by a hawser-drawn wooden carriage running on the rock ledges. It may work or it may not. If it does, then it means that my boats can unload in any weather. I'm not running any more cargoes by the old method. I tell you that so that you'll know just how determined I am for the blasting of the Mermaid gallery to be done now. I've got all the equipment you need, including compressor and pneumatic drills.' He paused, watching my face. 'Why don't you want to go back to Italy?' he asked.

I shrugged my shoulders. 'I was working in the lignite mines. It was all right at first. I wasn't getting shot at and the Italians respected me. But later — well, lignite mining isn't my line. And then again I don't like working with Italians. It's all right if you're the boss. But if they feel they've got you by the shorts — well, much more of their sneers and I'd have been involved in fights. And Italians don't fight the way men do in the gold mines.'

He smiled. *'Parlate Italiano?'* he asked suddenly.

'Si, si,' I answered. *'Molto bene.'*

He nodded. *'Benone.'* He leaned forward. 'Look, Pryce —

you seem a reasonably honest and dependable sort of fellow. I've got an estate in Italy. It's a big vineyard in the mountains behind Naples — near Benevento.'

'I know,' I said. 'That's where the strega comes from.'

'That's right. It's not far from Alberti's. That's where Mulligan's cargoes are coming from. We ship out things like lighter flints, contraceptives, Government surplus watches, rubber tyres and so on, things that fetch a high price out there. With the proceeds Mulligan brings back stuff like chianti, kummel, triple sec and strega. The rest of the cargo is made up of cognac, which is what my estate specialises in. Now then, what I need is an agent out there to look after my interests. It doesn't need any detailed knowledge. All I want is someone there on the estate to whom I can send instructions and know that they will be carried out. A man who'll keep an eye on things generally for me.'

'What about Dave?' I asked.

He shook his head. 'No,' he said. 'Dave's a crook. I need somebody honest. I've other plans for Dave. I'm going to open up trade between Italy and Greece. Mulligan's already got me a fair-sized schooner. It's now being re-fitted at Ischia. Well,' he said. 'What about it? It's a fair offer.'

'Suppose I say No?'

He laughed. 'You won't,' he said. Then he got up. 'Well, the sooner you get to work, the sooner you'll be out of the country and safe. And I'll see that Mulligan doesn't rob you on the way out. Get yourself shaved. You'll find a razor in their sleeping quarters. When you're ready I'll be in my office.'

He left me and I sat there, looking at nothing in particular, seeing the parched earth and brown hills of Italy. Christ, how tired I was of the sun and the dust and the flies! I sat there and cursed Mulligan for taking that money from my belt. If I'd had money I'd never have gone to see Tanner. I'd have been on my way to Canada now. And in Canada I'd have found my self respect.

I got up heavily and went into the bedroom. There was a glass above the washstand. I peered at myself. My eyes seemed sunk in black rings of strain and the two days' growth of stubble completed the picture of villainy. I got myself a razor and went through into the kitchen for hot water. The girl was there on her own. She looked frantically round as I entered as though seeking a way of escape. Then her gaze came back to me and remained fixed as though fascinated. 'What do you want?' she asked.

'Some hot water,' I replied, and the instant relief in her face was obvious. As she drew the water off from the tap, I said, 'Why was my mother shut up in that room?'

She didn't answer, so I repeated the question. 'Did they think her mad?' I asked.

She handed me the jug. The steam rose, clouding her eyes as she faced me. 'Did they?' I insisted.

'Please,' she said.

I took the jug and put it down on the table. 'Was it — because of what happened to your mother?' I asked.

She turned as though to run out of the room. But I caught her by the shoulders. 'Was it?' I repeated. I could feel her trembling just as she had done when she came to my room. 'Was it?' My fingers were digging into her flesh. She cried out. But I didn't care. I had to know.

Then slowly she nodded.

'What happened?' I cried. 'Tell me what happened?' I still had hold of her and she began to struggle. Then the door opened and the old woman came in. I let Kitty go and picked up the jug. The old woman smiled. I went back to the men's quarters then.

As I scraped at the stubble of my beard I fell to thinking of my mother again. And suddenly I knew I just had to find out the truth of what had happened in those years before the war when Kitty's mother had been killed and my mother had been shut up in that horrible attic room.

I finished shaving and went out into the yard and round to the front door. When I entered Captain Manack's office, the safe door was open and he was feeding papers into the fire. 'Won't be a minute, Pryce,' he said. 'Just checking through things —

in case.' He gave me a quick, secretive smile. I honestly believed the man enjoyed the situation. 'Have a drink,' he said. A tumbler of cognac stood beside him on the desk. He pushed a bottle with an Italian label across the desk to me. 'Pity to waste it,' he added. 'But we can't leave any of it around now. There's a tumbler on the mantelpiece.'

I helped myself and sat thinking about the girl and the house and the whole incredible set-up whilst Manack went through his safe. One thing I noticed as I sat there; the stack of notes from which he had paid Mulligan was gone. There was no money in the safe, not even my hundred and forty-five pounds.

At last he stood up and closed the safe. 'Okay,' he said. We finished the bottle between us and then went out into the damp blanket of the mist. As we left the house I glanced back at it over my shoulder. The little iron-barred window seemed to be watching us, the panes opaque with the white light of the mist. And at a lower window I caught a glimpse of the old man staring out at us, his bearded face thrust close to the panes. There was something very intense about that face at the window. It made me realise that I and his son were going to destroy what he had spent thirty years to achieve. And he'd offered me two hundred and fifty pounds to clear out.

The house suddenly seemed to recede and become a ghostly outline of a building. Then it disappeared, swallowed up in the mist. It was as though there had never been a house there — as though it were all a nightmare. The air was still and heavy and cold. Beyond the muffled drumming of the sea against the cliffs, I heard the distant moaning of the fog signal at Pendeen Watch, away to the north of us.

Captain Manack led the way down a slippery path where black slugs crawled and bracken stalks stood gaunt and brown between great heaps of broken mine debris. We passed an old engine house, its chimney thrusting a broken brick finger into the swirl of white vapour. Great stone arches were all that was left of the old blowing houses and here and there a coagulated mass of rotting iron marked the grave of once-active machinery. There were old shafts surrounded by circular stone walls and great concrete pits, all broken by frost, where the tin had been washed. The mist thinned as we went down towards the cliff top. From white it turned to gold. It was little more than a thin veil of moisture between us and the sun. The iridescence of it strained the eyes.

We joined a rough track. The tyre treads of heavy trucks had made deep ruts in the mud between the patches of broken stone. The track led us to a huddle of stone-built sheds with galvanised iron roofs. Manack took us into the nearest. It was full of tools and stores. In a corner was a small forge for resharpening drills. He took down an overall and handed it to me. 'Try that,' he said. 'You and my father are about the same size. There's a pair of his gum boots over there. You'll need them. The mine's pretty wet.' They fitted reasonably well and when we had equipped ourselves in overalls, gum boots and miners' helmets, and had primed our lamps, he led me across to the largest shed which housed the hoist. There were wide doors to this shed and the marks of trucks ran right up to the cage. 'We back the lorries in here so that nobody can see what we're loading,' he explained. I think he really enjoyed showing someone the way they worked.

The gig was not there. He rang a bell. 'If nobody answers then it means that the gig's not in use,' he told me. 'If you're using it and somebody rings, you must answer its ring. There's a bell-push inside the gig.' There was no answer to his ring and he pulled over a large lever. Deep down the shaft I heard the sound of water and an instant later the clatter of the gig coming up. 'It's a pretty rickety contraption,' he said. 'Worked by a water wheel. Push the lever over that way and the gig goes down, this way and it comes up. All very Heath Robinson. But it works. My father won't use it. Prefers the ladders. The gig's slow, but it's got plenty of power, and that's what we need for the stuff we have to bring up in it.'

'Where do you get the water to drive it?' I asked.

'Come Lucky. It's full of water. Adits blocked. No outlet to the sea like there is in Wheal Garth.'

'Bit dangerous, isn't it — standing right over you like that?'

He shrugged his shoulders and grinned. Maybe he got a kick out of working down there with a million tons of water towering above him in the flooded mine next door. But then he wasn't a miner. In this sort of country, honeycombed with old workings, how did he know what thickness of rock stood between him and the water in Come Lucky? The thought of it made my blood run cold.

The cage came up and we got in. Inside, was a similar lever to the one outside. He threw it over and in a moment we began to sink slowly into the ground. At intervals black gaps showed in the circular walls of the shaft, marking the entrance to the old galleries. He stopped when we had gone fifty or sixty feet down. The gates opened on to a gallery rather larger than the others I had seen. 'What level is this?' I asked as we stepped out.

'It isn't really a level at all. We use it as a store room.' Our lamps shone on dry granite walls. A few yards down the gallery he stopped. 'This is where you'll live now.' He was pointing to the rock wall.

'Where?' I asked.

He peered down as though looking for a mark. Then he pressed against the rock. A slab pivoted inwards. I pressed against the lower slab. That pivoted too. 'An example of Slim's stone masonry,' he grinned. Inside was a rock chamber about twenty feet by twelve. There were three iron bedsteads, an Elsan lavatory, tin wash bowls, cases of tinned food. 'It's ventilated, and the slabs bolt on the inside,' he added.

He pivoted the slabs back into place and we went on. The gallery had various cross-cuts and winzes leading off it. He shone his lamp into a raise which rose steeply. 'That's the way to the surface,' he said. 'You can only go up in the gig if it's standing at the gallery.' Quite soon the gallery opened out into a big chamber. It was stacked with cases. 'This is the storeroom,' he said.

'Liquor?' I asked.

He pointed to the label on the nearest case and his teeth showed beneath his moustache in a grin. It was marked in Italian — *Aranci*. Oranges. 'Cognac,' he said. Then: 'Come on. We'll go down now. Friar and Slim will be bringing the remaining cases up from the adit.'

As we went down in the hoist I was very conscious of the growing sound of water. It was not only the water driving the hoist wheels. It was the steady, persistent trickle everywhere. The walls of the shaft glittered with it. Green water-weed lined the slimy, circular surface of the rock. In places water was actually gushing out from crevices. The wooden frame in which the gig ran was green. At the bottom we stepped out into a broad gallery down which ran an ankle-deep stream of water. The air was damp, and a cold draught brought with it the sound of the sea. 'This is the main adit,' Manack said as we sloshed down it towards the boom and suck of the sea. I could feel the sharp ridge of rails below the water. Men's voices came to us on the salt wind and a moment later the gleam of their lamps showed round a bend.

As they approached, Friar's voice called out, 'That you, Capting?'

'Yes,' Manack called back.

They were dragging an iron trolley. The sound of its wheels on the rails filled the gallery as they came up with us. 'Only a couple more cases,' Friar said. 'Per'aps you'll come up then and see to the sealing up of the stores.'

'I'm just taking Pryce down to the end of the Mermaid,' Manack answered, 'I'll be right back.'

'Okay. We'll have the other two cases up by then.'

We stood aside to let the trolley with its load of two cases pass. The sound of it dwindled in a hollow rumble as the light of their lamps disappeared round a bend.

The sound of the sea became louder as we descended the sloping tunnel. The dank, salt-laden air grew colder. Round another bend we came suddenly on a patch of daylight — a cold, grey light that was barely strong enough to reveal the black, slime-streaked walls. 'One of the old shafts,' Manack said as we paused, looking up a sloping cleft in the wet rock. Green, half-rotten ladders were pegged to the rock, snaking up through the gloom to the bright light that filtered down from above. The rock cleft sloped so many ways that it was impossible to see the top. 'This is the way my father comes into the mine. Sometimes he uses the gig, but not often. Personally, I wouldn't trust myself on those ladders. They've been there since before the war. The shaft is part of the really early workings of the mine. It's not shown on any of the plans and was only discovered after — after a nasty accident.'

'You mean when Mrs Manack was killed? Was this the shaft?'

He looked at me quickly. His face looked pale in the grey half-light. 'Yes,' he said. 'You know about that?'

I nodded. 'Friar told me,' I said.

'Friar talks too much.' He stared up the shaft. 'She was my stepmother. I only met her once. A pretty little woman. They had to put ladders down to get her up. Her body was about halfway down. My father explored and opened up the rest of the shaft later. You wouldn't think a man would prefer the shaft where his wife was killed to the hoist, would you now? It's almost as though he dares the shaft to kill him, too.' He gave a harsh laugh and turned away.

As I followed him down towards the growing sound of the sea, I said, 'Your father is very interested in the mine, isn't he?'

'Interested! He's mad about it. He eats, sleeps and dreams Wheal Garth. He thinks of nothing else. Worked in it when he was a kid. Swore he'd own it one day. Now he does, every single share — except what the girl, Kitty, owns. That must have riled him.' He laughed. The sound of it echoed against the walls of the adit. 'The woman who was killed in that shaft was her mother. A few weeks before her death, Harriet Manack made a fresh will, leaving everything she possessed, which was mostly worthless holdings in Wheal Garth, to Kitty — or that's the story. My father never talks about it.'

I said, 'Your mother had holdings in Wheal Garth, didn't she?'

The beam of his lamp shone on me. 'How did you know that?' he asked.

'I didn't,' I answered. 'I was just guessing. A man whose sole interest is the acquisition of a mine might be expected to marry into a family that had holdings.'

'Yes,' he said. 'You're quite right. My mother's father was one of the original adventurers. He had quite a big shareholding.'

I hesitated. A question was on the tip of my tongue. But it stuck in my throat. It was too direct. I twisted it round another way. 'I suppose you hold an interest in Wheal Garth — from your mother?'

'No,' he answered. 'She left it all to the old man.' Again that harsh laugh. 'She was hardly likely to leave it to me. At the age of fourteen I ran away from school. Went to South Africa. Worked as a mechanic in a garage, opened up a tractor business, selling and delivering to Rhodesian farms, did a bit of engineering. I was a sad disappointment to them. They both wanted me to become a miner, you see. I don't suppose I'd written to my mother for a year at the time she died. And I was the only child. She died in 1924, just after I'd got to South Africa. I was fifteen then. After six years in South Africa I went to South America, trading in machinery along the western seaboard. Then I went to Mexico, fooling around in oil. I was in Persia, trying to outsmart the Arabs, when war broke out.'

The sea was very loud now. But I scarcely noticed it. I was thinking that if his mother died in 1924, she must have still been alive when my mother went off with Manack senior. The question that had stuck in my throat before came out suddenly. 'How did your mother die?' I asked.

He turned and the beam of his lamp glared in my eyes. 'Pneumonia,' he said. Then in that hard, quick voice of his: 'What made you ask that?'

'I just wondered — that's all,' I mumbled.

He went on then. All down the adit we had passed old galleries, leading off on either side, some of them so narrow that a man could scarcely squeeze his body through, others little more than holes through which a man would have to crawl on hands and knees. But at a bend a wider gallery ran off to the right, and as I shone my lamp into the gaping blackness I caught a glimpse of the top of a ladder poking up through a hole in the floor. The rhythmic thump and suck of a pumping engine sounded above the muffled thunder of the waves in the mouth of the adit. 'That leads down to the Mermaid,' Captain Manack said. 'There's a pump worked by a water wheel farther along that gallery. It clears the mine to a depth of twenty-three fathoms below sea level. You'll see the water running into the adit later.'

A pale glimmer of daylight showed round the next bend and in a moment we entered what looked like a large natural cave. The marks on the rock walls, however, showed that it had been hewn by hand. The cave was half-filled with water which slopped and heaved against the rocks as though seeking a way of escape. The sound of it was magnified by the rock walls so that it was scarcely possible to speak. Every now and then the shaft of daylight that came in through the narrow entrance of the cave was blocked as a wave heaved up and crowded into the cleft. Sometimes the sea spilled through in a white froth of surf and then the wind would whip a blinding sheet of spray across the cavern. Two packing cases stood on a flat ledge of rock which ran along one side of the water like a small landing stage. On the other side of the cave a stream of ochre-coloured water poured out of a hole — presumably the water pumped up from the lower levels.

'The entrance is quite wide below the surface of the water,' Manack shouted to me.

'Where's the barge?' I asked.

He pointed into the tumbled water. 'Down there,' he yelled. He went out on to the ledge by the cases and thrust his hand down into the water. He brought up a rubber pipe. 'She's fitted with tanks,' he called out to me. 'They're full of water at the moment. We empty them by compressed air.' He dropped the pipe back and shone his torch into a recess. There were half a dozen compressed air cylinders stacked there. 'We take her out submerged. The only thing above water is the man at the helm. Neat, eh? But it requires pretty calm weather.'

He went back up the adit to the shaft that led down to the Mermaid. 'You see now why I want the Mermaid gallery opened up. That submerged barge is all right, but it's cumbersome and too dependent on the weather.' We had reached the shaft and he led the way down. The rhythmic sound of the pump was louder even than the rumble of the sea in the cavern. As we reached the bottom, he said, 'Take my advice and just keep to the main adit, this shaft and the Mermaid gallery. Don't go exploring the other workings. God knows when the mine was first opened up. It was way back in the seventies. Father knows his way around. But he's the only one. And he admits that in all the years he's been here he doesn't know the whole mine. It's an absolute rabbit warren. The seaward side of the main shaft has most of the really old workings. There are dozens of ways out on to the cliffs. They used to tunnel in for the ore. The cliff face looks like a cave dweller's settlement in Sicily. Inland from the main shaft the mine squeezes itself between Botallack and Come Lucky. It's more recent than the old cliff workings, but it's still pretty old and the galleries have collapsed in places.'

'I shan't go exploring,' I said. I was thinking of all that water lying above us in Come Lucky.

'Maybe not,' he said. 'But I thought I'd just warn you. You're a miner, I know. But I don't imagine the mines in the Rockies are honeycombed like these old Cornish mines.'

'They certainly are not,' I said.

We were climbing up a narrow, sloping tunnel that twisted and turned as they had won the ore from the granite country that enclosed it on either side. In places the roof slanted up beyond the beam of my lamp. The remains of the timber used for stoping still clung in rotten beams to the rock. In other places the roof came down sharply and we had to bend almost double. Then suddenly we clambered over a shelf of rock and dropped into a much wider gallery that sloped gently.

Captain Manack stopped here and caught my arm. 'This is the upper end of the Mermaid,' he said. 'It runs direct from the main shaft. It's almost dead straight from the shaft to where it stops, half a mile under the sea. And it slopes up all the way so that at the shaft it's above sea level. See here. Look at this.' He directed his lamp on to the sides of the gallery. 'This is what Friar and Slim have been working at for over a year.' The sides of the gallery had been worked so that on either side there was a smooth-topped ledge. The work was recent. Down the centre of the gallery two steel cables rested in the sludge. 'We've built those ledges right the way out to the seaward end of the Mermaid,' Manack said. 'Most places we were able to hew it out of the rock, for the gallery is a pretty uniform width. Only occasionally we had to build it up.' His face under the glare of the lamp on his helmet was full of enthusiasm. He must have been the sort of small boy who was always blowing himself up with fireworks.

'I take it there's some sort of a truck going to run on these ledges,' I said.

'It's already running,' he replied. 'It's wood and galvanised iron with rubber tyred wheels and large sprung ball-bearings to hold it steady against the rock walls. The cables there run on to a winch. Come on. We'll go and have a look at the end of it.'

'Seems a hell of a lot of labour,' I said. 'And you don't know really whether it'll work or not.'

'It'll work all right,' he said.

'It may now,' I said. 'But it may not work when you break through the bed of the sea and the water comes roaring in.'

'That's your job,' he said. The gallery had levelled out and the walls were wetter. I guessed we must be under the sea now.

'You say you've had plenty of experience of blasting. Have you had any experience of blasting into the house of water?'

'Sure,' I said. 'But then I knew the amount of country I'd got to go through before I got to the water. And I'd some idea of the weight of the water, too. Blasting through the bed of the sea is a different matter.'

'I've got all the data you need,' he said. 'I've been over it with azdic. I know the exact depth of the sea above the blasting point and I know the exact depth below sea level of the end of the Mermaid. I'll explain in more detail when we get there. I've got scaffolding up and everything. I wanted my father to do it for me. He's an experienced miner. But he wouldn't, blast him. I'd almost persuaded him to about a month ago and, in fact, he did some preliminary blasting. That was how he struck the seam he was looking for. That finished it. He wouldn't dream of having the sea let into the Mermaid after that.'

'Well, it's a pretty rich lode,' I pointed out.

'He showed you a sample, did he?'

'Yes. And if that lode goes right down to the sixteen level, as he believes, you'd both of you be pretty rich men.'

He laughed. 'Father doesn't realise how much labour and machinery cost these days — that is, when you can get them. He's just on sixty-five, you know, and his brain's getting a little — well, he gets excited and he's not very realistic. It'd mean floating a company. The control would pass out of his hands. And he wouldn't stand for that. By the way, Pryce — he'll try to stop you from doing this job. I don't know just how he'll try, but he will. If he gets too troublesome, let me know. It'll mean a row. But I always get my own way in the end.' He said it with the hint of a chuckle, as though he got some devilish enjoyment out of rowing with his father. I thought of the two hundred and fifty pounds the elder Manack had offered me. And the face at the window watching us go down to the mine.

We were splashing through nearly six inches of water now. Occasionally I felt the outline of the cable through my gum boots.

The gallery was very quiet here. The distant sound of pumping was muffled and distorted so that it was like the steady beat of some giant's heart. Cripples' Ease seemed remote and far away. We were in a world of our own. We were rag worms burrowing under the sea. *It ain't natural.* That's what Friar had said. I'd never worked under the sea before. To keep my mind off the weight of water above our heads, I began thinking again of Cripples' Ease. The ghostly effect of the house fading away into the mist — that picture of it was indelibly imprinted on my mind. That and the little barred window. It all seemed so unreal. 'Has Cripples' Ease been in your family long?' I put the question to him more for something to say than out of any real curiosity.

'Father moved there in the early twenties,' he replied. 'I don't know much about it — I'd left by then. Some woman he'd taken up with gave it to him. Her father died and left it to her, together with a holding in Wheal Garth. You can see the name over the front door. James Nearne. He was landlord when the place was still a pub.' He caught my arm. 'Here we are,' he said. He bent his head so that his lamp lit the floor of the gallery. It dropped away into a great pit. Beyond the pit the gallery continued for perhaps ten feet and then stopped. In the blank wall at the end was fixed a great galvanised iron block round the wheel of which ran the cable we had been following.

There was water at the bottom of the pit. It lay like a still, black sheet some fifteen feet below us, its surface rippled by falling drops. Scaffolding spanned the hole and was built up into a shaft cut vertically in the roof of the gallery. Ladders climbed the scaffolding and disappeared in the black funnel of the shaft. 'We've cleared about ten feet of that shaft by blasting,' Manack told me. 'I reckon there's about another fifteen feet to go. Didn't dare go on without an expert. After each blow we cleared the rock. In the final blow I'm banking on all the loose rock falling down there.'

He indicated the pit.

'The weight of the water may carry rock into the gallery,' I said. 'I wouldn't like to say what'd happen when the sea breaks in here.'

'I've thought of that,' he said. 'My idea is this. You work up as near to the sea as you can. When you daren't go any farther, you fix your main explosives in watertight cartridges. Then you run a long drill through, put a small charge in and let the sea seep into the Mermaid. When the whole gallery is filled right up, then we blow the main charges by electric detonators. Okay?'

'Suppose the entrance gets jammed by rock?'

'Then I'll go down in a diving suit. Don't worry about it. That'll be my problem. What you've got to do is get to work on that shaft there. And remember, the sooner you get the job done, the sooner you'll be safe aboard the *Arisaig*. You take a look round now. I'm going back to the main shaft to see how Friar's getting on. I must remind him to get those compressed air cylinders up to the store room. I'll be back inside half an hour. Then maybe you'll be able to tell me how long the job is going to take and what your plan of operation is.'

'All right,' I said. 'I'll have a look round.' I watched his lamp bobbing along the gallery. It was surprising how straight that Mermaid gallery was. The levels of most Cornish mines twist and turn as they follow the sea. It was only later that I learned that the Mermaid was a development gallery. They had been looking for just what Manack had found.

As the glimmer of Captain Manack's lamp faded to a far-off pinpoint of light, I became very conscious of the sound of water all round me. The regular heart-beats of the pump were just a faint throb — a sound so slight that it might have been the pressure of blood in my ears. Dominating everything — the only definite sound — was the sound of the water. It trickled, it gurgled, it went *plop, plop, plop* in the pool at the bottom of the pit. I suppose it drained through to the lower levels, for there wasn't any more than a few inches on the gallery floor, and it had to go somewhere. I thought of all those levels, sixteen of them, thrusting out under the sea. And this was the top. The roof of the Mermaid gallery was the bed of the sea. It bore the whole weight of the water.

It felt chill and dank. The trouble was I didn't yet feel at home in the mine. It was different to any I'd been in before. And when things are different, that's when a miner worries. Whilst I had been standing there listening to the sounds of the water, the light of Manack's lamp had disappeared altogether. He must have reached the end of the gallery and turned up to the adit. I swung myself on to the ladders and climbed the scaffolding.

The shaft they had blasted was roughly circular and about ten feet in diameter. It coincided with the pit in the floor of the gallery. The ledges on which the carriage wheels would run must be a good eight feet apart. That gave plenty of room for the rubble from the breach in the sea bed to fall straight into the pit. I climbed until I reached the end of the shaft. For amateurs they'd done a pretty neat job. They'd kept the shape of the shaft, though it was a bit ragged at the edges. I felt the rock above my head. It was wet and in the light of my lamp I saw what looked like a shrimp scuttle into a crevice. The sides of the shaft streamed with water. I wondered whether Manack's calculations were right. The rock had a peculiar feel about it, as though it was part of the sea bed. It wasn't that it was soft, and yet that's the way it felt. It was granite all right, with streaks of basalt. But the surface of it was slimed over.

I climbed down and had a look at the pit. There was a ladder running down into it. As I peered down a change in the rock caught my eye. There were some tools on the lower platform of the scaffolding. I went down into the pit with a hammer and a cold chisel. It was about fifteen feet down to the water. The rock formation that had attracted my attention was across the other side. I put my gum boot down into the water. It was only a foot deep. I waded across.

Sudden excitement surged through me as I examined that dull rock. I got to work with hammer and chisel. All other thoughts were swept from my mind. I knew I was not making any discovery. The elder Manack had found it first. But God, if you've ever been a tinner — to chisel out almost solid ore like that!

After about a quarter of an hour's work I was streaming with sweat and my blood was thudding through my veins, for the air was not good down there. But I didn't care. I held in my hand a piece of mother tin about the size of my fist. And I had chiselled it out myself. I cleaned it on the sleeve of my overalls and peered at it, turning the jet of my lamp full on in order to see it better. Gold or tin — what did it matter? The ore content was such that the man who worked the seam couldn't help but become rich. If this were Australia now, I could have staked out a claim somewhere near Manack's. I stood there dreaming with the ore in my hand until a voice suddenly said, 'So you have found the lode, eh?'

The beam of a lamp flashed on me from above. I looked up. I could see nothing but the glaring disc of a miner's lamp. 'Now you understand why the gallery must not be flooded,' the voice added, and I knew then that it was the old man. 'Well? What have you decided?' he asked.

I didn't know what to say.

Perhaps he took my silence for acquiescence, for he said, 'You shall have your two hundred and fifty pounds. And when I start to work that lode, you shall be one of my bal captains.' He stared up at the scaffolding. Standing there above me on the edge of the pit he looked a magnificent figure of a man. If his helmet could have sprouted horns he would have looked like the old prints I had seen of the Vikings. 'My son is a fool,' he said. 'He doesn't know when he is rich. This will not work. And if it does — sooner or later he'll be caught. Then what good will it have done to have let the sea into the Mermaid? Before we could work that lode, this gallery would have to be sealed off, the mine would have to be de-watered to the two hundred level and the lode located there. Men are blind when they don't understand. All he knows about is machinery.' He leaned towards me again. 'Come on up, my boy. You shall have your money and then you can go.'

. I found my voice then. 'No,' I said. 'I'm not going.'

He peered down. 'You mean you intend to stay here and blast your way through to the sea as my son wants?' His voice quavered.

'I don't know,' I said. 'But I can't go.'

'Why?' His tone was tense.

I waded across to the ladder. I was at a disadvantage down here with him standing above me. I couldn't have it out with him like this. I began to climb. My lamp flashed on his gum boots. He was standing right at the head of the ladder. 'Why?' he asked again, and the echo of his question was flung back by the dripping walls.

'Because,' I said, 'there's too much I need to find out.' And I heaved myself out of the pit and leapt to my feet. We stood there facing each other, seeing the reflection of our mine lamps in each other's eyes.

'You mean about my son?' he asked.

'No,' I said.

He caught hold of my arm. For a man of sixty-five he was immensely strong. The grip of his fingers was like iron. 'Listen,' he said. 'I've found what I've been looking for all my life. Neither you nor anybody — not even my son — is going to rob me of that. Take my offer and go — before it is too late.'

'No,' I said again.

'Don't be a fool,' he cried. 'Take it and get out. If you don't —' He stopped and half-turned. The light of another lamp was shining on us.

'Take what?' It was Captain Manack's voice. The question was strung tight like a bow string. We must have been so lost in our altercation that we had not noticed him coming along the gallery.

'I have told him that I will not allow the sea to be let in here,' his father said. 'I have offered to pay him what you would pay him if he will go.'

'And what will you pay him with?' sneered his son. 'With

115

my money. Oh no. He stays until he's finished the job.'

'You intend to go through with this plan?' The old man's voice quavered.

'Yes,' his son replied.

'Then, sir, I must order you off my property.' The old man had a strange dignity. 'I have no alternative,' he added sadly. 'Though it is hard for me to say this to my own son.'

'Your own property?' Captain Manack laughed. 'I know how you got this property. If you want me to leave Wheal Garth then you'll have to get the police to shift me. And you won't do that, will you, Father?'

The old man's eyes glittered dangerously. 'Take care,' he said. 'One day you'll push me too far. Get rid of this man. That's all I ask. Get rid of him and let the Mermaid be.'

'That's all you ask.' His son laughed. 'Have you read this morning's paper?'

'You know I never read the papers. This is my world. I'm not interested in any other.'

'Well, to begin with, Pryce can't leave. The police are after him. There's a complete description —' He stopped then for he realised that the old man wasn't listening to him. He was staring at me — a look at once incredulous and fearful. Then suddenly his eyes were blank, giving no clue to his thoughts. 'I thought you said his name was O'Donnel,' he said to his son.

'Yes. But his real name's Pryce.'

'Jim Pryce,' I said.

The old man was trembling. He turned and stared at me. 'Pryce, did you say?'

'Yes,' I answered. And then I added slowly, 'Ruth Nearne was my mother.'

His eyes jerked wide and his whole body tensed. He was like a man under the impact of a bullet. 'No,' he said. 'No — no, it's impossible.' His eyes darted round the rock walls. Then he recovered himself. 'So you're Ruth Nearne's son. She was a fine woman — a fine woman.' He nodded in a fatherly way. 'She often spoke of you.'

The calmness of his manner roused me. 'How would you know?' I snarled. 'She was alone. You took her away from my father and then you deserted her.' I went towards him. 'You killed her. You drove her to suicide.'

The old man was watching me. His eyes had a cunning look. He edged away down the gallery. Captain Manack got hold of my arm. I flung him off. I was within a few feet of the old man now. I said, 'You think I'd help you to work this mine, knowing what I do of the way you treated my mother? No,' I shouted. 'Instead I'll blast a way through to the sea for you. I'll flood the place. All your life you've thought of nothing but that damned lode of tin. Well, you'll never touch it. You'll never touch it because of what you did to Ruth Nearne. When the sea comes roaring into this gallery, that'll be the end of your dreams. Then it'll be your turn to walk over the cliffs.'

The old man was trembling. 'Don't do it,' he said. 'Don't do it. The mine wants to be worked. It has the pride of a rich mine. It must be worked. And if you try to let the sea in, it'll kill you. I've warned my son. Now I'm warning you. The mine will kill you.'

He turned then and went quickly off down the gallery. And I let him go.

CHAPTER SIX

The Dog was Murdered Too

'So Ruth Nearne was your mother?'

I was gazing after the old man. The glow-worm light of his lamp was already some distance down the gallery. 'Yes,' I said. I was thinking of all the misery he had brought my mother.

'Is that why you came here?'

I turned to Captain Manack. He was watching me suspiciously. 'No,' I said. 'I didn't know it was your father she went off with. Not until last night.'

'What did you find out last night?'

'That he never married her. That she acted as his housekeeper. And that — she committed suicide.'

'Is that all you found out?'

'My God!' I cried. 'Isn't that enough? Your father drove my mother mad. He kept her shut up in that attic room where I slept. To leave a husband and a child and then find her lover married. Not only that, but when your mother died, he still didn't marry her. She remained here as housekeeper, and he married Kitty's mother. God — it was enough to send any woman mad.'

He shrugged his shoulders. 'Well, it's a strange world,' he said. His eyes seemed to laugh at me — or perhaps it was some trick of the carbon gaslight. It was almost as though he relished the situation. If so, he had the devil's own sense of humour. I felt angry and bitter — and frustrated. I should have thrashed that fiendish old man. It was what he deserved. Instead I'd let him walk away down the gallery telling me my mother was a fine woman. I could still see the yellow glow of his lamp bobbing along the gallery.

'Well, it's done now,' Manack said. 'There's nothing you can do about it. But it's a strange coincidence, you coming here like this.'

'Yes,' I said. 'It's a strange coincidence.'

'How long will it take you to blast through to the sea bed?' His voice was suddenly matter of fact.

'A day or two,' I replied vaguely. 'I hadn't given it a thought.'

'We'll go back now,' he said. 'You can start this afternoon.'

'I'll need help,' I told him.

'You can have Friar.'

'Okay.'

We started back down the gallery then. Nothing I could do about it. He was right there. I'd get the job done as quickly as possible, and then go back to Italy. I'd be able to forget about Cripples' Ease in Italy.

Back at the main shaft, whilst we were waiting for the gig to come down, Manack said, 'We'll run the air compressor and drill out to the Mermaid immediately after lunch. I've got about half a dozen sharp drills. I'll have Slim re-sharpen the rest.'

'I'll need an extra long drill when we get near the sea bed,' I told him.

He nodded. 'I'll get one,' he said. 'I'll borrow one from Wheal Geevor tomorrow.'

We didn't go straight to the surface, but stopped off at the store-room gallery. Slim and Friar had practically completed the job of walling up the stores. In half an hour it was done. When it had been covered with muck and dust it looked like solid rock. Slim knew his job as a stone mason. They knocked off for lunch then. Manack stopped me as we went along the gallery to the shaft. 'You feed here,' he said. He pushed back the slabs that formed the entrance to the hideout. 'You'll find iron rations in those boxes. I'll have milk and bread and other things brought down to you. It's not safe for you to feed up at the house now. Okay?'

I nodded. 'No harm in my coming up for a breath now and then?'

'I suppose you'll have to. But keep your eyes skinned.' He left me then and went down the short gallery to the gig. As it rattled upwards and their feet disappeared, I was overcome with a sense of loneliness. I'd never been so lonely in all my life. I heard the gig stop and the door opened. The sound of their voices died away. All sound ceased. It was deathly quiet. The drip of water in the shaft was no more than an echo in the stillness.

In the hideout I found spare lamps, carbide, electric torches, clothes, a clock and a radio. I prised open one of the boxes — corned beef, canned tomatoes, sardines, biscuits, Vitawheat, canned salads, apricots, jam, syrup, butter, knives, spoons, forks, even a can opener. I took some bully and biscuits and went up the narrow, sloping gallery that led to the surface.

This gallery climbed steeply and came out at the bottom of a short shaft. The circle of light at the top was blue and the sun was shining on one half of the protecting wall. There was no ladder to show that it was used, but stone footholds had been placed so that it was easy to climb up the rock wall. I blinked as I climbed over the stone wall into a patch of gorse. The mist had gone. The sky was blue. The light hurt my eyes. I switched off my lamp and looked about me.

I was about fifty yards inland from the main shaft of Wheal Garth. There was no one in sight. The world was very quiet and still, but it was a live stillness, not the deathly stillness underground. A corncrake chattered in a patch of scrub and there was the hum of bees in the blazing gold of the gorse bushes. The chaos of the mine workings, which had looked so grim in the mist, now blended pleasantly into the landscape of wild cliffs and grass green headlands. The debris of rock, which had before looked grey, was now a mass of colour from dark purple to russet brown. The workings sloped away in a riot of dark colour to the cliff tops, and beyond the cliff tops was the sea, calm and blue and shimmering with light.

I climbed up to a slight knoll and lay down in the warm heather to eat my lunch. Cripples' Ease was hidden beyond the rise of the hill, but I could see the track that wound down from it through the ruined mine buildings. And beyond was Botallack Head. There was a farm on the top of it. And down the near side of it were remains of the mine. An old chimney stood out against the shadowed darkness of the cliffs halfway down, and right at the foot, almost in the break of the waves, an engine house stood on a slab of rock. It looked like an aged fort. There were others strung along the cliff top to my left, out towards the headland known as Kenidjack Castle. Three, I counted, square and solid with thick granite walls and broken chimneys of warm red brick rising from one corner.

A girl's voice hallooed. It was far away, towards Botallack Head. I turned, rustling the dry bells of the heather. A lizard scuttled into a crevice of a rock. It was a moment before I could pick the girl out. She was almost at the foot of the Head, standing on the slab of rock on which the old engine house stood. Her hair was blonde and she wore a red shirt and white shorts, and she was waving. In the distance she looked infinitely attractive, infinitely desirable. A man's voice called in answer and I saw his figure scrambling down the rocky path to join her.

I lay back and closed my eyes. How nice to be on holiday. How nice to be on holiday down there with a girl. I'd never realised how beautiful Cornwall could be. My father had always said it was the most beautiful spot on earth, but when I'd arrived I'd thought it bleak and grim. I opened my eyes again — the boy and girl were climbing up a narrow path to the top of the cliffs. I watched them disappear over the top of the headland.

I closed my eyes again. The shimmer of the sea was very bright. But the sun hadn't the hard glare of the Italian sun — it was somehow soft and iridescent and the country was green and pleasant, not burnt an arid brown.

When I looked about me again, a figure was coming over the brow of the hill that hid Cripples' Ease. I sat up. It was a girl. She was not coming down the track, but striking across the heather above the mine. She was walking straight towards me, taking the direct route from Cripples' Ease to the shaft of Wheal Garth. It was Kitty. She was wearing a brown skirt and a green jersey. Her legs were bare and brown, and her hair was blowing in the wind.

I turned over on to my elbow and watched her as she came towards me across the heather. She had a basket in her hand and she was gazing out across the sea. She moved carelessly and with ease, as though she'd walked these cliff tops all her life. I wondered if she, too, were glad to be out of that house. Fifty yards from me she turned down the slope towards Wheal Garth. She didn't notice me in the heather. Soon I could see into the basket. It contained milk and bread and several packages. 'Are you looking for me?' I asked.

She stopped and glanced quickly round. 'Oh,' she said seeing me looking down at her. 'You startled me. Captain Manack asked me to bring these things down to you.' She held up the basket. 'I'll leave the basket here. One of the men can bring it back when they come up this evening.' She set the basket down. 'I brought it straight down because I thought you might need bread for lunch. Those biscuits must be awfully dry. The milk's fresh, too.' She started back the way she had come.

'Don't go,' I said. 'Come up here and sit with me for a moment.'

'No. No, I must get back.'

'Why?' I asked.

'I — I've a lot to do.' She stood irresolute, her face clouded.

'If you've got so much to do,' I said, 'why didn't you let Slim or Friar bring the basket down?'

'I've told you,' she answered quickly. 'I thought you might need some bread for your lunch.' She started up the slope.

'Kitty,' I said. 'Don't go — please. I want to talk to you.'

'No,' she said. 'I thought you'd be down the mine. I didn't expect to find you here.'

She was hurrying up the slope. I got to my feet. 'Well, if you won't come and talk to me, I'll have to come and talk to you,' I said.

'Go back to the mine,' she said. 'You oughtn't to be out here in the open.'

I caught up with her, 'Please,' I said. 'I must talk to you.'

She stopped and faced me suddenly. She was panting and her

cheeks were flushed. 'Will you have some sense? If you're seen out here you'll be recognised at once — anybody would recognise you from that description.'

'Oh, you know about that,' I said.

'I can read,' she answered. 'Now be sensible and go back to the mine. Besides, the milk will spoil out there in the sun.'

'Do you know everything that goes on here?' I asked.

'Enough to know you shouldn't be standing out here in the open like this.'

'Why the hell don't you leave Cripples' Ease?' I said. 'It's no place for a girl like you. Have you always been here?'

She nodded. 'Yes, always,' she said.

'Didn't you go to school?'

'No.'

'Then how did you learn to read?'

She laughed at that. And then suddenly her laughter died. 'Your mother taught me,' she answered.

'My mother?'

She nodded. 'She was almost my governess. You see, Mummy was a rather gay person. She hadn't much time for me, poor dear. I was a little girl in pigtails then.' She gave a quick laugh and turned. 'I must go now,' she said.

'No,' I said. 'Not yet. It's about my mother I want to talk to you.'

'I know. But I'd rather not.'

I caught her hand and pulled her round. 'Can't you understand?' I said. 'I never knew my mother. And now suddenly I'm in the place where she lived. You knew her. She loved you. Isn't it natural for me to want to hear about her? And I want to know why she was shut in that room.'

'I don't want to talk about it.' Her voice was angry and she wrenched at her hand. 'Let me go. I tell you I won't talk about it.'

'And I want to know why she committed suicide,' I added, holding her by the hand. 'I can guess. But I want to know.'

Her eyes widened. 'You can guess?' she repeated.

123

'Of course,' I said. 'My mother ran away with Manack in 1920. And Manack was still living with his first wife then. Even when she died he didn't marry her. He married your mother. And my mother went on living here, acting as housekeeper and as your governess. My God! That's enough to break any woman.'

'It wasn't that,' she said slowly. Then suddenly she pulled her hand free. 'I'm going back now.'

I caught up with her. She turned on me then, her eyes blazing. 'Will you let me be,' she cried. Her voice was shrill, frightened.

'Not until you've told all there is to tell about my mother,' I cried.

'Never,' she answered.

'Then I'll stay with you until you do,' I told her angrily. 'She loved you. She gave you that brooch. It was the only thing of my father's she had left. I have nothing of hers — nothing at all. And you, who have everything of hers that I as her child ought to have had — you haven't the decency to talk to me about her for a few minutes.'

'It isn't that,' she said, and her voice was sad.

'What is it then?' I asked.

'Can't you realise that I'd rather not talk about her? Can't you just leave it at that?'

'No, I can't,' I said angrily.

'Please,' she pleaded.

'For God's sake,' I said, catching her by the shoulders. 'Now come on.' I shook her. 'Why was my mother shut in that room?'

Her grey eyes were full of tears. 'No,' she sobbed. 'I can't. I mustn't.' I shook her violently. Then she looked up at me. The tears were trickling out of her wide eyes. For a moment she seemed unable to find her voice. Then she said in a whisper that I could scarcely hear: 'Don't you see — she killed my mother.'

'I don't believe it,' I said.

'Please let me go now.' She was sobbing quietly.

'No,' I said. 'I don't believe it. You're not telling me the truth.

Why should she do a thing like that? She loved you. She said so in that letter.'

'Perhaps,' she said. Her voice was suddenly sad. 'She was very sweet. She used to bring me out here on the hills and tell me fairy stories and teach me the names of the flowers and birds. I loved her very much. And then —' Her voice trembled and broke. 'Oh God! It was horrible,' she sobbed.

I sat her gently on the heather. 'What was horrible?' I said.

'You may as well know now,' she said quietly. 'She wasn't responsible for what she did. I'm sure of that. But afterwards — I was always frightened of her afterwards.'

'You mean she was mad?' I asked.

She nodded. 'I didn't want you to know. But I had to give you that letter. I'd promised to do that if ever I got the chance. I had to give it to you, didn't I?'

'Of course,' I said. 'Please tell me all that happened. I'd rather know everything. I know it's painful to you, but please — you do understand?'

She nodded slowly. But she didn't speak for a moment. She sat looking out across the sea. I sat on the heather beside her, trying to see in the profile of her face the little girl in pigtails who had wandered hand-in-hand with my mother across these cliff tops. She must have been a pretty child. She was pretty now. She had a broad, open face with high cheek bones and a short, stubby nose. It was the sort of face that made me think of a Chekov play. Perhaps she also had her dreams of a Moscow she was always just arranging to visit but never did.

'I was four years old when Mummy and I came to live at Cripples' Ease,' she said. 'I remember your mother — Miss Nearne she called herself — didn't like me at first. And I didn't like her. Probably she resented us and though I didn't know why then, I must have sensed that resentment. And then one day I fell inside one of those old engine houses. It was that one out there by Kenidjack Castle. I'd been chasing a lizard. I cut my knee and couldn't get out. There's a sort of well where the boiler used to be. It was quite deep with sheer stone sides. I cried and cried, but nobody came. I thought nobody ever would. Mummy was always out somewhere and there was only Miss Nearne. It was dark when she found me. She took me back and bandaged my knee and then she told me a fairy story to stop me from being frightened any more. But long before she'd finished I'd fallen asleep. So, of course, the next night I wanted to hear the rest of the story. And after that she always told me a fairy story at bedtime. And she started taking me for walks and telling me little stories about the animals and birds we saw. She told me about the piskies and the miners who'd worked these cliffs.' She looked at me and her eyes were sad. 'You see, we were both lonely. And she knew such a lot of things.'

'Yes,' I said. 'She was a school teacher before she married my father.'

She nodded and looked out towards the sea again. 'I know. And she used to tell me about her little boy who was a few years older than me. She talked a lot about you. She made up stories about you. She lived in a dream-world of her own, and she let me share it. And I loved it. Soon she began teaching me properly. I went everywhere with her. I helped her with the milking and with that little garden she made. I tried to keep it tidy after her death — as a sort of memory for the kindness she had shown me. But there was the war and I had so little time. Now, I'm afraid, it'll never be a garden again. I wish it had never happened,' she added, with sudden passion.

'Why did she stay on here?' I asked. 'I mean after the old man married your mother.'

'I don't know.'

'Was it because of you — because she was lonely and all the love that she had lost was concentrated on you?'

'Perhaps,' she said slowly. 'She treated me as though I were her own child. At first it was all right, whilst Mummy had her own car and was having a gay time. But then during the depression, I think she must have lost a lot of money. She sold the car and began to be at home much more. That's when the rows started. Mummy had to occupy her mind with something and she suddenly remembered she had a child. But I was always with Miss Nearne. I think she became jealous. Anyway, when they started to have rows, I – I'm afraid I took Mummy's side. You see, I was growing up then. I was less dependent on Miss Nearne and just beginning to be interested in the outer world. Mummy was always nicely dressed and her conversation was of people, real people – mostly men, I'm afraid. I saw less of Miss Nearne then and more of Mummy. And Miss Nearne gradually drew into herself.' She turned to me again. 'I'm sorry,' she said. 'I suppose, in a way, it was my fault. But I was only a kid. I didn't understand how people feel.'

She seemed to hesitate so I said, 'How long did this go on before your mother died?'

'Several years. It was on a Tuesday. I can't remember the exact date, but it was on a Tuesday in October the year before the war. Mummy was going to send me away to school. Miss Nearne objected. There was a terrible scene. Mummy called her frightful names. And then my stepfather came in and stopped them. That was after lunch. Miss Nearne went up to her room and stayed there. My stepfather took her tea up to her himself. That evening Mummy went out for a long walk with her dog, Peter. He was an old Labrador. She was very fond of him. Shortly afterwards Miss Nearne went out, too. I remember her going out. I was in the kitchen and she went past me without a word, her face very white and strained. I watched her going down towards the cliffs. I watched her because I was trying to make up my mind whether to run after her and talk to her. You see, I was to go away to school – it had all been decided that afternoon. And I felt sorry at leaving her.' Her voice dropped. 'Oh, how I wish I had gone after her!' She paused and then went on. 'An old shepherd we had then found her about an hour later out on the cliffs. He brought her back in a state of collapse. They took her up to her room. She was very ill and could remember nothing.

Mummy never came back. They were out searching for her all night. They found her next morning. She was at the bottom of an old shaft that was half-hidden in brambles. That one down there.' She pointed to a circular stone wall beyond the main shaft of Wheal Garth. 'The wall wasn't there then. Nobody knew about the shaft. I don't believe my stepfather knew about it — and he knew every gallery of the mine even in those days.'

'Who found your mother?' I asked.

'A miner. She'd never have been found if it hadn't been for the dog howling. Peter died when they tried to bring him up. His back was broken. The man who found her said the dog must have fallen down the shaft and she'd tried to get to him. The coroner took the same view at the inquest.'

'Then it was an accident?' I said.

She shook her head slowly. 'No. It wasn't an accident. That morning, after they found Mummy's body, Miss Nearne was sitting with me in the kitchen. She was terribly upset. She always felt everything very deeply, if it was only a sheep falling over the cliff. Mr Manack came into the kitchen. He didn't seem to notice me. He looked straight at Miss Nearne and said, "Does this belong to you?" It was a handkerchief. She took it, saw her initials and said, "Yes, where did you find it?" He said, "Just by the shaft where Harriet was killed." Then he ordered her to her room. Shortly afterwards I heard him going up. I was terribly puzzled — morbidly curious, if you like. I followed him. The door was ajar. I could hear what he said from the bottom of the stairs.'

'And what did he say?' I asked as she hesitated.

'He said, "I knew you'd done it, even before I found the handkerchief. There was no other explanation. The dog would never have fallen down that shaft. He knew them all. And Harriet always kept to the paths. She'd never have pushed her way through that gorse, unless someone had called her down that rabbit track." He told her then that she was not responsible for her actions.'

'But what about the dog?' I asked.

'Mr Manack found Mummy long before the miner did. He found her when he first went to look for her. He found her because Peter was standing over the shaft, whining.'

'Good God!' I said. 'Then —'

'Yes. He threw the dog down the shaft. There had to be a reason for Mummy going along that track. Peter was the only reason he could think of.'

'How horrible!' I murmured.

'Yes,' she said. 'He was a lovely dog. He used to bring me baby rabbits — he'd bring them back in his mouth alive and quite unhurt. But it saved your mother. And after that —' She hesitated and then added quickly, 'After that the bars were put in the attic window. You see, she couldn't remember where she'd been or what she'd been doing whilst she was out there on the cliffs. She was very ill for a long time.'

I was staring out across the cliffs. But I didn't see the sea. I didn't see anything — only that bare little room with the bars across the window and the hatch cut in the door. I was cold, despite the warmth of the sun. And when I did notice the sea, shimmering like gold, it seemed a mockery in this wretched place. 'But was she really mad?' I asked. I couldn't believe it.

'I'm afraid so,' she replied sadly. 'Loneliness does queer things to people. I know what loneliness is. Loneliness unbalanced her. She had fits of rages when she broke things. Sometimes she didn't remember what she'd done for perhaps a day or even more.' She suddenly put her hand on my arm. 'I'm sorry to have told you all this. I didn't want to. That's why I tried to avoid you, but I couldn't. You see, she told me so much about you. And I was very fond of her when I was little. Please — just remember that. She was a good, kind person. But things went wrong with her life and — well, it was too much for her.'

We sat quite silent then. I tried to think of something to say, but I couldn't. The whole story was so fantastic — so horrible. I wanted to be by myself. I wanted to think it all out. 'The milk will spoil out there in the sun,' I muttered, getting to my feet.

'Yes,' she said. 'The milk will spoil.'

I left her then and went slowly down across the rustling heather. I stopped by the basket and looked back. Kitty's figure was outlined against the blue of the sky as she climbed towards Cripples' Ease. I was sorry I had let her go then. I would like to have gone on talking to her about other things. I needed someone to talk to. The sound of voices made me turn. The girl in the red shirt and white shorts was coming back along the cliff top. She was holding her boy friend's hand and the sound of her laughter came to me on the light breeze. I went into the hoist shed and so back to the hideout. The light thrown by the inch-long jet of my lamp was very dim after the sunlight. But the gloomy rock walls and the dim light were better suited to my thoughts than the brilliant glare of a beautiful September day. I sat down on the bare springs of one of the beds and cursed Cripples' Ease as I had heard my father curse the place so many years ago.

I was awakened from my reverie by the sound of knocking against the slabs of the entrance. A voice called, muffled and faint. I got up and shot back the bolt. I couldn't remember having bolted it. But apparently I had. The stone slabs swung back and Friar poked his head in. 'Blimey, like chokey, ain't it?' He grinned. 'Still, it ain't got iron bars. It's seein' the daylight through iron bars wot used ter get me da'n. You ready? We got to load the compressor. Slim's gorn on da'n.'

'Yes, I'm ready.' I said.

We went up into the blue sunlight and down to the mine sheds. As we waited for the gig to come up I said, 'Where's Captain Manack?'

''E's still up at the ha'se. Be da'n later. 'E's 'avin' a ra' wiv the ol' man. Proper set to, they're 'avin'.'

We got into the gig and began to descend. 'What's the row about?' I asked.

'Same ol' thing — the ol' man don't want the Mermaid

flooded.' Friar laughed. 'But the Capting'll get 'is way. 'E always does in the end. Reck'n 'e's got somefink on the ol' man. Must 'ave, otherwise 'is father wouldn't stand for 'is monkeyin' ara'nd wiv the mine the way 'e does. There ain't no luv lost between them two. I went in after lunch ter find a't wot the Capting wanted doin'. Blimey, I could 'ear 'em at each other's froats before I opened the door. An' when I went in, there was the ol' man, white wiv rage an' quiverin' — actoolly quiverin'.'

We had passed the main adit level and the gig stopped of its own accord at the next gallery. The shaft went on down, but I could see that this was as far as the gig went. The place was full of the noise of rushing water. In a cleft behind the shaft I could see a big water wheel revolving slowly.

A lamp shone towards us, lighting up the arched rock walls of the gallery. 'That you, Friar?' It was Slim's voice.

'Yep,' Friar answered. 'Mind the cable,' he said to me as we went forward.

The cable was taut at about waist height. A dark bulk showed in silhouette against the light of Slim's lamp. It was a flat platform of wood about six feet wide, its wheels resting on the rock ledges on either side of the gallery. As we drew nearer I saw there was an air compressor standing just in front of it. Two planks were up-ended against the strange carriage. 'Is this the top of the Mermaid gallery?' I asked Friar.

'That's right, mate,' he answered. 'An we're goin' ter ride a't ter work in style. This 'ere is known as the Basket.'

'Why the Basket?' I asked.

'Lumme,' he said. 'You wouldn't need ter ask that question if you'd worked as long as Slim and me 'as ter get the thing workin'. A bleedin' year we bin cuttin' them ledges. An' you'd better go careful when you blast yer way up to the sea bed. 'Cos if this 'ere contraption don't work when the Mermaid's been flooded me an' Slim'll 'ave a word ter say ter you. Won't we, Slim?'

'You know my view,' Slim's voice answered.

'Bleedin' pessimist, you are,' Friar said. 'Fifty quid's the bet. An' don't you forget it.' He turned to me. 'Me an' Slim's got a bet of fifty quid on the Basket. 'E says the Capting's scheme won't work when the sea's in the Mermaid. I says it will. The Capting's no fool, Slim. You don't know 'im as well as I do. 'E's an engineer, an' don't yer forget it.'

'Even engineers get hoist with their own petard.'

'Wot the 'ell are you talkin' aba't? Wot's a petard?'

'A mine,' Slim answered with a sardonic laugh. 'Come on,' he added, 'let's get the compressor loaded on to the Basket.'

Levering with crowbars we manoeuvred the compressor on to the platform of the carriage. 'Better check that we got everyfink on that you need,' Friar suggested. I flashed my lamp over the platform. There was a pneumatic drill, steel drills, air pipe, drill-holder, picks and shovels.

'What about charges?' I asked.

'The Capting 'as 'em,' was the reply.

'Okay,' I said.

'Right. Up you get, then.' I climbed up beside the compressor. 'Any more for the Skylark.' Friar grinned and clambered up behind me. Slim went up the gallery to the bottom of the shaft. He threw over a lever. There was the sound of a gear engaging and I sensed the cable ahead of us sucking out of the mud. An instant later I was nearly jerked off my feet as the contraption began to move forward. The compressor swayed as the rubber-tyred wheels moved over the uneven surfaces of the ledges. The sprung bearings at the sides grated and clattered against the rock sides of the gallery. 'It's worked by the same wheel wot runs the hoist,' Friar shouted in my ear.

I nodded. It was impossible to talk. The gallery sloped steadily downwards, opening out before us to the extent of the beam of our lamps. The carriage swayed and clattered. And yet, considering that it was not on rails, but on rock ledges, it ran remarkably smoothly. The gallery began to level out. Water splashed on my hands and face from the roof and lay in dark pools that reflected the light of our lamps.

'We're under the sea now,' Friar yelled in my ear.

I nodded. But I wasn't thinking any more about the weight of water over our heads. I was becoming accustomed to the mine and my thoughts were engrossed in the ingenuity of Captain Manack's idea. When he had first told me that he was letting the sea into the gallery in order to provide an undersea route for contraband to be brought into the mine, I must admit I thought the whole idea quite fantastic. But now I was beginning to realise that it wasn't quite so fantastic as it seemed, only rather unorthodox.

The use of caves for smuggling, whether natural or hewn by hand, is as old as the hills. It had not surprised me, therefore, to find the underground workings of an old mine being used in this way. But an undersea entrance, with the contraband dropped over the side on wire slides on to an underwater truck — that was an entirely novel idea. True, the whole contraption, with its hawser-drawn carriage and rock ledge rails was crude. But then so much of mining is crude.

The carriage slowed up as the scaffolding at the end of the gallery came into view. It stopped directly beneath the shaft that had been begun in the roof. 'Well, wotjer fink of it, mate?' Friar asked in the sudden silence.

'Okay,' I said.

'Reck'n it'll work?'

'Yes,' I said, 'I think it will.'

He nodded and his cheeks cracked in a grin. 'It'd ruddy better,' he said. 'More'n a year we bin cuttin' they ledges. An' just over twenty-three 'undred kerb stones we made outa the rock we cut. So for Gawd's sake be careful when yer blast through to the sea. I got fifty pa'nd on it.'

'I will,' I said. I was looking up at the dark hole that showed between the scaffolding. I think at that moment I had forgotten everything else but the job of breaking through to the sea bed as neatly as possible. It's a ticklish job blasting through to what

Cornish miners call the house of water. I hadn't done it for a long time, not since I was in the Rockies — in the Coolgardie fields I'd always been working deep. The job only happens in hilly country. Your mine has been developed to the limit of the capacity of the pumps to remove the water. When you reach that limit you have to consider some alternative means of de-watering. If the mine is on the side of a mountain, as so many of the mines in the Rockies are, then the next thing is to drive an adit from the nearest valley up under the mine to act as a drain for the water that is preventing deeper development. It's quite a straightforward job, provided there's no underground river or reservoir of water — that's what makes it dangerous. You probe ahead with a long drill. And sometimes when you reach the house of water and the drill comes out with a gush of water pouring from the drill hole, the whole face of the adit collapses, drowning the miners. There'd been some nasty accidents like that at mines my father and I had worked in. But it had never happened to me.

In this particular case, drilling up to the sea bed, it was less dangerous in one respect — Manack had said he could give me accurate figures for the amount of country we had to blast through. On the other hand, the weight of water was likely to be much greater than one would ordinarily encounter. I stood there for quite a time, gazing up into the gaping hole and considering the problem.

'Come on, mate,' Friar said at length. 'Let's get crackin'.'

'Okay,' I said.

We removed the tools, fitted the air pipe to the compressor and got the drill up to the platform of the scaffolding. Friar then went down to the very end of the gallery where the giant block and tackle was fixed that held the hawser, pulled a rock out of the wall and lifted the receiver of a field telephone. He wound the handle and then said: 'Slim? Okay — yes, she's workin'. Pull the Basket back about four yards, will yer?' An instant later the hawser at the rear of the carriage drew taut and the whole thing, complete with compressor, backed away from under the scaffolding. 'Yes, that's fine,' Friar said as the carriage stopped. He replaced the receiver and climbed up on to the platform beside me, 'On'y fing we ain' got laid on da'n 'ere is room service.' He peered up at the shaft above our heads. 'Wot aba't when the ruddy sea comes in?' he said. 'It's the only fing as far as I can see that may gum the 'ole works.'

'You mean if too much rock comes in and blocks the carriage way?' I asked.

He nodded.

'That's my job,' I said. 'We'll keep to light blasts, clearing the rock after each blast, as you've been doing up to now. In the end there'll be a thin crust of rock between us and the sea. If the rock's sound it'll be all right.'

'An' if it ain't?'

'You won't be around to pay Slim the fifty quid you'll owe him,' I said.

'Gawd!' he breathed, and I could see his face was a shade paler. He wasn't a miner and I don't think he enjoyed working underground, anyway. But give him his due − he wasn't a coward. Only at the very end did he let his fear get the better of him.

By the time we'd rigged the clamp for the drill, screwing it like a bar horizontally across the face of the shaft, I had worked out where I was going to put my drill holes and the size of the blast I was going to use. I had forgotten about the rich lode that began in the pit below us, about Cripples' Ease and all that lay above ground. My whole mind was concentrated on the task before us.

By this you mustn't imagine that I hold with the idea of smuggling or wanted any part of the working and profits of the scheme. Mining is like any other job. Give a good miner a problem to work out and he'll become enthusiastic because of the job itself. And I figured I was a pretty good miner, even though I had been out of the game for six years.

Captain Manack came down shortly after four. We were drilling our third charge hole then. It was some time before we noticed him, for we were both of us right up in the roof of the shaft and the roar of the compressor and the clatter of the pneumatic drill and the sizzle of compressed air and water was shatteringly loud in that confined space. He clambered up the ladders beside us and when I saw the light of his lamp I turned off the juice. My ears were deafened. I could hardly hear what he said, though the only sound was the muffled roar of the compressor's engine and the hiss of escaping air. 'How are you getting on?' he shouted in my ear.

'Okay,' I said, and shone my lamp on the holes we had already drilled. 'We'll make about a dozen holes and put in light charges,' I shouted. 'It's more than usual for a face as small as this, but it'll be safer that way.'

He nodded, 'When will you be ready to blow?' he asked.

I looked at my watch. 'About seven, maybe eight o'clock,' I replied.

Again he nodded. 'I brought some tea down,' he said. He'd placed a canvas bag on the platform below. Out of the neck of it protruded the top of a Thermos flask. We knocked off then and the three of us had our tea seated on the platform of the scaffolding.

'I've just been going over my figures,' Manack said as he munched a jam sandwich. 'I reckon you've eighteen feet to go. How much headway will you make with each blasting?'

'About three feet,' I said. 'Maybe a little more.'

'It'll be the fifth or sixth blow, then?'

'Yes,' I said.

'Today's Friday. That makes it Sunday night or Monday morning if you do two blastings a day. Can you do two?'

'Yes, I can do two,' I told him.

'Good. Then I'll arrange for the *Arisaig* to take you and Dave off on Monday night.' He brought out a cigarette case and we sat smoking for a moment in silence. He leaned over the edge of the platform and shone his lamp down into the pit between the rock runways of the carriage. The dull surface of the tin in

136

the hole reflected back the light. 'Pryce,' he said, 'will letting the sea into the Mermaid prevent us ever working that lode?'

'What's the next level?' I asked.

'Undersea level?'

'Yes.'

'It'd be the two hundred level. That's nearly five hundred feet below us.'

I said, 'That's a hell of a gap. It'll mean de-watering the mine down to that level. You'll be able to gauge the probable position of the lode from the geological charts your father has, but even if the charts are accurate, there'll be a deal of development work to do before you strike the lode. And even then you can't be sure that it's the same lode he saw at the sixteenth level. It may be just a pocket. You'd need a lot of capital with no return for your outlay until you hit the lode. And she'd make a fair amount of water with the sea in this gallery.'

He nodded and shrugged his shoulders. 'Oh, well, it's just too bad.'

'The old man's pretty mad, is he?' I asked.

'Yes. Mad as hell. But you needn't worry. He won't interfere.'

I thought of what I'd do to any son of mine who insisted on letting the sea in on a lode as rich in tin as that, and I wasn't so sure the old man wouldn't interfere. 'It seems a pity,' I said. 'Why don't you throw up the smuggling racket and take to a legitimate business, mining that lode.'

'Because I'm not interested in mining,' he replied.

'But God,' I said. 'If that lode goes down like the old man says it does, you'd both make a lot of money.'

He peered at me, eyes suddenly narrowed. 'What's the idea, Pryce?' he said. 'You don't want to do that blasting job, that's it, isn't it?'

'I don't care what I do here,' I replied, 'so long as I get out of the place quick.'

'Then you stick to your job and leave me to handle my own affairs.'

I started to make some angry retort, but he got to his feet. 'You get on now. I'll bring the charges down soon after six. What size do you want them?'

I told him what size I wanted and he left us then. 'The Capting don't want advice,' Friar said as we watched Manack's lamp going down the gallery.

'He's a fool,' I said. 'If that lode goes on he'd make a fortune.'

'Wot, wiv taxation like it is na'?' Friar laughed. 'I can just see the Capting coping wiv forms and regulations and accounts. 'E just ain't cut a't fer it.'

We clambered back up the ladders then and continued with the drilling. At a quarter to seven Manack phoned up to find out what progress we'd made. There were still three more drills to do, so we knocked off for the evening meal. Friar went up to the house for his. I had mine alone like a badger in my rock-hewn hole. By eight-thirty we had begun drilling again and by ten I had inserted the charges and fused the detonators. We took the compressor and all equipment back with us on the carriage out of the way of the blast. The pit had been covered over with heavy timbers.

Slim left the capstan controls as the carriage came to rest at the bottom of the main shaft and came towards us. His face looked even longer than usual. 'Got some bad news for you,' he said to Captain Manack.

'What is it?' Manack asked.

'Dave's turned up.'

'Dave? At Cripples' Ease?'

Slim nodded.

'The bloody fool!' Manack was beside himself with fury. 'I warned him that if there was ever any trouble he wasn't to come near the place. God! Where is he now? Not up at the house, I hope?'

'No,' Slim replied. 'He had that much sense. He came straight to the mine. I put him in the bolt hole where Pryce is living.'

'Good. I'll go up and have a few words with Master Tanner. He's scared, is he?'

'Scared as hell.'

'That's the trouble with Welshmen,' Manack snarled. 'Too emotional. And they dramatise everything, like the Italians. Right now I suppose he thinks he's Gypo Nolan being chased all over the streets of Dublin.' He crossed over to the gig. As the cage rattled upwards, he said nothing. But his eyes gleamed in the light of the four lamps. He'd taken his helmet off and was running his long fingers through his hair.

We followed him into the bolt hole. Bedding had been brought down and put on one of the beds. Dave was leaning against the rolled-up mattress, smoking a cigarette as we came in. He leapt to his feet when he saw Manack. His quick dark eyes roved round the rock walls. He almost cringed away as Manack went up to him.

'Well?' Manack's voice was soft, but the tone abrupt.

'I had to come,' Dave said softly. He took a puff at his cigarette. 'It was the only safe place. I never thought the Coran girl would give me away like that. I was over at Clynt's farm near Morvah. Lizzie Clynt brought me the paper herself. I didn't trust her after that. So I came here. I had to, man – don't you understand?'

'You disobeyed orders and endangered the lives of the rest of us.' Manack's voice was cold and violent. 'You'll leave for Italy on the *Arisaig* Monday night. In the meantime you'll live here with Pryce. And you'll stay here, do you understand? No going up to the surface. You'll stay here and you'll keep the entrance closed. I'll give you instructions, money and papers on Monday.'

He turned to me. 'See he stays down here,' he said. 'I don't trust him in his present state.'

He went out, followed by Slim and Friar. The two slabs swung to behind them. 'What did he mean by *my present state*?' Dave's voice was pitched high and his cigarette glowed red. 'What did he mean, man? Does he think I'm scared? I didn't come here because I was scared. Indeed I didn't. I came here because' – he hesitated and trod out his cigarette – 'because I didn't trust Lizzie Clynt. Women are the devil, you know. I've no use for them, but the one — but you've got to trust them sometimes now, haven't you? But when she showed me that paper.' He opened his gold cigarette case. It was empty. 'Have you got a cigarette, man?'

'No,' I said. 'Perhaps there are some in the food cases there.' I searched in the case I had opened and found a carton of cigarettes. 'Here you are,' I said, and tossed him over a packet of twenty.

He lit one immediately. The flame of the match shook in his hand. He got up then and pushed open the slabs of the entrance. 'I hate being shut up, don't you? I like to be able to hear what's going on outside. We'd hear the gig coming down now, wouldn't we?'

'Yes,' I said.

He was crossing towards the bed again when a muffled roar came from the depths of the mine. The ground shook slightly. Dave swung round. 'What was that?' he cried.

'Blasting,' I said. 'We're blowing in one of the galleries.'

He went quickly over to the bed and sat down as though his knees ached. A blast of air swept dust in from the gallery outside. 'What are you blasting for? Manack isn't opening up the mine, is he?'

'Just a few structural alterations,' I said.

He didn't pursue the matter. He wasn't interested. That was outside himself and he was only interested in himself. He wanted to justify his presence at Wheal Garth. He wanted to prove — to himself most of all — that he wasn't frightened. 'You know when I left you?' he said. 'Up at the Ding Dong mine?'

'Yes.'

'I went down to Morvah. That's about two miles up the coast from here. Just outside the village, on the hills, there's a farm. Belongs to a farmer called John Clynt. His wife, Lizzie, is about twenty years younger than him, you know — a lovely girl she is. I met her at a dance once and I'd go up to the farm sometimes in the daytime when I was in port. Her husband's out farming all day. Well, I went there, you see. I knew she'd hide me away for the fun of having me during the day. But how was I to know the police would find out about that woman at Lamorna? She brought the paper up to me this afternoon. I was in one of the hay lofts, you know. And one look at her face told me she'd do what Syl had done. Syl was in love with me. That's the trouble, you know. They all fall in love with me, damn them. Why is it that women can't behave rationally? Syl was jealous. I knew that. But to go and give a man away to the police! That's what I can't forgive.'

'Oh! for God's sake, shut up,' I said.

'But, look you, man, she'd no cause to do a thing like that. I never told her I loved her. But a man needs a woman now and then. It was the same with Liz. She thrust the paper at me as I lay down there in the straw waiting for her to come to me and her face was set, you know, like a piece of sculpture in a church. But for the scandal if her husband found out, she'd have been down to Morvah village right away to fetch the police. But I couldn't stay. There was murder in her eyes as she stood over me whilst I read that story in the paper. The only place I could go was Cripples' Ease. What's Manack got to grumble at? It was the most sensible thing to do. Indeed, it was the only thing to do. I'd like to get my hands on Sylvia Coran now. I'd teach her not to go sneaking to the police. I'd —' He looked up and saw that I'd picked up an electric torch and was moving towards the door. 'Where are you going?'

'Up top — to get a breath of fresh air,' I told him.

'No,' he said. 'Stay down here and talk to me, man. I'm not used to these mines. I don't like —'

'I'm going up top,' I said.

His face looked white and scared as I closed the slabs upon the lamplit gloom of that little rock chamber.

There's something about a man who's scared that always seems unwholesome. They say a dog can smell fear. Maybe that's it. But I just couldn't stay down there with Dave Tanner. I went up the raise and climbed the shaft. At the top I poked just my head over the protecting wall. The night was bright with moonlight. There was nobody around and I climbed out. The sea was all silver and the stars gleaming palely behind the dark outlines of the old engine houses. A faint rhythmic beat pulsed in the still air, it was the sound of a ship's engines. The dark outline of her showed against the silver of the sea. She glided slowly along the rim of the cliffs like a phantom.

I strolled down to the sheds of Wheal Garth and in the shadows there lit a cigarette. It was so wonderfully still and peaceful. I drank in that stillness. This world of moonlight seemed so remote from that other world — the world in which Dave Tanner was scared and —. I pushed the other thoughts out of my mind. The moonlight and the stars and the stillness with the rhythmic beat of the ship's engine like a distant tom-tom — that for the moment was reality, not the rest.

The moonlight and the peaceful beauty of the place made me restless. I turned and climbed up the slope behind me. My boots rustled on the heather, scaring rabbits into their burrows. It was only when I came within sight of Cripples' Ease that I stopped to think why I was walking towards the house. Then I knew I was going to see Kitty. I needed her shy understanding. I wanted her sympathy. Not only that. There was more I wanted. The blood tingled in my veins. I wanted to see her smile, to make her aware that I was a man — not just Miss Nearne's son.

I went on, walking fast across the old workings. There was nobody about. The headland was all white in the moonlight. And the house, which had looked so grim in the storm that first night, was white too. I tried to avoid looking at that little dormer window in the roof. But it seemed to watch me as I went past the front of the house and into the yard.

I reached the kitchen by the scullery door. Kitty was sitting beside the open range, her head bent over a book. The old woman sat opposite her, mending some socks. They looked up as I came in. Kitty jumped to her feet. Her cheeks were red with the heat of the fire. 'What are you doing here?' she asked.

I hesitated. 'I came to see you,' I said.

'Came to see me?' She seemed surprised and her eyes dropped to the book in her hand. She put it down on the table. 'What do you want to see me about?' Her voice had a slight tremor in it.

'I just felt lonely,' I said quickly. 'It's such a lovely night and — and I wanted somebody to talk to,' I added lamely.

'There's Slim and Friar through there, if you want company,' she added. 'But you shouldn't be up here.'

'I don't want to talk to either Slim or Friar,' I told her. 'I want to talk to you.'

She looked down and her fingers turned the leaves of the book she had been reading. 'You shouldn't be up here,' was all she said.

'I know that,' I answered. 'Look — take a stroll down to the headland in a short while, will you? I'll meet you down by the mine.'

She didn't answer. But the old woman looked up from her darning and said, 'There's a nice moon, dearie, and the walk will do 'ee good.'

'Will you?' I asked again.

'Maybe,' she said very quietly.

Footsteps sounded in the corridor. She looked up, startled. They didn't turn off towards the front door but came straight on to the kitchen. The door opened. It was Old Manack. He stopped there in the doorway. His pale eyes glittered in the lamplight. My hands clenched automatically and I felt a violent desire to take him by his beard and fling him over Botallack Head where my mother had gone. He must have seen the violence in my eyes, for he stared at me as though fascinated by what he saw. A sound broke through my clenched teeth. It wasn't speech, it was just a sound. Fear showed in his eyes, but only for a second. Then they narrowed cunningly and I swear he smiled in his beard. I started towards him then. I don't know what I intended to do, but I wanted to get hold of him. Kitty caught hold of my arm and he quickly closed the door. I stood there, sweating in the warm kitchen, and listening to his footsteps going down the corridor to the front door.

'Don't do anything, please,' Kitty said. 'Go back to Wheal Garth. I'll come down to you there, just as soon as I've cleared the supper things away. I promise,' she added.

I looked down at her. I'd forgotten all about my need of her in that sudden surge of rage. I could feel her body close against me as she held my arm. She stepped back. I suddenly felt cold and drained. She was watching me, wondering what I was going to do. Her face was pale and her breath was coming fast through her half-open lips. 'Guess I'd better go,' I said. 'I'll wait for you at the mine.'

She nodded and turned away towards the range. I went out again into the moonlight. I could hear Friar's voice behind the curtained windows of the outhouse dining-room. I went round the house and started towards Wheal Garth. And then I stopped. Directly ahead of me, in black silhouette against the silver of the sea, I saw Old Manack going down towards the mine.

My muscles tensed. If the swine were going down the mine, I'd have him there. But he wouldn't be such a fool. Surely he wouldn't be such a fool. I waited tense with excitement, until his figure disappeared down the dip of the slope. I crossed the old mine workings then and from the top of the slope I watched him making for the sheds. Once he stopped and looked back almost as though he feared I might be following him. I dropped close to the ground. He hadn't seen me, for he went on and, when he reached the mine, he went into the store shed. I scrambled down the slope. When he came out again, I was concealed amongst the gorse that surrounded the shaft to the hideout. He had a helmet and overalls on and he carried a lamp. But he didn't go to the hoist. He went on down the slope.

He was making straight for the shaft he used — the shaft where his wife had been killed. The rim of its protecting wall showed like a ghostly circle amongst the brambles. I could have laughed aloud. To play right into my hands like this! I'd get the truth from him now. I'd wring it out of him down there in the bowels of his own damned mine.

The old man had reached the top of the shaft now. He turned and glanced about him. It was a furtive glance. He wanted to be unobserved. What the hell was he doing going down the mine at this time of night? And why did he use that shaft? What fatal fascination was there for him in that place? And then another thought flashed into my mind. *A man who could cold-bloodedly throw a dog down a shaft was capable of anything.* That thought was to recur more than once before the night was out.

Satisfied that no one was watching him, Manack climbed over the protecting wall. He stood for a moment on the inside, his head and shoulders visible as he looked up towards the house. Then he disappeared.

I didn't stop to think. I'd forgotten all about Kitty. I had my torch. I could be down in the main adit as soon as he was. I ran to the hoist and tumbled into the gig, flinging the lever over as I shut the door. And slowly the cage sank into the dripping darkness of Wheal Garth.

CHAPTER SEVEN

Pisky-Led

I stopped the gig at the main adit level and with my hand cupped over my torch so that it showed only a glimmer of red light, I hurried down the gallery. The air was very still. No wind blew up from the sea. There was no sound of waves. The only sound was the drip of water. The quiet of the place magnified the sound. The drip of water and the stillness both seemed merged. It was as though night had seeped down into the galleries and the mine slept.

The adit seemed longer than when I had come down it with Captain Manack. I was almost running. I was afraid I had missed the old man. But when I reached the bend that brought me in sight of the bottom of the shaft he used, there was his lamp glowing yellow against the walls of the gallery. I stopped then. The old man was going down the gallery towards the sea. I followed. I had switched off my torch. I could see the shape of the gallery against the distant light of his lamp.

A ghostly glimmer of moonlight filtered down into the gallery as I went past the shaft by which he had descended. Glancing up, I could see the ladders snaking up over the dripping rock walls. Ahead of me the light of his lamp disappeared. He had turned off to the right. The gallery was suddenly dark. I switched on my torch and almost ran to the point where his light had disappeared. He had turned up a cross-cut. I thought he must be going down to the Mermaid. But when I turned into the cross-cut and reached the shaft leading to the Mermaid, it was just a black hole with the rungs of a ladder sticking up out of it. I switched off my torch and stood there in the darkness, listening. All about me was the drip and gush of water. Behind was the sigh and gurgle of the sea in the adit. And ahead the rhythmic suck of the pump. The unearthly stillness of the mine was full of sound. No chance of hearing a man's movements.

The cross-cut forked just beyond the open hole of the shaft. I chose the right-hand one. It was little more than a cleft in the rock, about the height and width of a man. It sloped sharply down and then levelled off with ochre-coloured water ankle deep. My boots were full of it. The roof came gradually lower until I was bending almost double. I hit my head on a protruding rock and cursed. I uncupped my torch and shone the powerful beam ahead of me. The tunnel straightened out until I could see at least fifty yards along it. No sign of Manack. I knew then I had taken the wrong turning, for I had not been that far behind him.

I turned and hurried back. The left-hand fork was no wider than the other and it, too, sloped down. My water-logged boots squelched in the thick ooze that formed the floor. The sound of the pump grew louder till its rhythmic thump and suck filled my ears to the exclusion of anything else. With it was the gush of rushing water. The tunnel levelled off, heightened and broadened and, round a bend, I came upon the pump. A giant waterwheel turned slowly in a deep cleft. Water poured with the force of a small fall from the roof of the cleft. It fell with its full weight on the rear of the wheel, turned it and then disappeared into a black abyss below, sucking and gurgling in its haste to get to the sea. From the side of the wheel a big arm thrust up and down working the bob of the pump. The bob was a great beam, as big as a tree, pivoted at the centre. It rocked up and down like a see-saw, the farther end attached to a long rod which disappeared into the pump shaft. At each thrust there was a great gurgling and sucking. Then it would rise and a mass of water would surge into a narrow adit cut through the rock beyond.

It was a monstrous piece of mechanism. Groaning and sucking down there in the depths of the mine, it was like a prehistoric monster. It was part of the mine itself. It went on working night and day, automatically, without ceasing. It was the sort of contraption the old Cornish miners had used before the days of steam. I'd seen pictures of them in old mining books. But I'd never actually seen one before.

I took all this in at a glance as I dodged under the bobbing beam and hurried on along the tunnel. The rhythmic thumping of the giant pump became muffled and resonant as the roof of the tunnel closed down on me. At one place I had to crawl on my hands and knees through cold ochre-coloured water. Then the passage broadened out and the roof rose up and suddenly vanished. I shone my torch upwards. I was no longer in a tunnel, but in a great gap where a tin bearing seam had been ripped out leaving the bare rock on either side. Sloping all the way they must have cleared to a height of almost two hundred feet. The beam of my torch could just pick out the roof. It seemed as though the rock, which sloped up at an angle, must grind together at any moment, closing the two-foot gap.

A little farther on the roof came down again and I was bending low in a narrow, stuffy passage with the water round my ankles. Twenty yards or so farther on the tunnel ran out into a wider gallery that crossed it like a T-join. I switched my torch off as I looked out into this larger gallery. It was well that I did so, for not fifty yards up the straight, broad gallery to the right the light of a lamp showed the rock walls of a bend.

It surprised me that Manack hadn't got farther. But I didn't stop to think about that. I turned into the gallery and hurried after the subdued glow of his lamp. The floor of this gallery was much drier and sloped gently upwards. It was easy going, my mind had time to wonder what the hell Manack was up to. I would have expected him to go down to the Mermaid. That was the natural thing for him to do. That was where his precious lode was. But this way could only lead into the old part of the mine. I had kept my bearings — it was an entirely automatic reaction. And I knew that we were now going inland to the north of the main shaft. If he had kept straight on he would soon be in that part of Wheal Garth that narrowed and squeezed between Botallack and Come Lucky. At the thought of Come Lucky the hair prickled along my scalp. Come Lucky was full of water. Suppose the old man were going to blow a hole in Come Lucky?

All that weight of water would come flooding into Wheal Garth. That would stop his son's little scheme of letting the sea into the Mermaid.

I began to run. I had to keep close to him now. I had to see what he was up to. For all I knew he might have his charges fixed. He might be going to fuse them tonight. He'd do it at night. If he did it during the day, his son and Slim and Friar might be caught and overwhelmed in the Mermaid.

The gallery ahead suddenly became dark. I switched my torch on, shielding the beam with my hand. Round the next bend I found a narrow winze going off to the right. A faint gleam of light shone on the wet floor of it. The winze sloped down to a drift, which narrowed till it was no wider than my body. The roof came right down till I was bent low. Twice I cracked my head against the rock roof. I could have done with a helmet in these low tunnels. It got wetter as we descended until the water splashed around my calves. The passage twisted and turned, following the haphazard line of some old seam that had been worked. Round a bend I suddenly came upon him, not twenty feet away from me. He was standing with his lamp in his hand, looking straight towards me. It was almost as though he were waiting for me. I froze, wondering whether he had seen me. But apparently not, for he shone his lamp towards the roof. It was quite high where he stood and a ledge of rock ran up to a hole that looked no bigger than a rabbit's burrow. A stream of dirty liquid gushed from it. He fixed his lamp to his helmet, climbed the ledge and disappeared head-first into the hole.

I waited a moment and then followed. The hole was about three feet high and two wide. The air in it was stale. It smelt dank and rotten. I crawled on hands and knees for perhaps twenty feet through filthy water. Then the roof rose and I could stand upright again. The old man's lamp bobbed ahead of me like a will-o'-the-wisp. We turned right at a fork, climbed along a narrow ledge that dropped away to nothing, and then turned right, into another gallery.

I was beginning to lose my sense of direction in this maze. The tunnel curved away to the left. The light of his lamp grew brighter. He had stopped. I, too, stood still. He could not be more than twenty feet ahead of me. Then the light grew fainter. I followed. My torch was switched off. I was going forward by the diffused light of the lamp ahead.

Suddenly my right foot met nothing. I flung the weight of my body back as I fell. It was the only thing that saved me. I fell back with my left leg twisted under me and my hands braced against the rock on either side. I felt about with my right foot as I sat there. The floor of the tunnel dropped away. There was no floor there.

Manack's light was fading. Shielding my torch, I switched it on. I was sitting on the lip of a hole about two foot six across. I thrust the naked beam of the torch into the hole. It was a narrow shaft. Its aged rock walls were covered with slime and glistened with the water that seeped out of every crevice. It went down and down. I could not see the bottom of it, but I heard the faint sound of the sea above the steady drip of the water. There was a corresponding hole in the roof. It was an old shaft. Perhaps two hundred years old. Probably it had been cut when the mine was first being developed.

I was in a cold sweat. But for the fact that I had instinctively fallen back on to my other leg, I should now have been lying at the bottom of that black funnel, broken and crushed with the sea sucking at my body.

I got to my feet and stepped across the yawning circle of the shaft. It needed an effort of will to go on. It had been a near thing and I was badly shaken. I'd never been in an old mine before. At the next bend I had to stop, for Manack was standing by the entrance to another narrow gallery, his head cocked on one side as though listening. I could see his eyes glittering in the light of his lamp which was reflected from the streaming walls. Again I had the feeling that he was waiting for me.

This feeling became an obsession. I started to wonder whether he had deliberately chosen a gallery that led across an old shaft. But it seemed ridiculous. Why should the man think any one was following him? With the sound of water all round he couldn't possibly have heard me falling.

He disappeared into the dark cleft. Again I was following his lamp as it led me like a will-o'-the-wisp along a twisting corridor in the rock. I went more carefully now, using my torch where possible, and where not, testing in front of me with my feet at each step.

The light ahead suddenly vanished completely as though it had been blown out. I waited a second in the darkness, listening. I could hear nothing but the sound of water and a distant whispering that might have been the sea or a gush of water. It was an eerie sensation, standing there in the complete darkness, listening for the sound of a footstep that I could not possibly hear.

At length I switched on my torch and went forward by the red gleam that shone between my fingers. A few steps farther on I caught quite definitely the sound of the sea. It was a whispering murmur, like the sound of wind in trees. The gallery opened and the floor of it vanished again, sloping in wet rock into an abyss of watery sound. A whole seam had been hewn out here, leaving a blank space between the rock walls. And high above me a little circle of moonlit sky showed. It was a long way away, like a pin-point of light. It was hard to believe that up there was a world of gorse and heather with the lights of farmsteads shining out. Maybe at this very moment the girl and boy I'd seen earlier in the day were leaning against the circular wall that marked the shaft, gazing out across the sea to the silver of the moon track. It didn't seem there could be any world, but this nightmare maze of tunnels creeping tortuously through dripping, slime-covered rock.

The floor of the gallery didn't vanish like it had done before. It continued across the sloping surface of the rock in a wooden platform. Most of the lagging had decayed and fallen away. But the bare stulls, driven into holes in the rock, remained. They were green and rotten with age. I tested the nearest with my boot, clinging to a hand-hold on the rock before trusting my full weight on it. The wood broke with a soft crunch and I could hear it bouncing down against the rock walls until the sound of it was drowned by the sound of the water.

It was no use trusting my weight to those wooden stumps. Yet Manack had gone ahead of me. I shone my torch across the gap. It was about twenty feet and on the other side there was the dark cleft of the gallery continuing. For a wild moment I thought I was what old Cornish miners would have called pisky-led. Suppose that light I had been following wasn't Manack's at all? The old stories of the Knockers and the Hand of Dorcas came to me. And then I bent down and shone my torch along the line of the stulls.

Iron staples had been driven into crevices in the rock. That was how Manack had got across. No goblins. No piskies. Just solid iron staples. They seemed to bring a breath of sanity into that dank place. I went across then, holding my torch in my mouth and clutching to hand-holds with my belly flat against the slimy rock as my feet sought and found each staple, testing it before venturing my full weight on it.

But I was very thankful when I was across that gap and in the gallery beyond. I went on then. There was no light ahead now. A piece of rock fell out of the wall as I steadied myself against it. I shone my torch on the roof. The rock was no longer granite. It was softer and there were great gaps in it and crevices. More and more often my feet stumbled against broken chunks of it. It was a piece of bad country. Shortly afterwards I came to a fall, blocking the gallery. It was an old fall and the rock was so soft that the water pouring over it had moulded it into one slimy mass. The roof was higher here and a ledge in the left-hand wall ran back and up to a dark cleft. I climbed this and instantly saw Manack's lamp shining on the walls. Again I had the feeling he had been waiting for me

The rock was granite again now and so low that I was bent

almost double. It led to a place where several galleries met. They were all of them little wider than clefts. I plunged on after Manack's light. I was scared now of losing touch with it. This part of the mine seemed honeycombed. Every now and then I was passing openings in the rock — cross-cuts, winzes, raises, galleries — all higgledy-piggledy, the way the ore had been ripped out of the mine. And they all looked so much alike.

Twice I took a wrong tunnel, turned back and found Manack's lamp still quite near to the point where I had mislaid my way. I became obsessed with this idea that he was waiting for me, that he wanted me to follow him. And every time I thought of having to find my own way back, I broke out into a sweat of fear. I tried desperately to retain in my mind a mental impression of each new gallery, each turn and twist. But there were so many of them. It was utterly impossible. Not only that. I had to concentrate on following the dim light of the lamp ahead. And whilst hurrying, at the same time to test the ground under each foot.

I crawled through a long tunnel not three feet high. I was then only a few yards behind Manack. Some trick of the mine brought a fresh wind blowing up this tunnel and with it came the sound of the sea. The tunnel emerged into a narrow gallery. It was so narrow that at times I had to edge along it sideways. A part of the roof had come away in one place. And when I had scrambled over the fall, black darkness faced me. I switched on my torch and hurried after Manack. The tunnel climbed steadily, twisting and turning. There was no light ahead. All I had was the red glow from between my fingers. Here and there cross-cuts shot off at right angles. I kept on, going faster, becoming less cautious of the ground underfoot. I had to catch up with Manack.

Then suddenly the gallery ended. It was a fall. A bad one by the look of it. I shone my torch into the hole in the ceiling, blinking in the sudden glare of the naked beam. There seemed to be a dark hole. I scrambled up, thrusting myself right into the jaws of the fallen roof. But there was no opening. It had only been a shadow etching the face of the rock black. There was no way on along that gallery. A rock gave beneath my weight and I slid down the face of the fall, dropping my torch and skinning my hands.

In the sudden darkness I searched feverishly for my torch. All my hands encountered were cold rock and thick, clinging mud. God, I mustn't lose my torch. Supposing the bulb had broken. Why hadn't I brought a miner's lamp? A miner's lamp would last longer than a torch. It couldn't get broken. I knelt down on the floor, cursing, almost crying, whilst my hands searched frantically. Then I remembered my matches. Of course, I'd got my matches. Hell, what was I panicking for? I got a grip of myself. I felt the conscious power of my will loose the tension of my nerves. I realised that I was practically sobbing for breath as I put my hand in my jacket pocket. The matches rattled comfortingly in the box.

I struck one. The little yellow flare of light was like a beacon of safety. The torch had rolled farther down the gallery than the spot at which I had been searching. Its chromium-plated case twinkled as though hugging itself with laughter. I picked it up and thrust forward the switch. The beam shone out as bright as ever. I gave a gasp of relief.

Then I turned in sudden renewed fear and hurried back down that twisting, sloping gallery. I had to find Manack. I didn't know my way out. I knew I couldn't remember the twists and turns I'd come. I didn't even know what part of the mine I was in. All I knew was that I was in the old workings. I might wander here for days. Surely Manack would wait for me? He'd waited each time before. Or had I been wrong? Perhaps he hadn't any idea I was behind him. I rammed my head against a buttress of rock and cried out with the blinding pain. But I didn't stop. I peered up each narrow cleft that led off the gallery I was in. Some were cross-cuts. Others were just clefts that finished in nothing. In none of them did I catch sight of the friendly glow of Manack's lamp. I came to a fork. I couldn't remember it. I took the right-hand gallery. Before I'd gone twenty paces I was certain I hadn't come that way. I went back and tried the left. Again I was certain it wasn't the one I had come down. I stopped then. I was panting heavily. I must get a grip on myself. I had been wrong about Manack. He hadn't been waiting for me. It was all imagination. Why the hell had I come? And then a new thought struck me. Suppose Manack had known I was following him? Suppose he had led me up into these old workings on purpose? What a way to finish a man! What a perfect way to kill me — to lead me up here into this rabbit warren and then abandon me! Those stories I'd heard of the Roman catacombs. I remembered the priest who had taken me over the Santo Calisto — thirty-nine miles of underground passages, tier on tier of them, and all along the walls the niches where Rome's Christians had been buried in the early days of the persecution. I could see that priest, the lighted taper shining on his dark, foreign face and upstarting, wiry hair, as he backed away from us down gallery after gallery. He had told us that there were still galleries the monks had not explored, that Germans seeking escape after the fall of Rome had forced their way into the catacombs and never come out. That priest had scared me. And when at the top I had asked what nationality he was, for he did not speak with an Italian accent, he had smiled and said German.

I cursed out loud. I must stop myself thinking of things like that. *I must get a grip on myself.* I took a deep breath and held it, stopping my panting. Manack must be about here somewhere. I called him by name. I shouted at the top of my voice. But all that happened was that the sound of my voice came back to me as a hollow, muffled echo. I tried again. Again I heard my voice come whispering back along the galleries long after I had ceased to call. And then something like a laugh sounded. But it was just a trick of my imagination. It came again, a rustling, cackling noise. With it came a draught of air. Probably it was the sound of the sea wandering along the galleries.

The sea! I pulled myself together then and switched off my torch. I had to conserve the battery. No use wasting it whilst

I stood still, thinking. And I must think. I must reason this out. I mustn't panic. I was a miner, not a kid going underground for the first time.

I turned about in the darkness, searching for the direction of that faint breath of air that stirred along the gallery. It took me back towards the fall of rock. I followed it into a cross-cut. The cross-cut was low. I had to crawl through on hands and knees. The breeze was stronger in this narrow tunnel. I could feel it cool on my face. It smelt dank and salt. The tunnel opened out again and then descended steeply. Soon I was scrambling over fallen rock down an almost vertical funnel with water pouring between my legs, soaking me to the waist. It levelled out again. I could hear the sea now. The faint gurgle and lap of water came to me on the breeze which was strong and fresh.

Then suddenly the gallery ended. It wasn't a fall of rock that faced me. It was just empty space. I raked that space with the beam of my torch. It was a great cavern, whether natural or not I don't know. The sea slopped about in the bottom of it. I thought I could dimly see the black surface of the water on the edge of my torch's visibility.

There was no exit that way. The sides of the cavern fell away sheer. Even if I could have got down, there was no indication that there was a way out below. Water cascaded in little falls down the smooth, weed-grown rock. I scrambled back then, up the funnel and along the tunnel and back to the gallery from which I had started.

No good following the wind. I switched my torch out and tried to remember the way I had come. If I could just retrace my steps. I faced the gallery again and started walking. I took the left-hand fork. I went on, following my nose, selecting passages at random. Pretty soon I knew I was lost. There were falls I had not seen before, drifts knee-deep in ochre-coloured water, nothing I recognised. I found a weed-grown shaft that went up vertically and disappeared beyond the range of my torch without any circle of moonlight showing its pin-point light of hope at the top. Probably one of the old shafts that had been blasted in. Water became more evident. It poured from every crevice and ran knee-deep along a gallery I walked down. The roof of that gallery gradually lowered until the gallery was no more than a pipe down which the water poured, gurgling.

I went back again and tried another. This led me upwards, passing me from level to level. It had a plan. I could understand it. Then it suddenly petered out for no apparent reason except, of course, that the tinners had come to the end of the lode in that particular spot. I went back again, working my way down through the mine. If I could get within earshot of the pump — that would act as a guide for me. I followed the run of the water. The galleries were like narrow Gothic passages. And then suddenly they would open out into cathedral-like spaces where a broad seam had been worked. I worked my way down deep into the mine and the lower I went, the wetter it became. The black walls poured water. The air was dank and stale. There was no sound of the pump. No sound of the sea. Only the whispering trickle of water running over rock surfaces. A narrow winze took me down into a broader gallery. Here the water was almost up to my waist.

I struggled along it. I knew I should go back. I was too deep. But I couldn't face the thought of failure. The light of the torch was beginning to dim. For a time I refused to admit it. But down here in this swamped gallery with the dark surface of the water curving ahead of me I knew the battery was fading. The beam was no longer a white shaft of light. It had yellowed and lost its power. The change had been so gradual as to be almost imperceptible.

I forced my body forward through the weight of the cold water. Ahead the dark, polished surface was broken with water pouring in from the roof. And as I reached this point, my foot slipped from under me and I plunged forward, the water closing over my head. I came up gasping, holding the torch above my head and feeling about with my feet for the muddy floor of the gallery. I found it and climbed out of the hole, cold and dripping. One glance at the roof told me that I had stepped into a shaft for there was a gaping hole there out of which water poured in a steady stream.

I knew then that I was down to the water level of the mine. Below me were miles and miles of workings, all flooded. There was nothing for it, but to go back. I was scared now. Really scared. It was the yellowing beam of my torch that scared me. The battery had been stored too long. It might last five minutes. It might last an hour. But my time was limited. I had to find a way out.

I glanced at my watch as I waded back along that flooded gallery. The luminous hands showed five minutes to eleven. I'd been underground about an hour. I turned up a steep raise, dragging my mud-filled boots out of the water. My haste was almost frantic now. I must get as near to the surface as possible before the torch gave out. If I could find a shaft that ran up to a gleaming circle of moonlight — I could try and climb it. At any rate I could stay there until daylight and then start calling for help. There wouldn't be much chance of any one hearing me. But at least it would give me some hope. Or if I could find one of the galleries that led out on to the face of the cliffs.

As I climbed, I began to search about with my face for a sign of a breeze that would indicate the direction of the sea or shaft. But the air was still and lifeless. The galleries were like a tomb. I began to think of the catacombs of Rome again. No, I mustn't think of that. I'd lose my head if I thought of that. There was that story by Edgar Allan Poe. What was it? *The Cask of Amontillado*. Damn Poe. He was the last writer I ought to be thinking of if I was to preserve my wits.

Then suddenly I stopped. A gentle throbbing sound was in my ears. Was it my blood beating in my temples? I was panting like a lunatic. Was it the blood, or was it the sound of the pump? I tried to forget the beating of my heart and listen. But I couldn't be sure. Fear and the still, damp air could play all sorts of tricks.

I went forward slowly, concentrating all my energies on

listening. The gallery roof rose. A rock ledge ran up to a dark hole. The sound seemed to come from there. Or was it my imagination? It was so ephemeral. I climbed the ledge and crawled into a narrow tunnel that was comparatively dry. God, how dim my torch was getting. The tunnel broadened and lifted to a gallery. The throbbing sound became louder and sharper and turned to a dripping. The rock was softer here. Part of the floor had caved in. Water dripped there resonantly. That was the sound I had heard.

I switched the dimming torch off and leaned against the wall, closing my eyes so that the darkness would not be so apparent. That sudden spark of hope had vanished. I felt exhausted. I put the torch in my pocket and leaned my whole tired weight against the wall. I had to think. I hadn't long now before I should be in darkness. The gallery was utterly still. The only sound was the steady drip of the water. There was no breath of air to guide me.

And then suddenly I realised that my hands were touching, not granite, but a softer rock. I got my torch out again. Yes, it was softer rock. That was why the floor had caved in. This was the same sort of rock that I had encountered shortly after Manack had led me across that stoping. Of course, this bad bit of country might extend over a wide area of the mine. But it was unlikely. The mine was predominantly granite. Soft stone would be only likely to fill in a fissure in the granite country.

I went on again. I came to a winze and peered down it. My torch barely showed me the outline of the walls. But a breath of cool air seemed to caress my face. I went down the winze and turned left into a narrower gallery, following the air. The walls were granite here and the roof was low. At the next bend the gallery finished in nothingness. I stood in the gap and looked out into what at first appeared to be a cavern. But I could just make out a wall of rock rising opposite me.

And then with a gasp of joy I saw a ledge running down to a fall of rock. The rock of the fall was soft and the water pouring over it had welded it into a solid mass. I slid down on to it. Surely this was the way Manack had led me? Surely I wouldn't be mistaken? There couldn't be two falls so identical. As I went down the gallery I became more and more convinced that I had stumbled on to the track by which I had come. The rock walls were soft. The roof was full of crevices and great cracks. Lumps of broken rock lay on the slime-covered floor.

And then I was suddenly at the stoping. I could hear the water pouring down the slope of the rocks to the sea far below. And right above me was that little pin-point of light that marked the top of a shaft.

The relief made me feel weak at the knees. I stood there for a moment, steadying myself and gazing up at that distant circle of light. What a difference it made to feel that I was in contact with the world above ground! It made even the darkness bearable.

Then I switched on the torch again and felt with my boot for the first of the iron staples. I found the wooden stump of the sloping timber. The staple was just above it, but I couldn't seem to find it. Perhaps in my excitement I was feeling in the wrong place. I took a firm grip at the handhold I had and felt farther out. But there was nothing, only the rotten stump of timber. I stepped back into the arch of the gallery then and leaned out with my torch glowing dimly against the rock above the stull.

There was no staple. Nor was there a staple above the next baulk of timber.

At first I thought this stoping must be different to the one I had crossed before. But there was the tiny pin-point of light high up above me and the slopping of the sea below. The rock formation was the same, too. I might be in the same cutting, but higher or lower than when I'd crossed before. But surely that fall of rock would not have been duplicated with the ledge running back and up to the narrow cleft that ran into granite country? I went back down the gallery to see. It was the same fall all right. When I returned to the stope I knelt down and leaned out, shining my torch on to the place in the rock where I thought a staple should have been.

A ragged hole showed in a cleft. The iron of the staple had marked the rock and dirt was pressed back on either side. The staple had been knocked back and forth until it had fallen out.

It was then that my torch began to flicker. It hardly gave any light at all. I switched it off. Here, thank God, was not complete darkness. I could look up to that little circle of moonlight. Remote though it was, I derived some comfort from it.

I got a match from my pocket, struck it and leant far out. Its flickering light showed me that the next staple was also missing, and the next after that. They had been there when I had followed Manack across the stope. Now they had been prised out. It could mean only one thing. Manack had known I was following him. He had been waiting for me at each bend. He had deliberately taken me up into the old part of the mine. Then he had doubled back and crossed the stoping, knocking the staples out behind him. My God, what a devil! That was murder. It wouldn't seem like it. But that's what it was. And I remember thinking again — *a man who would cold-bloodedly throw a dog down a shaft would do anything.*

I sat down on the floor of the gallery with my legs dangling over the abyss and considered what to do. I was quite calm now. I wasn't lost any more. I knew my way back to the pump and the main shaft from here. All I had to do was get across that twenty foot gap. That was a problem I could understand. I wasn't scared any more. There was nothing to frighten me about it. I wasn't facing the unknown now. This was a reality, something I could understand. Manack had tried to kill me. Indirectly he had attempted to murder me. And all that stood between me and safety was twenty feet of bare, sloping rock. It was my wits against his.

When I had rested a while I started out to do the only thing possible. I switched my torch on, I found a foothold and a handhold and swung out of the gallery on to the rock face, the torch gripped in my mouth. The rock was not quite sheer — an angle of about eighty degrees, I should say — and pressing

161

my body close to the wet face of it, I was able to relieve the strain on my limbs. The trouble was that the rock was slimy with water and fingers and boots were inclined to slip. Below me the sea slopped about noisily as though licking its lips in expectation of my fall.

I worked steadily out across the gap from handhold to handhold. Sometimes my feet were firmly set in a crevice or on a jutting rock, sometimes they dangled uselessly. At the fifth handhold I could find no place for my foot to grip. I hung there by my hands, searching in the dim flickerings of the torch for the next hold. But I couldn't see one. I searched about with my feet. There was nothing but smooth rock. I hung by one hand and felt out with the left. There was no handhold and no foothold, just the slimy surface of the rock. I had to go back then.

I tried climbing up. I got a little way and nearly stuck. My elbow joints were quivering with the strain by the time I regained the gallery. I sat down then with my back against the rock wall of the gallery. I'd try again later. But first I had to rest. I felt utterly exhausted. I seemed to have been stumbling through the workings of this mine for a lifetime. Yet it was only half-past eleven.

I tried to relax. My clothes were wet and uncomfortable. I wasn't cold. The air, though dark, was quite warm. I just felt dirty, wet and tired. Damn that blasted old man! What was the idea? Why had he wanted to kill me? What was he afraid of?

My limbs soon began to grow stiff. My clothes clung to me in a sodden mass. I began to shiver. I wasn't consciously cold, just wet. I got to my feet. I had to get across that gap. I tried climbing down and along under the stoping. But again I reached a point where there were no hand or footholds. Coming back my foot slipped and the sudden strain on my hands caused one of them to slide on the wet rock. I hung for a moment by one hand and only just managed to find a crevice with my boot. It was with great difficulty that I climbed back into the gallery.

After that I knew it was no use. I had to find a way round. But my torch was finished now. The pale glimmer of light was only sufficient to reveal the rock face when held a few inches from it. I felt my way back to the fall of soft rock, from the ledge, climbed it, crawled into the tunnel and took the first cross-cut to the left. Creeping along with my hands on either wall, I took another turning to the left. It sloped down and a moment later the floor fell away from under my feet. I risked one of my precious matches here. The gallery dropped almost sheer for about fifteen feet and then levelled out again. I scrambled down and went on. The gallery forked and I took the left and was brought up in a few yards by a fall. I struck another match. There was no way through. I went back and tried the right fork. Again a fall and at the cost of still another match I discovered the gallery was completely blocked.

I went back, scrambling up the steep part in the dark. I tried another gallery and another. One ended in a shaft, the other in a blank wall of rock. I had only five matches left now. And suddenly I got scared I wouldn't find my way back to the stoping. At least there was a gleam of hope there. I took a wrong turning first time. I tried again in a sweat of fear. This time I came out through the tunnel on to the fall of soft rock. And so back to the stoping with that little pin-point of light high, high above me.

I sat there, shivering and listening to the sound of water. Perhaps daylight would show a gleam of light on the sea water below. If not . . . That didn't bear thinking about. Nobody knew I was down here. I could just stay here and rot.

And then suddenly I sat up. I thought I heard a voice, very faint and distant. There it was again. A long, echoing call. I must be going mad. It was like a woman's voice. I listened, but it didn't come again. I sat back. It was possible to imagine all sorts of sounds in the dripping of the water. I thought of the stories old tinners had told up in my father's shack in the Rockies, stories of goblins working underground, of the spirit of Gathon and sudden flares and lights. 'Wherever there do be a lode o' tin, thee's sure to hear strange noises,' I remember one grizzled old miner saying. But they never spoke of a woman's voice.

Then suddenly I sat up, my nerves stretched taut to a stifled scream. There was a light in the gallery beyond the stoping.

I tried to tell myself I was seeing things, that the darkness was playing tricks on my eyes. But I could see the cleft quite plainly, like an old doorway and it was all yellow with light. I stood up. Perhaps it was Manack coming back. The light seemed to be getting stronger. Then a long-drawn out cry curdled my blood. It was a soft wailing sound that dragged itself through the galleries and came echoing back in wail after wail, growing fainter each time. It came again. It was a woman's cry — a mad, wailing, echoing cry. And slowly the light grew brighter in the shaft beyond the stoping.

CHAPTER EIGHT

Mad Manack

I don't know what I expected to come along that gallery. I stood there, clutching at the wet rock of the walls and my blood pounded in my ears. But for the darkness of the gallery behind me, I think I would have run. The light grew steadily brighter till the walls glistened and I could see the rotten stulls of the stoping thrust out like arms from the sloping rock. If it were human I knew it couldn't cross that gap. But I don't think I thought it was human. No man brought up on the old tinners' tales could possibly have thought that wild cry human.

At last the light itself appeared. It was attached to a miner's helmet and the miner himself came steadily on towards the stope. I thought of all the men who must have lost their lives down here. The mine was old. Two or three centuries of tinners must have worked down here, burrowing down from above and in from the cliffs. Many would have been killed.

I waited in a sweat of fear to see what the thing would do when it reached the rotten lagging. Would it come on — or would it stop?

The figure reached the gap, stopped and then swung itself against the rock, feeling for the staples.

It was human.

But it wasn't Manack. It was much smaller than Manack. It wasn't his son either, or Slim or Friar. I hesitated. I hadn't been seen. I was in the shadow of my part of the gallery. The miner failed to find the expected foothold, drew back and bent down, looking for the staples that should have been there. The beam of his lamp shone like a disc of light straight at me. Then I found my voice. 'Who are you?' I asked.

The figure jumped back with a startled cry.

It was a woman's cry.

'Is that you, Jim?' asked Kitty's voice.

Relief, surprise, humiliation — they were all mixed up. 'Yes,' I said, coming out into the light of her lamp.

'Oh, thank God!' she said.

'What in the world are you doing down here?' I asked her.

'I came down to find you. Thank God you're all right.' The softness of her voice whispered back at me as though it had wandered through countless galleries.

'Didn't you think I would be?' I asked.

'I don't know,' she replied. 'I didn't know what to think. I saw Mr Manack come up. I was down by the sheds where you said you'd meet me. I waited. But you didn't come up. And then I got scared. I went down to the hideout. Mr Tanner hadn't seen you. I went out to the Mermaid then. I thought you might be down there. But you weren't, and when I got back you hadn't returned to the hideout. I was really scared then and decided to come up into the old workings. I thought you might have got lost — or something. But I see I needn't have bothered,' she added with a trace of sharpness.

I said, 'Is this the only way into the old workings?'

'No. There's one other way. It's a very low tunnel. You have to crawl flat on your stomach. A stranger wouldn't find it.'

'I see,' I murmured. 'But this is the way you'd normally come?'

'Yes. My stepfather drove staples into the rock.'

'Well, your stepfather's just knocked them out again.'

'What do you mean?'

'You won't find any staples now.'

'I was just looking for them when you spoke to me.' She peered down. 'No, you're right. They've been knocked out.'

'Yet less than an hour ago when I followed the old man across this gap, they were there. What do you know about that?'

'You mean —' She broke off, unwilling to put the thought into words.

'That's right,' I said. 'He led me up into a rabbit warren of galleries, then doubled back and cut off my only line of retreat. A nice fellow, your stepfather.'

'And he knew you were following him.' She said it slowly, stating it as a fact. 'He knew that, didn't he?'

'How did you guess?' I said, surprised.

'It's not a guess. I knew he meant you to go down the mine after him. When you left the kitchen I looked out of the window to — to see if there really was a moon. He was standing on the slope that leads down to the mine. He was looking back to the house, waiting. As soon as he saw you come round the house, he started on down towards the mine. I left the kitchen and followed you. I saw you hiding in the gorse, waiting for him to come out of the store shed. Then, when he disappeared down that shaft, I saw you run for the hoist. I waited and waited. At length Mr Manack came up — alone. I thought you'd be up soon after him. But you didn't come, so I went down to the hideout. It was then I got worried and decided to look for you in the mine. It's not a place for a stranger to be wandering in — even if he is a miner.'

'It certainly is not,' I told her. 'My torch has gone dead on me, I'm down to my last five matches, I've scrambled miles and had the fright of my life. I was just sitting here, thinking that this place was likely to be my tomb. Look, what about showing me that alternative route?'

'Yes,' she said. 'Wait there. I won't be long.' The light of her lamp faded down the gallery. Then suddenly all was dark again as she turned out of the gallery.

I became conscious once more of the unending drip of the water. That infernal darkness almost had me convinced Kitty had never been there, that I had imagined it all. I waited there in the darkness for five, maybe ten minutes. Then a light glowed in the gallery behind me. A moment later she was standing beside me and the great cleft where the tin had been stoped out showed clearly in the beam of the lamp she held in her hand.

The relief of having light and company! I found her hand in the darkness. 'I'd like to thank you,' I said.

'It's all right,' she said, and drew back timidly. 'I just felt there was something wrong, so I came down.' Her voice had fallen to a whisper.

'Well,' I said, 'I don't know what would have happened if you hadn't turned up. I'd have just stayed here till I rotted.'

'Somebody would have come to look for you.'

'I don't know,' I said, 'They might not have thought of looking for me up here. And I'd never have got across that gap. And I wouldn't have found the other way. I'd no light. It was only by luck I found my way back as far as this. He lost me in the farthest reaches of the old workings.' I turned her towards me. 'You saved my life, Kitty.'

'It's nothing,' she said, nervously.

'Well, it is to me,' I said with an attempt at a laugh that got stuck in my throat.

We were silent for a moment, neither of us knowing what to say. I turned her face towards me. She wouldn't look at me. But she didn't turn her head away. I bent and kissed her then. Her lips were warm and soft. I drew her close to me, but at the touch of my body she thrust away from me. She was panting and I caught the gleam of her eyes. They were wild and scared looking, like an animal's. But I needed her. I needed her close to me — to prove that I wasn't alone any more. I caught hold of her by the arms and drew her towards me. Her helmet fell clattering to the floor and her hair tumbled loose, hiding her face as she fought me off.

Suddenly she stopped struggling. The next instant her body was pressed close against me and her lips sought mine. They were open, inviting lips and she thrust against me with an abandon of passion that was quite wild. Then she drew quickly back and bent to pick up her helmet. I could hear her breath coming in quick pants. She turned back along the gallery. 'I'll show you the tunnel,' she said in a whisper as though she did not trust herself to speak to me.

I followed her. We came to the fall of soft rock, climbed the ledge and entered the hole that had led to the next gallery. She took the third cross-cut to the left and almost immediately turned left again. This gallery opened out to some height. She stopped and directed the beam of her lamp high up to a black hole in the rock. 'There you are,' she said. 'I don't think you would have found that.'

'I certainly wouldn't,' I said.

She led the way up a series of ledges in the wall and disappeared head first. I followed her. We crawled along on our stomachs for perhaps twenty yards. All I could see was her legs and buttocks humped against the light of the lamp which she held out ahead of her.

At last we emerged into another gallery and were able to stand upright. A few minutes later I could hear the rhythmic suck and thump of the pump. We turned left into a wider gallery that was full of noise — the noise of the pump, mingled with the gurgle and rush of water. At the end of the gallery we passed under the great bob as it see-sawed up and down. Ten minutes later we were in the gig clattering to the surface.

It's difficult to describe the utter relief with which I looked out upon the moonlit headland. There was the sea, all silvered, and the stars — and the old workings looked white and pleasant in the ghostly light. My whole body relaxed to the sight of it and I felt desperately tired. The fear I had felt down there in those twisting galleries, the sense of being lost, the darkness — it was all like some ghastly nightmare. I could not believe that it had really happened. It was as though I had just woken up. It just didn't seem real.

I suppose I was looking a little dazed, for she caught my hand, and said, 'You'd better come up to the house and get dry. You're wet through.'

'Yes,' I said.

She left me and went into the store shed. I just stood there, gazing at the moonlight. When she came out she had discarded her overalls. She had the skirt and jumper on that she'd been wearing that morning and her hair blew free about her face. 'How come you know your way around the mine?' I asked as we started up the slope to the house.

She laughed. 'I've lived here nearly all my life. You don't expect a young girl not to go exploring. And then, when my stepfather found I liked going down the mine, he used to take me with him. I was the only person he'd got to show his property to.'

'Why didn't you get away from the place?' I asked. I was thinking of this girl alone in the house with old Manack, alone with him except for the woman.

'I don't know,' she said softly. 'I've only been to Penzance once. That was to give evidence about —' She stopped then and added quickly, 'I didn't enjoy that visit. And then my stepfather was alone except for old Mrs Brynd and there was the war. Somebody had to look after the bit of a farm we've got.'

The thought of old Manack had brought the strength pouring back into me in a flood of anger. I'd have it out with him when I got up to the house. There was something more to it than just a desire not to have the sea let into the Mermaid. He was scared of something — scared of me. I'd seen it in his eyes down there in the Mermaid when he'd learned that I was Ruth Nearne's son. My hands clenched and I strode up that slope with the great sense of power that anger brings.

The girl understood my mood, for she said, 'You won't do anything hasty. Just dry your clothes and go back to the mine. You'll be clear in your mind about what's happened when you've slept on it.'

'I'm clear enough in my mind about it now,' I answered, and went on in silence.

A thought was gnawing at my brain. A man who'd commit murder like that, the way he'd tried to kill me — a man who'd do that must have a streak of madness in him. I remembered how his eyes had glittered down there in the Mermaid gallery. That was it, the man was mad. The sight of that rich lode had driven him crazy. And he'd seen that lode as a kid. He'd only had one idea after that — to own the mine and work that lode himself. That was the reason for his first marriage, and for his second. And if he'd to kill a man to prevent the sea being let into the mine, then he might have killed before. The thought in my mind was so horrible that I tried to throw it out. It would make my mother's madness more ghastly by far than I had ever dreamed.

I tried not to think about it, but strode on with my hands clenched. I'd have it out with him right now. I'd get the truth out of him if I had to kill him with my bare hands to do it.

We had come in sight of the house now. I could see the bars on the little dormer window. They stood out sharp against the panes, which were white with reflected moonlight.

The girl caught hold of my arm. 'You won't do anything, will you?' she asked again.

I didn't answer. I didn't want to talk to anybody about it. I just wanted to get at old Manack.

'Please,' she said. She was panting with the effort of keeping up with me. 'It won't do any good. He thought you were going to destroy the mine. He loves it. It's his only child. Please.'

We had reached the house now. I made straight for the front door, the girl clinging to my arm. I tried to shake her off. But she held on, pleading. The door was not locked. I went in. Then I turned and tore her hands loose from my arm.

'Please, Jim,' she cried. 'Please.'

But I got myself clear of her.

'You go back to your kitchen,' I said.

'No good will come of this,' she cried.

Her face was distraught in the moonlight and her breath came in sobs. I left her there, with her great eyes watching me in despair, and went down the dark corridor. It was dank and chill, like the galleries of the mine. My wet clothes clung to me and my boots squelched on the stone flags. There was a light shining under the door of the old man's study. I turned the handle and pushed the door open.

The old man was sitting at his desk. He looked up and when he saw me standing there in the doorway all dripping from the mine, he started to his feet, the lamplight shining on his pale eyes.

For a moment we stood there, staring at each other. I don't know whether he thought me a ghost or was just too startled to speak. Whatever it was, he just stared at me with his mouth opened like a cavity in his head. I turned and shut the door. Then I started towards him. And at the same moment he made a dive for a little iron pick-axe that stood on a shelf among some relics of early mining.

I reached him as his hand closed on the deadly weapon. He fought me off with a strength that was incredible in a man of his age. But I was stronger than he was. I twisted the pick from his grasp and flung him back. He fetched up against his desk, overturning the big swivel chair with a crash.

He was frightened now. I could see it in his eyes. His tongue showed through his beard as he licked his lips. He was breathing heavily. 'What do you want?' he asked. 'If it's about your mother, you know all there is to know. She was mad.'

I felt an itch to get my thumbs into the grey stubble of his neck. 'I'm not sure it isn't you who are mad,' I said, keeping a hold on my anger. His eyes stared at me. They didn't blink. It was as though they had no lids to them. And they were pale — paler than I'd ever seen a man's eyes. I said, 'You thought I wouldn't get out of those old workings, didn't you? You thought I'd die, trapped down there beyond that stoping. You wanted me to die.'

His hands had tightened on the edge of the desk. 'I don't know what you're talking about.' He made an attempt at aloofness, but his voice trembled.

'Yes, you do,' I said. 'You knew I was following you. You deliberately led me into the old part of the mine. And then you went back and knocked those staples out.'

'How was I to know you were following me?' he asked.

'Why did you knock those staples out?' I asked him.

'I didn't want any one going up into those workings.' He stood up. 'What I do on my own property is my business, Pryce. Wheal Garth belongs to me. And no damned deserter of a miner is coming letting the sea into Wheal Garth.'

'Deserter of a miner, is it?' I roared. 'And what are you then? A murderer.'

At the word he seemed to shrink back, his face pale. The skin of his cheeks tightened across the bones so that his beard seemed to grow out of his skull. 'No,' he said. 'No.' His beard lifted. 'That's a lie,' he almost screamed.

'It's not a lie,' I thundered. 'You left me to die, buried alive in your damned mine because you were afraid of me. You had no more consideration for me than you had for the dog you flung down that shaft after your wife — or than you had for my mother.'

He seemed to have shrunk in stature. He looked bent and old. 'I did it to save your mother,' he said. 'I tell you I did it to save her.'

His vehemence brought the horrible thing that had been in my mind crawling to the surface. I tried to dispel it. It just wasn't possible. And yet . . . 'Your wife, Harriet, left you all her holdings in Wheal Garth, didn't she?'

He seemed to sense the drift of my question, for he began to tremble and didn't speak.

'Didn't she?' I shouted at him.

He nodded. He seemed mesmerised. Those pale, unblinking eyes were fixed upon me as though — yes, as though they saw some horror.

'Did my mother have any holdings in Wheal Garth?' I asked him.

His eyes flickered. I don't think he was capable of answering my question. He was dumb with fear.

'James Nearne, my mother's father, owned this place,' I said. 'He was landlord here when it was a pub. When the mine was still working. Now you own Cripples' Ease. My mother made it over to you, didn't she? She must have done.' I went towards him then. 'Did James Nearne also own shares in Wheal Garth?' I asked him.

And when he didn't answer, I said, 'So my mother made those over to you, too, eh? And your first wife left you her holdings in Wheal Garth. Three women — and they all owned shares in Wheal Garth. And they all died,' I added.

Still he was silent.

'I understand now,' I said. 'You killed them. You and your love of that cursed mine. You got their holdings and you killed them.'

'I didn't,' he shrieked, suddenly finding his tongue. His lower lip was trembling visibly. Stark madness stared out of those pale eyes. He leaned forward then. 'They would not work the mine, you see. A mine has a soul. A derelict mine is a devilish thing. It kills people, unless they take notice of it. It kills them, I tell you,' he cried. 'That's why Harriet died. It was the mine. And your mother. And you,' he screamed. 'Wheal Garth'll not let you destroy its riches by letting in the sea. It'll kill 'ee. You see if it don't.' There was a froth of spittle on his lips and his eyes glittered as he stood there screaming at me like a monkey. And I faced him, dumb with horror, appalled at his admission.

Then the door was flung open. 'What the hell's going on here?' It was Captain Manack.

'You keep out of this,' I said.

'Get back to the mine,' he ordered. 'You've no business to be up here, anyway. What'd happen if the police paid a visit? There's gossip enough as it is.'

'Who cares about the police?' I answered. I was angry at his interruption. I wanted time to work it out. The mine had killed them, he had said. And he was the mine. That meant that he had killed them. He had killed his wife — he, and not my mother. My God, what a fiend! He'd killed his wife and made my mother think she had done it. 'You crazy swine,' I muttered.

His son came forward and caught my arm as I moved towards the old man. I flung him off. There was murder in me at that moment. The Captain must have seen it in my eyes, for he cried out, 'Pryce!' His voice rang as though he was calling a platoon of infantry to attention. 'Stand back, will you.'

I said, 'This is between your father and me. You keep out of

174

it. And when I've finished with him,' I added through my teeth, 'you can look after the bits.'

'Get out of here,' he ordered. 'Do you hear? Get out!'

'Not until I've finished with this murderous swine,' I said.

But as I started for the old man, who was cowering against the desk, the Captain suddenly called out, 'Stay where you are, Pryce — or by God I'll shoot you.'

I stopped then, for he had a gun in his hand.

'That's better,' he said. And his teeth showed angrily beneath his moustache. 'Stand back against the wall. Go on — stand back.' Reluctantly I did as he ordered. 'Now then, what's the trouble?' he asked. His voice was tense.

'This,' I answered hotly. 'Your father's a murderer. He's just tried to kill me down in Wheal Garth. And he killed his second wife. He pitched her down that shaft and then persuaded my mother that she'd done it. He killed my mother and Kitty's. For all I know he killed yours as well.'

'No. My mother died naturally. But he did kill his second wife.' The son's lips were drawn in a tight little smile. 'That's why I control what happens in Wheal Garth,' he added.

At that there was a terrific crash. We all swung round. Kitty was standing there in the open doorway, her face ghastly white and the broken remnants of the tea tray on the floor at her feet. 'I — I was bringing you some tea,' she said in a pitifully small voice.

'Better go back to the kitchen, Kitty,' I said.

She looked at me with staring eyes. Then she nodded slowly and went out as though in a daze.

Seeing her go so stunned by what she'd heard made me realise the pathetic tragedy of it all. This old man crazed with the lust for tin, and Kitty living here and not knowing he had murdered her own mother.

The old man saw the open door and suddenly darted towards it. I thrust out my foot and he pitched headlong to the floor. I'd have been on to him if his son hadn't suddenly barked at me to keep back. There was something in the way that man held a gun that made it clear he wouldn't hesitate to use it. The old man was scrambling to his feet. He reached the door, mumbling incoherently to himself. Then he vanished into the corridor.

'Let him go,' said Captain Manack. 'I'll look after him in a minute.' He motioned me to a seat. 'See here, Pryce,' he said. 'This has been a bit of a shock to you. But there's nothing you can do about it — not now. Killing him' — he jerked his head towards the open door — 'won't bring your mother back. He's mad. I've known it ever since I came back. The mine has driven him crazy. What happened this evening? What started all this?'

I told him. When I'd finished, he nodded slowly. 'I was afraid of that,' he said. 'But I thought his guilty conscience would keep him clear of you.'

'What are you going to do now?' I said. 'There must be some justice in the world.' I got to my feet. 'My God, Manack! I want the swine brought to justice. He *drove* my mother mad. The sheer, calculated cruelty of it is horrible. I want justice,' I cried, thumping the desk. 'And by God I'll have it, even if it means giving myself up and standing a court martial.'

'Listen,' he said. 'What good will that do you? None. Absolutely none. I'll look after the old man. I'll lock him up. From now on he'll be out of harm's way. You do the job you have to do. Then you clear off. He'll get his desserts. He'll spend the rest of his life wandering forlornly through the galleries of Wheal Garth watching the sea slopping about in the gallery that might have brought him a fortune. He's mad enough now. He'll die a crazy, pathetic old man. You'll have your revenge, if that's what you're seeking.'

'I'm not seeking revenge.' I told him. 'It's justice I want.'

He shrugged his shoulders. 'You can do what you like when you've finished this job for me,' he said. 'But he won't hang, even if you can prove it — which I doubt. They'd send him to Broadmoor. And you'd serve a sentence for desertion. You'd drag your mother's name through the courts — see her wretched history plastered all over the pages of the Sunday press. And destroy Kitty entirely,' he added.

He was right there. I leaned against the desk. The anger had gone. I felt flat and tired. 'I guess you're right,' I said. The thought of Kitty, who had only once been as far as Penzance, giving evidence from the witness box at a murder trial — it was unthinkable. 'Okay,' I said. 'I'll let him be.' And I went towards the door. Then I stopped. 'But see he's locked up safe. I'm not working down in the Mermaid if he's loose — not with all that water standing over us in Come Lucky.'

'Don't worry about that,' he answered. 'I don't trust him any more than you do.'

I hesitated. I wanted to tell him I was clearing out — leaving the place — getting right away from the whole rotten business. But he sat there watching me, the gun in his hand and his eyes narrowed. He wouldn't let me go. I knew that. He'd too much to lose. He'd kill me rather than let me get clear of the place.

I went out and closed the door behind me. Now that my anger was gone I felt adrift. I had no purpose. Disgust for the whole rotten business filled my mind. I felt the way Hamlet must have felt. The manner of my mother's death called for vengeance. And yet I could not do it. I could not just kill the old man in cold blood. He was mad. And disgust, not anger, filled me. I'd go away. I'd get clear of it all.

Then I saw the kitchen door facing me. And through it came the sound of a girl sobbing. It was a wild, uncontrolled sound. I opened the door and went in. Kitty was alone. She was sitting by the fire, her shoulders racked by sobs so violent that it seemed impossible for her body to stand it. Her face was white even in the ruddy glow of the flames. She didn't see me. She was staring into the fire and her eyes were dry.

'Kitty!' I said.

She didn't hear me.

I went over to her and took her by the shoulders. She looked up then and saw me. The sobbing stopped. She seemed to be holding her breath. Then suddenly she bent her head against my body and the tears came. Her body trembled and shook in my hands. 'Don't cry,' I said. 'It's past now. It couldn't be helped.'

'It could,' she cried out wildly. 'It could. Oh, Jim — how can you forgive me? She was so good to me. And I believed him. I believed what he said of her. I should have known she didn't do it. I couldn't have saved my mother. But I could have saved her.' She looked up at me wildly. 'Say you forgive me, Jim. Say you forgive me. I couldn't have known, could I?'

'Of course not,' I said, stroking her hair. The poor kid was beside herself.

'Oh God!' she breathed. 'It's so horrible. All that year. She was in that room a year. And she believed she'd done it. She believed she was mad. Oh, if I'd only known,' she sobbed. 'It's my fault. I shouldn't have believed it of her. If I hadn't believed it, then she wouldn't have.'

'Then he'd have killed her a different way,' I said gently. 'Don't worry, Kitty. It wasn't your fault.'

She clutched at my hand and held it tight against her wet cheek. 'She used to tell me fairy stories when I was a little girl with pigtails,' she said in a stifled voice. 'She loved me. I should have known. Her face looking at me through the hatch . . . Oh, God!'

The door opened and Captain Manack came in. 'The old man's not in his room,' he said. He came up and caught hold of Kitty. 'Did you hear my father come out?'

She gulped and then nodded.

'Which way did he go — upstairs?'

She shook her head. 'He went out the front door,' she said slowly.

He let her go then and turned to me. 'He's down the mine. You come down with us.' He turned quickly and went out through the scullery. I heard him shouting for Friar and Slim.

'Listen, Kitty,' I said, seizing her by the shoulders and forcing her to look at me. 'You can't stay here. Do you understand? You must go away.'

She nodded slowly. And then she said in a small, lost voice,

'But where? I've nowhere to go. I hate this place. But I've never been anywhere else.'

'You're coming away with me.' I said it without thinking, my mind suddenly made up.

She stared at me. Voices sounded through the open scullery door. They were coming nearer. 'Meet me down at the mine at three o'clock in the morning. There's no time to talk about it,' I said quickly as footsteps sounded on the cobbles of the stables. 'Meet me at three o'clock. Understand?'

She nodded slowly. She was too dazed to think it out. She would have agreed to anything I said at that moment. 'Promise?' I said.

'I promise,' she answered.

I heard Friar's voice saying, 'Ruddy lark, this is — I don't fink. We bin on the job since six this mornin', yer know, Capting. I didn't aim ter spend the night playin' tag wiv your old man down that bleedin' mine.' They stopped in the scullery.

'We've got to find him,' Captain Manack answered sharply. Then he came through into the kitchen. 'Come on, Pryce,' he said.

'I'll stay up here for a bit,' I said. 'The girl's had a shock.'

'To hell with the girl,' he snapped. 'Come on now.'

'I'm staying with the girl,' I told him.

'You're coming down the mine with us.' There was an implied threat in the quietness of his voice. 'Don't start any trouble up here,' he added, and glanced towards Kitty.

I had half a mind to defy him. But it wouldn't do any good. He'd got his gun. I could see the shape of it bulging in his pocket. 'All right,' I said. Then I turned to Kitty. 'Promise?' I asked her again.

She nodded slowly. 'I promise,' she said as though repeating something she'd been taught.

I left her then and went out with Manack. As he shut the door behind us, I saw her sitting just as she had been when I had come in, her eyes staring straight in front of her without seeing anything. I think it must have been then that I realised that I loved her. I know it suddenly seemed quite natural that I'd decided to take her with me when I left in the morning. And the sight of her suffering tore at me as though it were myself that was suffering.

Outside, I was surprised to see that the moon was still shining. It seemed such a long time back that Kitty and I had gone into the house.

We walked hurriedly and in silence, Manack beside me. Slim and Friar behind. We reached the mine buildings. They went into the store shed and got helmets and lamps and clothes. Then we went into the hoist. 'Suppose 'e's wanderin' aba't the cliffs?' Friar said. ''E might be anywhere. Don't yer fink one of us better stay on top?'

'No,' Manack answered and we got into the gig. 'He's down the mine. It's the place he'd naturally go.' He flung the lever over and we began to descend. But he stopped at the store room gallery. 'This is where you get off, Pryce,' he said.

'You don't want me down the mine?' I said.

'No.' He stepped out beside me. 'I'm not taking any chances with you, my lad — not after what's happened. Dave!' he shouted. 'Dave! Where is that damned Welshman? Dave!'

The light of a torch flickered. 'Yes. Yes, what is it?' Dave Tanner's voice sounded agitated as he suddenly appeared in the gallery.

'Oh, there you are. Have you got a gun?'

'Indeed I have, Captain. I always —'

'Then keep an eye on your chum, Pryce. You're not to leave him — understand? If he tries to get away use your gun. I hold you responsible for him.' He turned to me. 'Don't take this amiss, Pryce. I don't mean you any harm, but I'm taking no chances. A couple of days and you'll be through. Then you can go.'

His action had taken me so completely by surprise that I said nothing for a moment. Dave had reached us now. The whites of his eyes showed in his swarthy face. 'What is the trouble, Captain?' he asked.

'There's no trouble,' Manack replied sharply. 'Just see that he's here in the morning, that's all.' His voice dropped. 'If he's not — well, you won't get your passage to Italy.'

The menace in his voice brought sudden suspicion to my mind. 'When I've done this job for you,' I said, 'what guarantee have I that you'll let me go then?'

'My word,' he answered. 'I've never gone back on my word, Pryce. You'll sail on the *Arisaig* Monday night if the Mermaid's opened up by then.'

'And get murdered by that swine Mulligan,' I said.

His face darkened and he caught hold of my arm. 'I told you I never went back on my word, didn't I? He'll have instructions to land you at Naples.'

He met my gaze and I knew that he would do what he said. 'All right,' I said.

He nodded and stepped back into the gig. Friar put the lever over and it rattled out of sight down into the bowels of the mine.

'Whatever's happened, man?' Dave said. 'I waited and waited. I thought you'd never come back. I don't like it here at all — not on my own. There's the sound of the water, you know, and it's so quiet.' And when I didn't say anything, he said. 'Is it a row with the Captain you've had?' The sound of the gig ceased. Everything was quiet — only the drip of the water. I shivered and turned towards Dave. He started back. 'It is a ghost you've seen, man?' he said. 'You're as white as a sheet. And your clothes — they're all wet.'

'Yes,' I said, 'I'm cold and wet.'

I went along the gallery to the hideout. Dave stepped aside to let me pass, his hand in his jacket pocket. He was scared of me — scared of Manack — scared of himself. He made me nervous.

As soon as I was inside the hideout, he pulled the slabs to and bolted them. Even then he kept his distance. I stripped and towelled myself down. All the time he plied me with questions. In the end I told him how old Manack had tried to kill me.

'Ter-rible!' he said. 'Ter-rible!' He sat there shaking his head, living the fear that I had suffered with all the emotionalism of his race. 'But why did he do it, man?'

'He didn't want me letting the sea into his beloved mine,' I told him.

'You should have stayed here with me,' he said. 'Worried to death I was about you. I thought maybe the police had come. I went out once. But then I was afraid that if they came, they'd search the mine. I bolted myself in. Like being in a coffin, it was. I got scared. It was so quiet and me not knowing what was happening in the world outside.'

And so he went on whilst I sat and tried to think. The old man was loose in the mine. And Kitty up there alone in the house. How was I to meet her at three in the morning with Dave Tanner sitting there, nervous as a kitten, and his hand on the butt of a gun? And if I did meet her, where were we to go! I was a fool. All I'd been thinking about when I'd told her to meet me was getting out of the place. I'd forgotten I was wanted by the police — forgotten that a description of me had been published. And whilst I tried to sort it out in my mind, that damned little Welshman went on talking. I tried to shut him up. But it was like telling water to stay in a bottle with a broken bottom. He just had to talk. He had to talk because he was scared to sit silent.

In the end I could stand it no longer, 'I'm going outside,' I said. I had to know whether they had located the old man. I got to my feet. In the same instant Dave had leapt to the entrance, the gun in his hand. 'No, you don't,' he said.

'Listen, Dave,' I said, 'I need some fresh air.'

'So do I,' he answered. 'But the Captain said I was to keep you here. And it's not going against the Captain's orders I am.'

'I can't stand this place,' I said. 'It's like a tomb.'

'It is indeed. But —' He shrugged his shoulders.

I said, 'You realise that the old man means to kill me. He's tried already and he'll try again. He's loose in the mine at this moment. For all I know he's outside in the gallery right now. One charge and he could have us walled up in here by a fall of rock.'

Dave's eyes dilated in horror. 'You really think that?'

I nodded. 'And they'd never get us out in time,' I said.

'You think he'd try?'

'He might. You don't want to be trapped down here, do you?'

'Indeed I don't. I've always hated being shut in anywhere, you see.'

'Well, then, let's go up top,' I suggested. 'I won't try and escape if that's what you're scared of. Where the hell would I go? I'm wanted by the police the same as you.

'That's true enough.' He went over the entrance and shot back the bolt. 'We'll wait in the gallery.'

'Why not up top?' I suggested.

'The Captain may return.'

With that I had to be content. At least I could watch for the gig to come up. We dragged a couple of boxes out into the gallery and sat there. Dave was taking no chances and stationed himself well behind me. For a time he talked incessantly. But gradually he grew silent. I felt tired and sleepy. The time dragged by. I think I must have dozed for I started awake and heard the rattle of the gig coming up. Dave turned out his lamp. A faint glow showed at the end of the gallery. It grew bright and the sound of the gig grew louder. Then for a brief instant I had a glimpse of miners' lamps and the bearded skull of the elder Manack standing between Friar and his son.

A match flared in the darkness and Dave relit his lamp.

'I'm going up top,' I said.

'Stay where you are.' Dave's voice was nervous again.

'I want to see the old man safely clear of the mine,' I said. 'For God's sake, man, what's the matter with you; I shan't run with Captain Manack within call.'

That seemed to satisfy him and he followed me without further protest as I went up the cross-cut to the shaft and climbed the ladder to the top. The moon was sinking towards the sea, throwing long shadows across the white landscape. I breathed in the fresh air and, as we sat down on a patch of bracken among the gorse bushes, I sensed that Dave was less nervous up here in the open air.

We hadn't been there a few minutes before figures moved out of the black shadows of the sheds. There were four of them. Friar and Slim each had hold of one of the old man's arms. His son followed behind. They climbed the hill towards us. As they came within earshot Slim was saying, 'Bloody lucky, I call it.'

'It fair makes me sweat ter fink aba't it,' Friar said.

'Well, see that you don't mention it to Pryce,' Captain Manack ordered. 'I don't want him getting scared.'

'I'm all fer goin' back ter the nice peaceful life of makin' kerb stones,' Friar said. 'Wot you say, Slim? Kerb stones is a sort o' restful thing ter be makin'.'

'You didn't think much of the job when we were cutting those ledges,' Slim answered sourly.

'Well, yer can 'ave too much of a good thing. Nah all we fink of is liquor.' He spat. 'Some o' these 'ere ruddy Black Marketeers oughter come an' get their liquor the 'ard way — like we does.'

The sound of their voices died away. I watched them disappear over the brow of the hill, four dark figures against the moon-filled sky. 'What about going up to the top of the hill and seeing him safely inside the house?' I said. 'I won't be happy till I know the old man's safely locked up.' The time was two-thirty. I had to keep him above ground till three.

He hesitated. 'All right,' he said.

We went slowly up the hill. I bore away slightly to the left where there was a gulley that ran up close to the house. We went up this and came out within fifty yards of Cripples' Ease. There was no one about. The house stood square and unbeautiful, looking out with pale eyes to the sea. 'Come on,' Dave said. 'He's safe enough now.'

A light flickered suddenly in the little dormer window. The bars showed clearly against the orange glow. Then the light vanished as though cut off by the closing of a door. Dave was plucking at my elbow. I shook him off impatiently. Something told me what I should see and it fascinated me. For a moment the window remained as blind as the others. Then suddenly I saw what I was waiting for.

Pressed close to the panes was Manack's bearded face. I can see it now — haggard and drawn. He was looking out to the mine and his face caught the light of the sinking moon so that it was white as the face of a ghost.

CHAPTER NINE

Blasting Operations

The sight of the old man's face peering out from between the bars of that little window gave me a horrible sense of satisfaction. I had wanted justice. This was vengeance. I thought of how my mother had looked out from behind those bars and how it drove her to suicide. And now, the man who had made her believe she had killed Kitty's mother, the man who had shut her in there away from the world, was himself locked in that room — and mad, really mad. I started to laugh. The sound of my voice jarred and frightened me. It was a harsh laugh, but I couldn't stop it.

Dave looked round. 'Ssh!' he said. 'Somebody might hear you.' But I went on laughing. 'Man alive, what's got into you?'

I shook my head. Gradually my laughter died away and I felt weak and exhausted. 'You wouldn't understand, Dave,' I said.

We had reached the shaft now. Dave stood aside and motioned me to go first. It was then that I remembered Kitty. It was two forty-five. I'd only quarter of an hour to wait. 'You go on down,' I said. 'I'll stay up top a bit.'

He looked at me quickly, his eyes suddenly suspicious. His hand came out of his jacket pocket. The blue steel of his gun glinted. 'Go on,' he said. 'Get down the shaft.' His voice had the high pitch of tension. He was scared of me.

'For God's sake, Dave,' I said. 'We came up for a breath of air, didn't we? It won't hurt to stay up top a little longer. You don't want to go down to that stuffy little hole again, do you?'

'No,' he said. 'But I'm taking no chances, see. You heard what the Captain said. He said if you weren't here in the morning, I'd get no passage on the *Arisaig*.'

'But, good God,' I said, 'I'm not going to run away.'

'Bloody right, you're not,' he answered sharply. 'Now get going.'

'Listen,' I said. 'I just want to stay up here for a few minutes more. I won't run away. I give you my word.'

'Think I'd take your word. It's daft, you are, to talk of such a thing.' His dark eyes watched me narrowly, the gun gripped in his hand. 'It's up to something, you are, man,' he said excitedly. 'And I'm taking no chances. I'm wanted for murder. And the only man who can get me out of the country safely is Captain Manack. Now, get down that shaft. Try anything and I'll shoot you.'

I laughed. 'You wouldn't dare,' I said. 'Captain Manack needs a live miner to open up that gallery. A dead one's no good to him. Look, Dave — I'll tell you why I want to stay up top a little longer. There's a girl up at the house. She used to know my mother. I've arranged to meet her down here. There, will that satisfy you? She's coming down at three o'clock — that's in ten minutes' time.'

'You're lying,' he breathed excitedly. 'I don't believe a word of it. It's up to something, you are. I know it. You want to get away on your own — turn King's Evidence, maybe. If you hadn't turned up the other night, I'd have taken Sylvia Coran with me and the police would never have known I'd survived the disappearance of the *Isle of Mull*. Your fault it is that I'm on the run. Do you understand? Your fault. And now you want to get away from me. Now you think I'm dangerous.' He was quivering with the violence of his feelings and there was a murderous gleam in his eyes. 'Well, I am dangerous,' he added. 'I'm not afraid of using a gun. And I don't want any more talk about girls. You're not meeting a girl. You're trying to get away. All that nonsense about seeing the old man safely up to the house. Lies, all damned, lousy, bloody lies. You're trying to get clear of us. Well, you're not going to do it, see. Now, get down that shaft or I'll start shooting.'

He was all worked up. The gun literally quivered in his hand as he brought it up. I believe he wanted to use it. I think he wanted to feel the power that firing a gun gives a man. He needed that sense of power, for he was scared — and that made him dangerous. I sat down on the protecting wall of the shaft. I did it with an assumption of ease which I certainly did not feel. 'Have some sense, Dave,' I said. 'Fire that thing and it'll be heard for miles. Kill me and —'

'It's fitted with a silencer,' he interrupted with a tight-lipped grin.

'All right,' I said. 'But if you kill me, Manack won't do anything for you. Right now he needs me.'

'I shan't kill you,' he answered.

'All right,' I said. 'But if you wound me, it'll be just as bad. Captain Manack needs that gallery opened up right away. A wounded miner is no more use to him than a dead one.'

Dave laughed. 'It's a good shot, I am. And a miner can work all right even if he has no toes.' His voice suddenly became almost strident. 'For Crissake, man, get down that shaft or do I have to hurt you?'

He raised his gun. He meant it. I could see that. I shrugged my shoulders. What was the good? I'd need my feet if I was to get Kitty away from this place. He was raising the gun now. His whole body trembled with the desire to fire it. His eyes were almost glazed. I had broken out into a sweat. 'All right, Dave,' I said quickly, as the black barrel of the gun pointed at my left boot. 'I'll go down.' He didn't seem to hear. I could see the white of his first finger knuckle as he squeezed at the trigger. 'All right, Dave,' I shouted.

His eyes lost their glazed look and met mine. Then he looked down at the gun in his hand. Slowly, almost reluctantly, he lowered his arm to his side. The sweat glistened on his face. He seemed dazed. 'Get on down, then,' he said in a voice that was strangely husky. He was like a man drained of all energy.

I went down the shaft. The rock holds were wet and slimy under my hands. Darkness and the sound of water closed me in. The world above was reduced to a white circle of light. The moon was so low that no light came down into the shaft. Then the circle of light was filled with Dave's dark figure and the yellow gleam of his torch shone on the rock walls.

Back in the hideout, he closed the entrance and bolted it. Then he had me sit on one side of the dugout whilst he squatted on a box on the other side, the gun across his knees and his black eyes watching me ceaselessly. I lit another miner's lamp and sat there thinking of Kitty. The hands of my watch moved slowly round to three o'clock.

Blast that frightened little Welshman! She'd be up there waiting for me. She'd think I wasn't coming because I was angry with her. My God, she might do anything if I didn't turn up. The picture of her seated by the kitchen range, dry-eyed and shaken with fearful sobs, leapt to my mind. She had blamed herself for what had happened. She was in no fit state of mind to be left alone. If I didn't meet her, she might . . . I thrust that thought out of my mind. She'd come down to the hideout as she had done before. No good imagining things. She was upset — terribly upset — that was all. It was quite natural. She wasn't the sort of girl who would go and do anything foolish.

But as the time drifted by I became more and more worried. I kept on seeing her standing up there all alone as the moon's shadows lengthened and lengthened. And then when I didn't come . . . There were the cliffs straight ahead of her. She'd think of the cliffs and how my mother had ended her life. She was bound to.

I kept on glancing across at Dave Tanner. And every time I did so, his black eyes would meet mine watchfully. Once he said, 'It's no good. I'm watching you and I'm not sleepy.'

I fancied I could hear the tick of my wrist-watch. It was so still. It *was* like a tomb. Suddenly there was a new sound. Dave started to his feet, the gun in his hand. It was the hollow sound of rock on rock. It came from the entrance-way. 'Somebody's trying to get in,' Dave whispered. His eyes were dilated and his whole body tense. 'It's the police. It's tapping, they are — searching for the entrance.'

'Nonsense,' I said. 'It's the girl. Open up, Dave.'

'No,' he cried. 'No. Stand back.'

His gun was pointed at my stomach. He was so strung up I

didn't dare move. If I'd moved he'd have fired. 'I didn't tell the Captain,' he whispered. 'But when I was coming here I ran slap into the local bobby. Up on the main road, it was. I came that way because it was quicker than going round by the moors. He was standing quite still fiddling with his bike. I didn't see him until he shone his torch on me.'

The tapping ceased. There was a far-away, distant sound. It might have been water or it might have been somebody calling. The thickness of the rock slabs deadened all sound. It came again. After that there was silence. I looked at Dave, measuring the distance for a sudden spring. I had to get to that girl. But he saw my intention in my eyes and retreated to the far corner, the gun levelled at me. 'Dave,' I said, 'I must speak to that girl.'

'You stay where you are,' he ordered.

'But good God,' I said, 'what makes you think that was the police? I tell you it was the girl. She came to find me, like she did earlier this evening.'

'Indeed, I hope you're right.' He sat down heavily on one of the cases. 'My God, I hope you're right.' He wiped the sweat from his face with a dirty rag of a handkerchief. 'If that was the police —' he didn't finish. 'What makes you think it was the girl?' There was a note of hope in his voice.

'Look,' I said, 'the kid's had a hell of a shock. She's just discovered that old Manack murdered her mother.'

'You don't say?'

I told him the whole story then. It was the only way. I told him everything. And when I had finished, he said 'Jim, bach, that's ter-rible.' It was incredible how emotional he was.

'Now, will you let me go up and see the girl?' I asked. 'I'm scared she may do something silly up there on her own.'

He hesitated. Fear and love of the dramatic and the emotional were at odds in his mind. I said, 'For God's sake, can't you see what's in her mind? She feels that it's her fault my mother went over the cliffs that day. She needs me to tell her it's all right. If I'm not there —' I stopped then, loath to put the thought into words.

190

He nodded and got up irresolutely. 'I give you my word not to try to escape from you,' I said. 'And if the police are around we'll come straight back. Okay?'

He went over to the entrance and quietly eased back the bolts. Then he pushed back the top slabs and peered cautiously out. I was right beside him. The gallery was dark save for the light of our lamps on the rock wall immediately opposite the hideout. It didn't take me long to go up the cross-cut to the shaft and climb the stone sets to the top. The moon had just set. The sea's horizon stood out sharp and black like a ruled line against the vague light left in the night sky. The cliff tops were full of dark, huddled shapes, impossible to tell whether Kitty was there or not. I ran stumbling down to the sheds of the mine. She wasn't there. I started calling her name. It came echoing back to me from stone heaps and ruined mine buildings. But she did not answer. I went down along the cliffs towards Botallack Head. Time and again I thought I saw her. But it was only a bush or an old stone wall.

I didn't like that place at night. It gave me the creeps. It had been all right in full moonlight. But in this half-light it seemed hostile and withdrawn into some primitive past of its own. All those workings! The sweat of thousands of men had gone into honeycombing these cliff tops. Ignoring Dave's protest, I stumbled up and down along the top of those cliffs, calling her name. But never an answering call, save for a distant owl. I was beside myself. Kitty suddenly became very precious to me. I needed her. And I was afraid I'd lost her. Dave, limping along behind, caught up with me as I stood once again on the brink of the dark cliffs of Botallack Head. The place fascinated me. The long rollers marched in endless straight lines against the base of the cliffs. Black rocks showed in the boiling surf. Away to the left the old engine house stood like a castle outpost, its brick chimney half-smothered in spray. I thought I saw a body down there on a sloping slab that gleamed dully with the water that poured off it. I blinked and when I looked again it had gone.

The light played tricks. I stepped back. I don't suffer from vertigo, but there was something about those cliffs — they drew me.

Dave caught hold of my arm. 'It's back to the house she's gone, I'm thinking,' he said, with all the quick sympathy of an emotional nature.

'Yes,' I said. 'She's back at the house.' I turned away. 'We'll go up and see,' I added, and strode off inland to the track that ran up to Cripples' Ease.

He raised no objection. I could hear him limping along after me. The light was fading out of the western sky. It was getting darker every moment. The ruin of the old mine workings seemed to jump at us out of the night; strange, blurred shapes that had no substance. The lights of a car moving along the main road through Botallack village threw Cripples' Ease in sudden dark relief. Once more I felt that sense of unreality the building had conveyed that first night. It had no right to be occupied in the midst of all this desolation. It should have been allowed to disintegrate with the rest. It was part of the past.

The lights of the car beside it swung in a great arc. For a second I was looking straight into the beams of the headlights. Then they disappeared behind the house. 'Get down, man,' Dave called as I stood there, dazed by the brilliance. I dived behind a wall of ruined stonework. The car was coming down the track towards the house. Dave crawled up and lay panting beside me. 'What would a car be wanting here at this time of night?' he muttered. The tremor of his voice betrayed the state of his nerves.

'Trippers coming back late from a dance,' I suggested. 'Not a bad place for necking.' But I don't think I believed that myself. Somehow I didn't see a young couple coming out here after the moon had set.

The headlights swung clear of the house. The stones gleamed on the great heaped-up piles alongside the workings. I looked at Dave. I could see his face quite clearly. It was white and his breath came quickly. The car slowed down to a crawl as it came level with the house not fifty yards from where we lay hid. The headlights swung away from us as the car turned. Finally it stopped, its lights blazing full on the dark façade of Cripples' Ease. Two men got out and went to the front door. One wore uniform.

'Police,' Dave whispered. 'The bloke in plain clothes is a detective.'

I nodded.

'If they'd got anything on the Captain they'd have brought more men and surrounded the place,' he added. 'It's suspicious they are, that's all.' Relief and fear showed themselves in his voice.

The two policemen waited in the doorway. At last the door opened. It was Captain Manack. He had a dressing-gown on over his pyjamas and he carried a lamp. A few words and the two police officers went inside. The light entered one of the front rooms. I could see right into it for there were no curtains and the shutters were not closed. It had apparently been the bar. It did not appear to have been altered since the days when the house had been a pub. Even at that distance I could see the bar counter with shelves for bottles behind and a dartboard hanging on the wall above the fireplace. Captain Manack went out. A few minutes later he came back into the room and shortly afterwards Slim entered, followed by Friar. They were both in their night things. Then the old woman came in. And finally Kitty.

A great weight seemed lifted off my mind at the sight of her standing there in the doorway in her dressing-gown. She seemed heavy and tired. Her face was white and expressionless. I couldn't bear to watch her being interrogated. 'Maybe we ought to get back to the hideout,' I suggested.

'Lie still, man,' Dave whispered urgently. 'Lie still and don't move. They may have men posted all round with night glasses. Just lie still and wait.'

For the better part of half an hour we lay there, our stomachs pressed to the cold stones that became sharper as the minutes lengthened. At last there was no one in the room but Captain Manack and the two officers. All three were smoking. Then they went on. The door closed and the house was black again. The light appeared next at the front door. The two policemen went across to their car. I heard the plainclothes man say in quite a cheerful voice. 'Good night, sir. Sorry we called so late.'

'That's all right,' Captain Manack answered. 'Good night.'

There was the slam of doors as the policemen got into their car. Then the engine roared into life. And at the same time a face appeared at the little dormer window at the top of the house. I could see it quite clearly in the blaze of the headlights. It looked white and strained and the beard was thrust between the bars. I could see the old man's eyes.

Then the car began to move, the headlights swung away from the face of the house and I could no longer see the window. The house was no more than a ghostly shadow in the sudden blackness.

We watched the car turn right on to the main road. We followed its headlights all the way to St. Just and traced its movement right out along the Penzance road. Only then would Dave agree to move and return to the hideout. So much had happened my brain was dazed. The girl was safe. To that extent at any rate my mind was at rest and I fell asleep with my clothes on.

I awoke at the faint sound of metal striking rock. I was sweating and the air in the dugout was stale. I rolled over and looked at my watch. It was eight-thirty. Dave was sitting on his bed, rubbing his eyes. His face was pale and beaded with sweat and there were dark rings under his eyes.

The slabs of the entrance were being struck from outside in the gallery. It was a regular beat to the form of a signal. Dave went over and drew back the bolts.

The slabs swung back and Captain Manack came in. He too, looked tired and his hair stood straight up like fine wire. He glanced quickly from one to the other of us. 'Had breakfast yet, Pryce?' he asked.

'No,' I said. 'I overslept.'

'So I see.' He was like an officer on a foot inspection. His eyes took in the frousty disorder of the dugout. At length they fixed themselves on Dave, who had retired to the farthest corner, and sat biting his nails and casting surreptitious glances at his master. Manack moved towards him. His eyes had a strange look. I began to get my things together. Those eyes of his scared me. I wondered how much of his father's madness he'd inherited. He caught hold of Dave by his collar and jerked him to his feet. 'The police were here during the night.' The words were bitten short between his clenched teeth. 'I thought you said nobody saw you coming here?'

'Well, you see —'

'I don't want any more of your lies,' he almost screamed, shaking the little Welshman to and fro. It was amazing the strength he had in those thin arms. 'You said you met no one. But the local policeman, of all people, swears he saw you coming along the main road just outside Botallack. Is that true? Answer. Did he see you?'

'Yes. I was going —'

'God in heaven!' Captain Manack cried and flung Dave against the rock wall. 'You fool! Why the hell didn't you tell me? At least I'd have known what to expect.' He turned to me. 'Pryce,' he said, 'you've got to be through to the sea bed tonight.'

'That's impossible,' I told him.

'Nothing's impossible,' he barked. 'Make the preliminary charges bigger. The *Arisaig* will be off the adit at four tomorrow morning. If the job's done you sail with her. If not —' He shrugged his shoulders. 'Then you take your chance in this country. Understand? You'll have Friar to work with you on the drilling. Slim, Tanner and myself will clear the loose rock after each blow. Now get moving.'

I took a can of bully, some bread and a bottle of milk and joined Slim and Friar in the gallery outside. As we went towards the gig I heard Dave's voice, pitched high on a note of fear, cry out, 'That's not true. I swear it isn't. I didn't want to scare you unnecessarily, look you. It was dark and —'

'Scare me?' Captain Manack laughed harshly. 'I suppose an unexpected visit from the police at four in the morning is one of those little surprises that are expected to act as a sedative. Well, now I'm going to do some scaring.' There was a sudden scream and then silence.

'What the hell's he done?' I asked Friar.

He pushed me into the gig. 'You don't want ter worry yer 'ead aba't that,' he said. Slim threw over the lever and we rattled down into the depths of the mine. ''E ain't killed 'im, if that's wot's worryin' yer,' Friar shouted in my ear. 'Though Gawd knows it's wot 'e deserves. Four o'clock in the bleedin' mornin' the police turns up. That's a bastard hour fer hinterrogation.'

'How did Captain Manack explain my visit?' I asked.

The gig slowed up and came to rest at the bottom of the shaft. 'Easy,' Friar answered as we stepped out. 'Told 'em the truth. Said yer was a deserter from Italy wot'd just come into the country. Told 'em you'd come ter 'im fer 'elp because you'd bin wiv 'im fer a short time in Eighth Army. 'E said 'e'd 'ad ter refuse yer and you'd gorn orf in the direction of St. Just.'

'And Dave Tanner?' I asked.

'There wasn't nuffink ter prove 'e'd ever come da'n ter Cripples' Ease. Believe it or not, the coppers 'adn't even got a search warrant. They just questioned us and then left. I was scared the old man would let somefink slip, but when they 'eard 'e was ill, they let it go at that. But they'll be back. That's why the Capting's so keen ter get the 'ole thing finished an' the *Arisaig* away tonight. An' ruddy glad I'll be when it's done, too. I ain't too keen on coppers in and a't of the place like trippers.'

We climbed on to the carriage. Slim pulled back on the lever and we started down the gallery. I opened the can of bully and started my breakfast. 'What was it you discovered last night, Friar?' I shouted through a mouthful of bread and corned beef.

Friar glanced at me quickly. 'Wot d'yer mean?' he asked.

'Last night — whilst you were down the mine looking for the old man,' I shouted to him. 'You discovered something. "Fair makes me sweat to think about it" — that's what you said. What was it?'

"Ow d'you know wot I said?' he asked. 'You wasn't wiv us.'

'No,' I answered. 'But I went up for a breath of air. I heard you talking amongst yourselves as you took Old Manack up to the house. What had you found?'

'Oh, nuffink much.' Friar turned his head away and made a pretence of being interested in the movement of the bearing against the rock walls. 'There was more water comin' into the Mermaid than we'd reckoned, that's all.'

'That wouldn't scare me,' I shouted.

'Wot?' He gave me a quick glance. 'Let it go, mate. It ain't important.'

'Where did you find the old man — up in the old workings?'

He nodded. 'Yep.'

I fell silent then, watching that crazy contraption move steadily down the wet gallery that ran out under the sea. My guess was they'd never been down the Mermaid last night. Captain Manack had known where his father had gone and he'd made straight for the old workings. I felt uneasy. They'd discovered something; something the old man had been up to. *Fair makes me sweat to think about it.* I glanced closely at Friar, wondering whether he was thinking about it now. He was staring in front of him, his big, calloused hand clenched on the guard rail. Well, whatever they'd found, the old man was out of harm's way now.

The carriage slowed. The great timber beams of the scaffolding showed in the lights of our lamps. I went to have a look at the effect of the previous day's blast. The trickling sound of water was loud now that the carriage was not bumping and swaying along the ledges. There were several inches of water on the floor of the gallery. We sloshed through it. The timbers across the pit were piled high with rubble. The charge had blown out more than I had expected. I directed the beam of my lamp to the roof. Everything was covered with a thick film of rock dust. It had mingled with the water to form a slimy grey paste. One of the scaffolding timbers had been split by the blast. Water streamed down from the shaft. I picked up a piece of rock from the floor.

It was granite all right. But it was streaked with basalt.

'Wot's up, mate?' Friar asked.

'The rock's weaker here,' I told him.

'Dangerous?' he asked.

'Maybe,' I said. 'Let's go up and have a look.'

We set ladders up into the freshly blown section of the shaft and clambered up. The rock was faulty. You didn't need to be an expert to see that. It was streaked with veins of basalt and cracked with the force of the explosion. Through a thousand minute crevices the water was seeping. It splashed on our helmets, on our upturned faces and sizzled as drops struck the naked flames of our lamps. It streamed down the walls so that they glistened like burnished steel. 'Don't look too safe to me,' Friar said. ''Ow much rock is there between us an' the sea?'

I glanced at the rock walls, measuring with my eye the height added to the shaft by last night's blow. 'About fifteen feet according to Captain Manack's reckoning,' I told him.

'Fifteen feet don't seem much,' he muttered.

I examined the rock again. The roof of the shaft was no longer neatly cut out by the force of the charge. It was broken and jagged. 'Two more blasts should do it,' I said.

'Two more!' His voice sounded doubtful. 'Blimey! I ain't sure I cares very much aba't doin' one more. Look at that crack there, mate. Wide enough fer me ter put me fist into. Looks ter me as though the 'ole bleedin' lot'll fall away soon as we get the drill goin'.'

'Looks worse than it is,' I told him. 'We'll drill the charge holes and then probe ahead with the long drill.'

He caught hold of my arm and peered up into my face. 'You 'ave done this sort o' thing before, ain't yer? I mean, yer do know wot yer up ter?'

'Scared?' I asked.

'Wot, me?' He drew back angrily. ''Course I ain't. I just like ter know I'm workin' wiv somebody wot knows his onions, that's all.'

Within ten minutes we had the drill clamp fixed across the shaft. Then Friar started up the compressor and the whole undersea gallery reverberated to the roar and chatter of the pneumatic drill. By the time we'd done two holes, Captain Manack arrived with Dave and Slim. They off-loaded the compressor and then set to work loading the broken rock on to the carriage. Manack climbed up beside us. 'How's it going?' he shouted.

I shut off the air. 'Getting pretty wet,' I said. 'Have you got the long drill?'

'Do you want it immediately?' he asked.

'No,' I replied. 'But I'll probe ahead as soon as we've finished the charge holes.'

He nodded. 'I'll bring it down next time I come. I want to get this rock clear now. When will you be ready to blow?'

I looked at my watch. It was nearly ten. 'Midday,' I told him.

'What are the chances of being through to the sea bed tonight?'

'All depends how quickly you can clear the debris,' I said. 'Reckon I can blast faster than you can clear. Trouble is it may not be a very neat job. Rock's faulty here.'

He nodded and climbed down. I turned on the air again. The drill leapt in my hand and bored into the rock. Pieces flaked off. Nose, eyes and mouth were full of rock dust despite the spray of water that hissed into the drill hole. Every few seconds I paused to examine the rock. I was scared of a fall. Down below us Captain Manack, stripped to the waist, drove himself and the other two. They were clearing the pile of rock fast. He brought me two long drills when he returned from disposing of the first load of rock. By eleven-thirty I had finished the charge holes and Friar and I started to drill the probing hole. When the drill was only three feet in, water began to trickle along my hand and down my upturned arms. By the time the drill was full home there was a steady flow from the hole, running out of it as though from a tap only half turned on.

I called to Captain Manack. 'I think your figures are wrong,' I told him when he'd clambered up on to the ladders beside us. 'It may be due to the flaws in the rock. But I'd say we'd drilled pretty near to the sea bed.'

He nodded. 'Asdic wouldn't take into account a deep fissure in the rock,' he said. 'It gives you the general level of the sea bed. You think we'll be through at this blow?'

'No,' I answered. 'But we may come pretty near it, and that may make it unsafe to do any more drilling. I don't like this rock. If you want my advice,' I added, 'you'll start the whole thing again somewhere else where the rock isn't faulty.'

But he shook his head. 'No time for that. If I'm to run any more cargoes I must have this undersea route open. I'll take a chance on it opening with a clean break.'

'Okay,' I said. 'Got the charges?'

He went down and brought up the charges. I tamped them into the charge holes. The rock had all been cleared, except for one great jagged piece too heavy to lift. They were rigging a pulley. We loaded the compressor and the tools. I fixed the fuse and we tramped back along the gallery to the main shaft. Then Manack thrust over the lever that operated the carriage haulage gear. The hawser lifted out of the mud with a sucking sound, tightened and began to reel in on the drum beside the water wheel. We waited until the carriage appeared out of the gloom of the gallery. Then we went up to the surface in the gig. As we went up, I said, 'Supposing the police arrive and start searching the mine. Who's to warn us?'

'The girl,' he answered.

'What makes you think she wouldn't give you away?' I asked him. 'After what she heard last night she must hate the place.'

He looked at me and smiled beneath his moustache. 'She'll warn us all right,' he said.

'I don't see why she should,' I persisted.

'Don't you?' He laughed. The harshness of it sounded above the noise of the gig wheels on their wooden runners. 'She'll do it for your sake.'

'My sake?'

'Yes. Good God, man — don't say you haven't realised she's in love with you? Why else do you think she went searching for you up in the old workings last night?' He put his hand on my arm. 'You don't have to worry about that,' he said. 'By daylight tomorrow you'll be beating out past the Scillies on the *Arisaig*. She doesn't know that, of course. And see you don't tell her. Not that you'll be seeing her before you leave. But if she heard about it. Well, women are funny creatures. Look at the mess Dave got himself into.'

The callous way he spoke of it . . . I could have killed him. Perhaps he saw how I felt for he said, 'You stay down here till the job's done. The *Arisaig* will be off the adit at four o'clock. I fixed that this morning. And Mulligan has his orders. He'll not interfere with either you or Tanner. I'll bring you letters for the manager of my estate this evening. Believe me, the sooner you're out of the country the better for you.'

The gig stopped at the store gallery. We all got out with the exception of Captain Manack. He went on up to the surface. I followed the others into the dugout. I was thinking of Kitty. I had to get a message to her somehow. But it was no use asking Manack to take it. Friar was sorting through one of the cases of rations. 'Wot aba't bully an' apricots?' he suggested.

I caught hold of his arm. 'You going to the house, Friar?' I asked.

He looked up. 'No,' he said. 'My orders is ter stay da'n 'ere. We starts work again soon as them charges is blown.'

I sat down on the bed. What the hell would Kitty be thinking of me? Manack was right. If she heard I was leaving on the *Arisaig* in the early hours of the morning, anything might happen. I couldn't leave her here. And he'd said she loved me. My God! I needed somebody to love me. I needed her. I couldn't go on like this — alone. I thought of the hot moonlit nights in Italy. The women there were easy enough. But a man needed something more than that of a woman. If Kitty were with me . . . I got up and started pacing up and down the dugout. I suddenly knew that I had to have Kitty with me. I wouldn't go without Kitty. It wasn't only that I needed her — that I loved her. It was the thought of her staying on up there in the house. She'd go mad. She'd brood and brood on what had happened. And then . . . It didn't bear thinking on. I had to get her away from the place. I'd refuse to go on with the job unless Manack agreed to her leaving with me. Yes, that was the answer. I'd refuse to do the job for him.

'Ain't yer feelin' 'ungry?' Friar asked me.

'Eh?' My mind was so full of my thoughts that I scarcely understood what he said.

'Wot's got into yer — pacin' up an' down like that? Yer ain't worried aba't that shaft, are yer? Yer don't think it'll collapse on us?'

'No,' I said. 'No, I wasn't thinking about that.'

'Then s'ppose yer come an' 'ave somefink to eat?'

I took the plate of bully and bread that he offered me. And at that moment there was the distant, muffled sound of an explosion. Once again the dust rose with the blast of air that swept through the mine. Friar stood up. 'The Capting said we was to start again as soon as the charges 'ad exploded.'

I said, 'The dust would choke you. We wouldn't be able to see a thing. Give it time to settle.'

He hesitated. Then he shrugged his shoulders. 'Okay, mate. But you'd better do the explainin' ter the Capting.'

We finished our meal and then prepared to go down again. I was just refilling my lamp with carbide when Captain Manack entered. 'Has the charge gone off yet?' he asked.

'Yes,' I said. 'About twenty minutes ago.'

'Then why the hell aren't you down there, getting on with it?'

'Waiting for the dust to settle,' I told him.

'To hell with the dust,' he cried angrily. 'Go on, get on with it. We haven't time to waste worrying about dust.'

'You can't do much till the dust has laid a bit,' I answered.

He was about to make some angry retort, but he thought better of it.

'Is the ol' man still safely locked up?' Friar asked.

'Yes,' was the reply.

We went down then. I was still thinking about Kitty. I'd have to have it out with Manack. But I put it off. I'd wait till we came to the last blow. He'd be easier to handle then.

When we reached the end of the Mermaid we found it wetter than ever. The fall had not been as heavy as I'd expected. I climbed up into the shaft and found the reason. We were through the faulty rock. The roof was solid now with the exception of several deep fissures through which the salt water poured in a steady stream. Manack clambered up beside me. 'How many more blastings?' he asked.

'Two at least,' I said.

'The second going through to the sea bed?'

'Possibly,' I said. 'You can see the rock is more solid here.'

He nodded and went down to help the others clear the rubble. Friar took his place beside me and we began to drill the charge holes. It took longer this time and before we'd finished the fifth hole the rock had all been cleared, including the big piece. We were alone with the roar of the compressor and the chatter of the drill as it ate into the rock face.

Friar, I noticed, kept looking down. And every time I switched off the air he'd cock his head on one side, listening. 'What are you expecting?' I asked.

'Nothing,' he said quickly. 'Nothing.' His face was running with sweat. He wiped it off with a brightly coloured handkerchief. ''Ow many more ruddy 'oles are yer goin' ter drill?' he asked.

'Three more,' I said. 'Why?'

'Oh. I just wondered.' His manner was a little too off-hand. There was something on his mind.

'What's worrying you?' I asked.

'Nothing.' He turned back to the rock face. 'Come on, fer Gawd's sake. Let's get on with it.'

I put my hand on his shoulder and turned him towards me. 'What's on your mind, Friar?' I asked.

'Nothing,' he replied savagely. 'Nothing. Come on. Let's get crackin'. Sooner the sea's in this 'ere ruddy gallery the better I'll be pleased.'

We drilled the remaining three holes and I fixed the charges. Then we drilled to the limit of the long drill. Water poured down the drill and on to our arms. But it was not a steady stream, only a trickle. We weren't through to the sea bed.

As I tamped down the charges, Friar stood back and gazed down to where Manack and the others were replacing the timbers that covered the pit. 'Wish ter Gawd 'e'd 'ave somebody stay up at the 'ase,' he muttered.

'What are you worried about?' I said. 'The police?'

'Yep. The perlice an' that crazy ol' man. I don't like it. I tell yer straight, I don't like it. 'Ere we are cooped up da'n 'ere an' nobody up top to give us warnin' 'cept the girl. Anything might 'appen.'

I stopped then and looked at him. He turned away and pretended to adjust his lamp. 'What's on your mind, Friar?' I asked.

'There ain't nuffink on me mind.'

I took hold of his arm. He was getting on my nerves. 'There's something you know and I don't,' I said. 'What is it?'

'It ain't nuffink.' He pulled his arm free. 'It's me nerves, that's all. All very well fer you — you're a miner. I ain't used to this sort o' work. Gives me the willies, that's wot it does. It ain't natural like ter be standing 'ere breaving God's air when we're right underneath the sea.' He handed me another charge. I tamped it home. But my mind wasn't on the job. He was scared. Not just scared because he was working down here under the sea. He was scared because he knew something — something that threatened us. I thought of the conversation I'd overheard the previous night. '*See you don't mention it to Pryce. I don't want him scared.*' That's what Manack had said. I glanced at Friar. The sweat glistened on his neck as he bent to unscrew the drill clamp. His eyes met mine and turned away quickly. His hands fumbled. He was a bundle of nerves. And when we'd fixed the charges his haste to get out of the Mermaid gallery was so marked that it would have been funny had I not felt the threat of something I did not know about.

The gig stopped as before at the gallery leading to the hideout. We all got out with the exception of Manack. 'I'll be back in a few minutes with some tea,' he said. The others went on up the gallery. I hesitated. Then I turned to Manack. 'Will you be seeing Kitty?' I asked.

He nodded, his eyebrows lifting slightly.

'Then tell her to be ready to leave with me tonight,' I said. 'I'm taking her with me.'

'You'll do nothing of the sort,' he snapped, his eyes flashing angrily. 'The *Arisaig* isn't a refugee ship. Mulligan wouldn't stand for a woman on board.'

'I'll look after Mulligan,' I said.

We faced each other sullenly for a second, neither speaking. I was cursing myself for putting it the way I had. I should have flattered his sense of power by appealing to him to allow her to come with me. Instead I'd imposed it on him as a decision already made. I'd have to make it an ultimatum now. 'Either she comes with me,' I said. 'Or else —'

'Or else what?' he snarled.

'Or else the Mermaid stays like she is.'

'I see.' His eyes were furious.

'See here, Captain Manack,' I said, 'the girl can't stay on in that house — not after what she's heard. It wouldn't be safe for you in any case. I'm offering you the easy way out. What about it?'

His face relaxed. He hesitated. Then he nodded. 'All right, Pryce,' he said. 'Maybe it's all for the best. But it's up to you to make your peace with Mulligan. All right?'

'Thanks,' I said. 'You won't forget to tell her, will you? And tell her I'm sorry about last night. I was going to meet her down by the mine buildings. Explain why I couldn't, will you?'

'All right,' he said. And the gig rattled up to the surface.

The charges exploded just after five-thirty. A few minutes later Captain Manack returned with two big Thermos flasks of hot tea. 'Police been around at all?' Slim asked.

'No.'

'Wot aba't the ol' man?' Friar put in. 'Did yer see 'im? Was he locked up orl right?'

'Of course,' Manack answered sharply, and out of the tail of my eye I saw him jerk his head significantly in my direction. He was clearly angry with Friar for putting the question.

As Slim poured out the tea, Manack came over to me. He had a bulky envelope in his hand. 'There you are, Pryce,' he said, handing it to me. 'There's letters of instruction there to Mulligan and Carlo Forzala, the manager of my estate. There's also two hundred and fifty quid in pound notes.'

'Thanks,' I said. 'What about the girl? Did you see her?'

'Yes,' he said.

'What did she say?'

'She said she'd like to see you before you go.'

'Is that all?'

He nodded.

'Didn't she make any comment? You did tell her that I wanted her to come to Italy with me?'

'Yes, I told her.'

'How did you put it to her?' I didn't trust him. 'You tried to put her off,' I accused him.

'Don't be a fool,' he answered angrily. 'What did you expect? The kid's scarcely been out of Botallack. It'd suit me if she did go with you. She's good looking enough to cause trouble sooner or later. See her before you go. Maybe you'll be able to make her change her mind. It'd help if you were offering to marry her.'

'But —' Hell!! I hadn't thought about it. He'd turned away now and I sat down and glanced through the package. The letters seemed okay. I folded the envelope and tucked it into my body belt.

As soon as we had finished tea we went back to the Mermaid. The fall of rock was about the same as before. The water was seeping in faster and the pit below the boards was a small lake. Friar and I re-rigged the ladders whilst the others cleared the rock from the timbers covering the pit. As I worked away with the drill, I noticed Friar getting more and more nervy. And when the others had left with the first load and we were alone up there on the torn scaffolding, he became really scared.

At length I shut off the air and said, 'For God's sake, Friar, what's wrong with you?'

'Wot yer mean?' he asked, his eyes darting towards the gallery below us. 'There ain't nothing wrong wiv me.' But his eyes were wide and his breathing heavy. And all the time I felt he was listening for something. Though with the roar of the compressor it was impossible to hear anything.

'Go on,' he said. 'Get on wiv it, can't yer?'

'What's the hurry?' I asked.

'I told yer — I don't like workin' da'n 'ere. The sooner I'm hup top again, the 'appier I'll be, that's all. Is this the last blow?'

'I don't know,' I said. 'Maybe.' Then I caught hold of him by the shoulders. 'Listen, Friar,' I said. 'There's something worrying you that I don't know about. Suppose you tell me what it is.' And when he didn't reply, I said, 'I'm not doing any more drilling till I know. It isn't the water above us you're scared of. It's something back there in the mine. What did you discover last night?' I shook him angrily. 'You discovered something. What was it? And why are you worried about the old man being locked up safe? It's something to do with the old man, isn't it?'

Slowly he nodded his head.

'Well, come on — out with it,' I said. 'You can't expect me to work down here with you knowing what the danger is. Come on. What are you scared of?'

'I ain't scared,' he whimpered. 'Honest, I ain't.' His Adam's apple jerked up and down as he swallowed. 'It's just that —' He hesitated. Then his eyes looked straight at me. 'You won't tell the Captain, will yer?'

'Of course not,' I said.

'Okay. Well, this is wot 'appened las' night. We came da'n the mine ter find the ol' man — remember? The Capting seemed ter know where 'e'd be. 'E took us straight up into the old workings. We 'ad ter crawl on our bellies through a ruddy tunnel no bigger'n a tree trunk. 'E led us right back where the mine narrers between Botallack and Come Lucky. That's where we fa'nd the ol' man. 'E'd got a biddle an a pile o' drills an' 'e was 'ammering 'is way into the rock face at the end of a gallery. Fair swimmin' in water that gallery was. "Wot are you doin'?" the Capting asks 'im. "Making sure you'll not be lettin' the sea into the Mermaid," the ol' man answers wild like. We took him a't then. Mad as a coot, that's wot 'e is. Slim ast the Capting wot 'e reckoned the ol' man was up ter. The Capting said 'e didn't know. But 'e did, an' so did I. So did Slim, too. We was right under Come Lucky in that gallery. Wot the ol' man was doing was breaking a way fru' into the flooded mine. Water was fair rushin' da'n that gallery. If 'e'd made a breach it'd 'ave come roarin' right through the mine, A't 'ere we wouldn't 've stood a chance.'

So that was it. No wonder he was scared. I lit a cigarette. 'Yer won't say anyfink aba't it to the Capting, will yer?' he said. 'I didn't oughter've told yer.'

'No, I won't say anything,' I told him.

The carriage came rattling back along the gallery. We could hear it even above the roar of the compressor. We started drilling again. By the time the debris had all been cleared and the compressor loaded on the carriage we had finished the charge holes and were working with the long drill. But still we weren't through to the sea bed, though there was plenty of water about. Manack climbed up beside us. 'Well?' he shouted. 'Shall we make it this time?'

I pulled the drill clear and told Friar to go and shut the compressor off. 'No,' I told Manack, 'It'll be the next blasting.'

He glanced at his watch. 'You'll be running it a bit fine,' he said. 'It's past nine already.'

I shrugged my shoulders. 'Can't be helped,' I said. 'Even if I put heavy charges in I don't think it'd break through. It wouldn't be a neat job, anyway.' The compressor engine slowed and coughed into silence. The sudden quiet was uncanny. The trickling sound of water whispered through the gallery. We went back to the dugout then and waited for the blast of the charges. Manack didn't go up to the house this time, though Friar suggested twice that he ought to. We were all a bit jittery.

At last it came — a dull, distant thud. Then the blast of air. We only waited ten minutes. Then we went down in the gig and stumbled along the Mermaid gallery through choking clouds of dust. It clogged nose and mouth and hurt the eyes. I could feel the grit in my teeth and on my tongue. We were walking this time, leaving Slim behind to run the carriage out. I don't know what I expected. We must be very close to the sea bed now. I wouldn't have been surprised to find the gallery blocked by sea water.

But it wasn't. We went on down till the dripping walls told us we were under the sea. The gallery was still open. I don't know how the others felt. But my nerves were strung taut as I walked down that gallery. I didn't know what thickness of rock now stood between us and the sea, and that's a frightening thought to a miner.

At length we reached the new fall. I flashed my lamp up into the dark hole of the shaft. Water was seeping through from a number of places. It glistened silvery in the light. Our gum boots stood six inches deep in a muddy grey lake. Captain Manack rang Slim and told him to send the carriage down. The hawser sucked clear of the muddy stream as it pulled taut, water dripped from it.

Friar and I set the ladders up and climbed into the shaft. A loose bit of rock crashed down, narrowly missing my head. Water poured over me. The rock looked pretty thin. Friar, close behind me, said: 'Gawd! An' ter think there's fishes and things swimmin' ara'nd just above our heads.'

I didn't say anything. No need to tell him I didn't like it. The carriage arrived with the compressor. Manack came up as we were getting the drill clamp fixed. He looked at me. He was enough of an engineer to realise that the creviced roof of rock wasn't any too safe. There were great cracks in it and the water came through in a steady stream. I sent Friar down to start up the compressor. 'Better take it easy when you start drilling,' Manack said.

I nodded. 'I'll put double charges this time,' I said.

'Right. I'll have this rock cleared as fast as I can. This is no place to hang around.' He grinned and clapped me on the shoulder. 'Don't take any risks,' he said. The compressor started up, drowning all other sound. I watched him climb down the jagged rent of the shaft. Crazy, reckless and unscrupulous he might be, but he knew how to handle men.

Friar climbed up beside me and we started drilling. The time was then just eleven. For two hours we worked in that cramped space, thrusting that bucking drill into the watery rock face. Each time I thrust it home to the hilt my heart was in my mouth. Once a whole section of rock broke away, crushing the ladder on which Friar stood. He only saved himself by hanging on to the drill clamp. If I'd any sense I'd have refused to go on. But then Manack wasn't the sort of man to stand for that. He came up to have a look more than once. And each time I sensed the intense excitement in him. This was the sort of thing he enjoyed.

By one o'clock they'd finished clearing the debris from below the shaft. Once when I looked down I caught Dave's eyes glancing nervously up at the shaft. The water was rising. It was almost to the top of his gum boots. His face looked white in the orange glow of the lamps. They cleared the planks from above the pit. Friar glanced nervously down at the black expanse of water below us. 'Ain't we nearly finished yet?' he asked. His face was streaked with wet rock dust and his eyes looked fever bright with nervous exhaustion.

'Only one more,' I said.

Then somebody shouted down below. I could just hear it above the roar of the compressor. I looked down. Captain Manack was on the far side of the pit, the side where the telephone was. He seemed excited and he was giving orders to Slim, who glanced quickly up in our direction. Friar suddenly pulled at my sleeve. 'Somefink's up,' he yelled. His voice was high pitched, almost a scream.

Manack scrambled along one of the ledges. Slim turned and vanished into the gallery. Dave followed, casting one quick, frightened glance in our direction. Manack scrambled up the scaffolding and on to the ladders in the shaft. 'How many more?' He shouted the question into my ear. His voice was steady and controlled.

'One,' I told him.

'Okay,' he said. 'We'll get everything ready. As soon as you've placed the charges, ring Slim at the bottom of the shaft. He'll bring you in on the carriage with the compressor.'

I nodded.

He patted me on the shoulder and disappeared down the shaft. Then I started the airflow again and began to drill the last hole. I was halfway through when Friar began tugging at my arm. I stopped the drill. 'Somefink's wrong,' he said. Sheer terror showed in his eyes. He was trembling. He was sweating so much that the water ran off his face as though it had a film of oil on it. 'I don't like it,' he screamed. 'They've all gone.'

I looked down. The gallery was dark. There was nothing there but the roar of the compressor. 'Why've they left us?' he cried. 'It's a trap.' He swung round on me, shaking with fear. 'I tell yer it's a trap.' He started down the ladder then.

I caught him by the shoulder. 'Don't be a fool,' I said.

'Leave go of me,' he shouted. 'I tell yer he means ter kill us. He's goin' ter let the sea in wiv us da'n 'ere.'

I pulled him back. 'We're the only people who can let the sea in,' I shouted. 'Now pull yourself together.' I shook him till I was afraid I'd throw him off the ladder. At length he quietened down. His eyes became more normal. 'Nothing can happen to us so long as this rock stands between us and the sea. Understand?'

He nodded.

'All right then. Let's finish this hole.'

When the drill had gone in up to the hilt, I sent him down to stop the compressor. In the sudden silence he called up to me. 'The water's rising,' he said. 'It's over two feet deep.'

I said, 'Bring the charges up.' I wanted to get it over.

'No,' he said. 'No. I ain't stayin' any longer. You stay if yer like. But I've 'ad enough. I'm going back up the shaft.'

'Come back, Friar,' I shouted.

'No,' he shouted. 'No. I ain't never comin' back da'n 'ere.' His voice faded away down the gallery.

I climbed down. The charges were lying on the carriage alongside the compressor. I picked them up. Then I hesitated. The place was deathly quiet save for the sound of the water. There was no light but my own. Far away down the half-flooded gallery Friar's lamp flickered in the water. The stillness and the sense of being deserted was overwhelming. I put the charges down and climbed on to one of the ledges. When I dropped off the ledge on the other side of the pit the water came in over the top of my gum boots. I pulled back the rock and wound the handle of the field telephone. There was no answer. I tried again and again. No answer. And all about me the water trickled and dripped. I glanced up at the dark hole of the shaft. Should I go up there again and fix the charges? I thought I could feel the rock splintering under the strain. My nerves sensed the weight of the water on that thin shield of rock. I was sweating and I wanted to start running down the gallery.

I got a grip on myself. It had held for two hours. And all that time we'd been drilling. If it held then, it'd hold now. I was being a fool. It was just that fear was catching. If only Slim had answered the phone. But probably they hadn't had time to get back to the main shaft.

I literally forced myself to go back along the ledge, get the charges and climb into the shaft. Twice I paused. Every nerve in my body screamed at me to go back. But each time I made myself go on. At last I was up there with the thin sheet of rock pouring water over my face and hands. I started tamping the charges home. They were double charges this time. The work quietened my nerves. I concentrated all my mind on the task of fixing those charges.

Suddenly a new sound invaded the dripping stillness. I stopped my work and listened. There it was again. It was like a bell ringing. Had the air pressure suddenly increased, making my ears sing? Suppose the gallery leading up to Come Lucky had given way? The old man had been drilling into the face of it, Friar had said. He might have weakened it. If the water from Come Lucky was flooding into the Mermaid gallery the air pressure would rise, making my ear drums sing. My hands trembled at the thought. I could feel the sweat forcing its way out through the pores of my skin. I listened for the distant roar of water pouring down the gallery. But everything was quiet, only the drip of water and the insistent sound of that bell. Some trick of the rock perhaps. I flashed my lamp on the roof of the shaft. The fissures gaped wide. Water hissed on the flame of my lamp. I licked my lips. They were wet and salt from the water that fell on my face. And still that bell kept ringing in my ears. It was so indistinct that it was scarcely audible above the sound of the water. Imagination perhaps . . . And yet . . . I thought of all the cases I'd heard of miners being warned of disaster. Often it was a noise that warned them. Some sixth sense. Some change of the air pressure making their heads sing. The sound was still there, insistent, urgent, as though it had a message for me.

And then suddenly I remembered the telephone. I dropped the charge I was holding and scrambled down the ladder. I fell the last few feet, splashing into the water below me. I staggered to my feet. There at the end of the gallery a red light glowed just above the place where the telephone was concealed. I laughed out loud so that the sound of my own voice startled me. The relief made me feel light headed. I waded to one of the ledges, my gum boots heavy with water. I climbed along it to the telephone.

But it wasn't Slim's voice who answered me as I picked up the receiver. It was Kitty's. 'It's you, Jim?' she said. 'Oh, thank God. I didn't know what had happened. They all came out except you and Friar. I've been ringing and ringing.'

Her voice sounded nervous and she was panting. 'What's happened?' I asked.

'Nothing,' she said. 'It was only that I got worried when I saw them coming up out of the gallery. Captain Manack seemed almost — almost scared. I wanted to make certain that you were all right.'

'Yes, I'm all right,' I said. 'Why did Manack come up?'

'I rang him — about ten minutes ago.'

'Anything wrong?'

'Nothing serious. Only that old Mrs Brynd let his father out of that room. The old man came straight down the mine. I saw him going down —'

'You mean old Manack's escaped?' I shouted. 'And he's in the mine?'

'Yes,' she answered.

The strength drained suddenly out of my joints. I glanced into the dark tunnel that stretched away ahead of me. Any moment I expected to hear the roar of water. 'Listen, Kitty,' I said urgently. 'Go straight up to the surface. Understand? Get straight up to the surface.'

I didn't wait to hear her reply. I dropped the receiver and scrambled back along the ledge. Beyond the pit I dropped to the floor of the gallery and ran splashing and stumbling through the water down the long tunnel that led to safety.

CHAPTER TEN

Come Lucky

I thought that gallery would never end. My breath came in great gasps. I ran as I had never run before. The sweat poured from me. I got clear of the water as the gallery sloped upwards. But my gum boots were like lead. I had to stop and tip the water out of them. Those precious seconds wasted seemed like years. Any minute I expected to hear the distant thud of an explosion and the rumble of water tearing into the mine.

Suddenly a light showed ahead. I hadn't the strength to call out. It remained stationary as I pounded up the slope of the gallery. A voice called out, 'Is that you, Jim?' It was Kitty's voice. The little fool had stayed down.

'Get to the surface,' I gasped.

She didn't move.

'Get up to the surface,' I shouted again. The effort of speech hurt my throat. The blood was pounding in my ears and my chest heaved.

Still she didn't move. 'What's happened?' she asked as I came up with her. 'You look as though you've seen a ghost. What is it?'

'Come Lucky,' I answered, seizing her arm.

I saw her eyes widen as she realised what I meant. Then we were running side by side along the gallery. We reached the shaft that led up to the adit. I hesitated. But the desire to make height was overwhelming. I thrust her to the ladder. We climbed at a furious rate. Even so, she outstripped me. My limbs felt weighed down with a great weight. I'd been working steadily all day, and now this sudden demand on my strength. I felt so tired I thought I'd never make the top. The steady beat and thud of the pump coincided with the throbbing of the blood in my ears.

We made the top. At the same moment a voice shouted. A miner's lamp showed the great bob of the pump swinging rhythmically up and down. Then the lamp ducked under the bob and came running towards us. I have a fleeting recollection of old Manack's face, streaked with sweat and dirt and pallid with exertion. Then he brushed past us and another lamp appeared beyond the great bobbing beam of the pump. 'Stop him!' It was Captain Manack's voice.

His face was set and his eyes wild as he dashed past us after his father. I took Kitty by the arm and rushed her down the narrow cross-cut and out into the main adit. I could hear the sea slopping about in the adit cave, and behind me the pump beats thudded like the beating heart of the mine.

I turned up the adit towards the main shaft. Ahead of us the lamps of the two Manacks bobbed as they turned a bend. We followed. I couldn't hear the pump any longer. All I could hear was the heaving gasps that came from my mouth as I strained my last effort.

We rounded the bend. The lights had vanished. But a faint orange glow showed in the shaft that the old man used. We reached it and peered up. The lamps showed like glow-worms in the shaft. The old man was about forty feet above his son. Water glistened on the weedgrown rock. They were climbing at a furious rate. I thrust Kitty towards the ladders. She began to climb. I followed her.

I had barely set foot on the slimy rungs of the ladder when deep within the mine there was a muffled roar. It was far away, remote as the echo of a minor earthquake. I paused, listening for what I dreaded. A blast of air struck my face. It smelt stale and dank. It was like air that had been imprisoned long under ground. And then I heard it — a faint, rumbling roar. Another, lighter blast of air swept up the shaft behind us, bringing with it a choking cloud of dust. Deep in the mine the rumbling went on. It was like the rumblings of some giant's belly. It was crude and terrifying.

Something fell past me and hit the ground below with a splintering of wood. I glanced down. A length of ladder lay broken at the foot of the shaft, its rotten timbers shattered by the fall. High above us I saw the old man still climbing. But below his son had stopped. A great strip of laddering had been torn away.

And in that instant a sudden gush of dirty water spurted from the side of the shaft. I saw Captain Manack swept from his hold on the ladder, like a fly brushed off by a hose jet. Then the water hit me and I fell. A body crashed on top of me as my feet hit the ground. I fell, rolled over and fetched up with a terrific crack on my helmet against a rock wall.

Everything was black. The whole place was full of the sound of water pouring from a height. And behind that sound was the deeper, more distant rumbling of water tearing through the mine. Something heavy lay across my legs. It stirred. 'Jim?' It was Kitty's voice, strained to a shriek.

'Are you all right?' I shouted.

'Yes. Oh, thank God you're all right.'

I found her hand and we got to our feet. The noise of the water was terrific. 'Quick,' I cried. 'That main shaft. Have you got a match?'

'I've got a torch,' she shouted back. The beam leapt out in the darkness, showing a solid fall of water pouring down the shaft. There was no sign of Captain Manack's body. He must have been swept away in the brown flood that poured down the adit. 'Run,' I shouted, and we started off up that adit to the main shaft.

As we ran the sound of the water pouring down the shaft lessened. Instead, the muffled roar of the Come Lucky flood ripping into Wheal Garth became louder. As we came to the main shaft a soft glow showed in the darkness ahead. I heard the rattle of the gig's wheels. The glow brightened. 'The gig's coming,' Kitty shouted. I flung myself at the lever which would stop it at our level. I threw all my weight on it, but it wouldn't budge.

The gig reached our level. I had a glimpse of Friar, Slim and Dave huddled together in the light of their miners' lamps. Slim had hold of the lever which kept the gig moving. That was why

I hadn't been able to shift the lever at our own level. 'Stop,' I shouted. 'Friar! For God's sake stop.'

They saw us. I could see their eyes bright with fear. They saw us, but they didn't stop. Slim kept hold of the operating lever. Friar made a move towards the lever. Then he stopped, staring out at us with his mouth open and his eyes staring with horror. Dave stood there, biting his nails and making no move. The gig rattled past. The glow faded.

Rage dominated all other emotions. It swelled up inside me so that I felt I could tear down the timbers that formed the runway for the gig up the shaft. I stumbled to the framework and tore at the wood with my bare hands.

Then as the light of their lamps slowly dwindled up the shaft my rage subsided and cold fear took its place. I turned to Kitty. She was standing quite still as though stunned by what had happened. 'They've left us to die,' she said.

'Isn't there some other way up?' I cried. 'There must be some other way.'

She shook her head. 'There must be, but I don't know of any. There are plenty of shafts but none that we could climb without −' She suddenly broke off, listening.

The sound of the gig had ceased. Down the shaft came shouts. I peered upwards. The lights of their lamps were still visible. The gig was motionless. 'Pryce! Pryce!' one of them was calling.

'What is it?' I shouted back.

'The gig has stuck,' came back the answer faintly. 'Try to work it your end.'

I thrust over the lever. It went over quite easily now. But nothing happened. 'What's wrong?' Kitty asked. I tried the lever again. 'The water's got down to the bottom of the main shaft,' I told her. 'It's stopped the wheel from turning.' Then suddenly an idea burst upon me. Fool! Why hadn't I thought of that before? Except for odd shafts there was only that one way into the old workings by Come Lucky. I listened. The distant roar of water pouring through the mine seemed fainter. It was finding its way direct to the lower level. 'Quick,' I said, catching hold of Kitty's arm. 'The sea.' We started running down the adit. The shouts of the three men trapped in the main shaft faded. 'Can you swim?' I gasped out the question as we ran.

'Yes,' she answered.

We stumbled on, the beam of her torch cutting a swathe in the darkness of the tunnel. The sound of water grew louder. Then we saw it, coming down the shaft we'd tried to climb. The volume was not so great now. The main weight of the water was probably finding other outlets. We waded into the brown flood that swept down the adit.

I gripped Kitty's hand. She didn't say anything, but I felt the answering grip of her fingers. My God, when I think of it now. It needed nerve to go down and not up — to go down into the race of swirling, brackish, ochre-coloured water. But she didn't hesitate. I'll admit my heart was in my mouth. The noise of water closed in around us, blocking out the sound of the flood breaking through the mine.

We reached the cross-cut that led to the pump and the shaft down to the Mermaid gallery. Vaguely I heard the pump beats. They were slow and laboured. I stumbled and almost fell. Kitty shone the torch down into the ochre stream. A piece of ladder was jammed across the tunnel, and by the wall to my right a hand was thrust up from the water. I caught it and pulled. Captain Manack's head rose above the level of the water. It lolled loosely like some frightful doll. The teeth were bared and the eyes glazed. His neck was broken.

We went on then. There was no smell of the sea. I was scared the weight of water had already filled the adit. The floor of the tunnel dipped sharply down to the adit mouth. The brown flood through which we waded deepened and moved faster. The sound of it became like a roar of a waterfall in that confined space. I kept tight hold of Kitty's hand. It was difficult to prevent our feet being swept from under us. At any moment the weight of water pouring into the lower levels of the mine might flood it to sea level. Then the full volume of it would come pouring down this adit.

The tunnel widened and the torch suddenly showed the dark cavern where the sea came in. But there was no sign of the flat rock slab of the landing place. It was covered by a bubbling froth of filthy liquid. And where a narrow opening should have led through to the sea there was only the sloping roof of the cave. I looked at Kitty. She met my gaze. I made a motion with my hand indicating we'd have to dive and swim under water through the adit mouth. It was impossible to speak in that din of roaring water. She nodded. Her grip tightened for a second on my hand and then released it and slipped off her overalls and gum boots. I did the same. Then we stood there, hesitating. She was looking at me, her eyes wide. 'Hurry,' I shouted.

She couldn't hear, but I think she must have understood from the movement of my lips, for she nodded again and handed me the torch. As our hands touched, she suddenly came close to me and kissed me. Then she stood back, looking at the brown froth of water that filled the cave. She stood hesitating for a second and then quickly spreading her hands, dived in.

I saw her head for a second in the scum as the water bore her towards the exit. Her hair hung like strands of seaweed in the bubbling froth, and her face was white against the dark, heaving bulk of the water. Then she dived.

I waited, but she did not reappear.

My ears suddenly began to sing. There was a great roaring behind me. I half-turned. I knew what it was. I knew that the water had risen above sea level, that it was in the adit and roaring down towards the sea. I crammed my helmet tight on my head and with the torch still in my hands, dived straight out for the entrance.

As I hit the water there was a great roaring sound in my ears. I could see nothing, though the torch was still in my hands. I kept my head down, thrusting deeper with my legs and let the water do the rest. I felt myself flung forward. My head fetched up with a terrific jolt against rock. Only my helmet saved me from having my skull stove in. My back was keel-hauled along a slanting face of rock. I felt myself being sucked down and down. My hand struck a rock. The pain of it jarred along my arms. Then I seemed quite stationary, yet I knew I was being thrust along by the weight of water behind me. My ears stabbed with pain. A great band tightened about my chest. The desire for air became my whole world.

Then I was being pushed upwards. I thrust up with my hands and feet. An instant later I was gasping on the surface. A wave lifted me and broke with a crash. The backwash of it carried me clear of the dark shadow of the cliffs, gasping in a smother of foam. I swallowed water and choked with the salt of it. The next wave bore down on me, broke and carried me struggling towards the cliff. My feet touched rock for an instant. Then the backwash carried me clear again.

I tore off the helmet which was still jammed tight on my head. Then I took a deep breath and, burying my head in the surf, summoned my last ounce of energy to crawl clear of the break of the waves. One, five, ten minutes — I don't know how long it took me to get clear. My clothes clung to me, hampering my movements and the seething welter of water seemed intent on flinging me against the cliffs.

But at last I was clear and trod water, gently rising and falling with the waves. Behind me the dark wall of the cliffs towered into the night, frilled at the base with a raging inferno of surf. I began to shout, but my voice was lost in the roar of the surf spilling across the rocks.

Then I found I still had the torch. It was in my trouser pocket. When I'd put it there I don't remember, probably just before I started to swim clear of the break. I switched it on. It still worked. The friendly beam swept across the heaving seas. An instant later I heard a faint cry. An arm showed upthrust from the top of the wave a little further out. I swam on. Kitty met me. She had a cut on the side of her head and one shoulder was bleeding. But she was treading water easily and smiled as I swam up.

'All right?' I asked her.

She nodded. 'You're bleeding,' she said.

'So are you,' I answered and got a mouthful of water from a broken wave cap.

We laughed. We were alive. It was good to laugh. We laughed till a wave rolled right over us. Then we didn't laugh any more. The tide was setting towards Kenidjack Castle and we were being swept in towards the headland. I stripped off all but my pants. Kitty got out of her skirt, and then we settled down to swim for it.

The tide was setting fast and we were tired. There was no chance of going with the current. That way we should have landed on the jagged rocks at the foot of the headland. We swam straight out to sea.

Kitty was a strong swimmer and she was fresher than I was. We kept a steady pace side by side. And all the time I watched the surf boiling at the foot of the headland. It was astonishing how rapidly it seemed to come towards us. The ugly black teeth of rock grinned at us. The surf slavered through them as though waiting to tear our bodies to pieces.

It came nearer and nearer. Then we were in the break of the waves, diving through them and swimming for our lives. For a moment I thought we wouldn't make it. I could feel the undertow clutching at my body as wave after wave thundered down on us. Then we were out of the surf and treading water with the headland receding slowly from us. Kitty swam up beside me. I think she must have realised how tired I was for she said, 'Can you make the shore now? There's a little beach right in under the headland.'

'Okay,' I said, and we began to swim again.

That was the longest swim I ever did. The current was not so strong now, but it was still setting south along the coast and we were trying to swim straight in on the lee side of Kenidjack Castle.

At last we were in the break of waves again. But there was no strength in them now and they carried us the way we wanted to go. I trod water between the waves and then went in with a crawl as each one broke over me. At last my hand, down-thrust to drive me forward, touched rock. I caught hold and clung to it as the surf receded. The next wave carried me in and I felt pebbles under my feet. A moment later I joined Kitty up the narrow beach, clear of the sea. I lay down on the cold pebbles, my chest heaving as though it would burst.

A cold wind blew in from the sea. It was damp and chill under the cliffs. I sat up. The waves thundered in long lines of broken surf. The water sucked and gurgled in the rocks. The moon had set, but there was still light enough in the clear sky to see the outline of Kenidjack Castle hunched against the stars. I looked at Kitty. She was breathing heavily and her teeth chattered. Her slip clung close to her body, emphasising her strong build. Her breasts rose and fell. I reached out and took her hand. She smiled, but didn't say anything. There was nothing to say. We'd been lucky — damned lucky.

I suddenly remembered those three men going up the shaft in the gig. I struggled to my feet. God I was weary! 'Come on,' I said. 'You'll get cold here. And we must see if we can do anything about the gig.'

She nodded and rose to her feet. 'You don't think the water will reach them there, do you?'

'I don't know,' I said. 'Depends how high the water level was in Come Lucky. Has it been wet here during the past week?'

'Yes,' she said, 'very wet. And Come Lucky's a big mine, much bigger than Wheal Garth.'

'Only that one adit to drain Wheal Garth?' I asked.

'Yes, that's the only one.'

'Come on then,' I said. 'We must hurry. That water will rise fast.'

We went along the beach, climbed a shoulder of rock and then struggled up a long, grassy slope to a path that led to the rock crest of the headland. At the top we passed an old rifle range and then reached the first of the ruined engine houses. Kitty struck away to the right up the slope of the worked hillside to another track. A few minutes later the huddled shape of the sheds at the top of Wheal Garth rose up out of the darkness.

We went straight into the hoisting shed. I forced open the doors and peered down the sloping shaft. Far below a glow of light outlined the top of the gig. And out of the shaft came the sound of men singing. They were singing 'Good King Wenceslas.' It was a strange choice. Dave was leading them. His voice came floating up the shaft, clear as a bell. He had a nice voice. I shouted down to them, but they went on singing. I waited until they came to the end of a verse and then called down to them again. The singing started up again and then subsided. I called again.

A voice answered. It was very faint. I called down, 'What do you need?' The answer came floating back up the shaft. The words were indeterminate. I think they said that the water was rising, but I couldn't be sure. I turned to Kitty. 'Is there some rope here?' I shouted.

'Yes,' she said. 'In the stone shed. I'll get it.'

I followed her. There were tools, too. I took two saws and an axe and with a coil of rope over my shoulders, ran back to the shaft. I lowered the tools on the end of the rope, but the shaft was at an angle and they kept on getting caught on ledges of rock and on the timber framework of the hoist. The men below started shouting and banging on the wooden cage of the gig. Then one of them began to scream. It was a horrible sound. It ceased suddenly and Dave's voice began to sing 'Jerusalem'. The sound of the lovely hymn floated up the shaft with a thousand distorting echoes so that it sounded like a choir singing in a cathedral.

Then suddenly the sound tailed off and vanished. A man's voice began to shout. It rose to a scream and then vanished in a gurgle as though he had been throttled. Leaning out, peering down the shaft, I saw the light had faded to a faint glow. Then it was suddenly snuffed out like a candle. I called, but there was no answering cry from the black depths of the shaft. I stood up then and closed the wire mesh gates. 'We'd better go up to the house now,' I said.

Kitty nodded. She seemed dazed with the horror of listening to those men being drowned by the rising water. I took her arm and we went out into the cool, salt wind.

The house was in darkness as we topped the rise. It was just a black shadow sprawling there in the blackness of the night. I felt the girl's body tense as she saw it. God, how she must loathe the place! Cripples' Ease! It was a name that suited it. It must have been a bitter and cynical landlord who called it that in the days when the miners from Botallack used it as a pub.

We came to the track and started across it to the front door of the house. And then I stopped. The door was wide open and a figure moved in the darkness of the passage. It vanished. We crossed the track, close to the desolate little garden that had once flowered under my mother's hands. A light showed in the passage. We both stopped then, rooted to the spot. It was old Manack. He held a lamp in his hands and was gazing out of the doorway towards us, his mouth open and a wild look of horror in his eyes.

I started to move forward. 'No,' he screamed. 'No.' He leapt back and the door swung to, blotting out the light. There was the rattle of a chain and then the bolts were shot home.

I turned to Kitty. 'Maybe he thought we were ghosts,' I said.

She was trembling. She looked like a ghost, her hair hanging in sodden strands over her pale face and the slip clinging like a white shroud to her body. 'Come on,' I said. 'We need dry clothes. Then we'll go.'

'Go?' she said. 'Where to?'

'Italy,' I said. 'Didn't you get my message? I asked Captain Manack to tell you I was leaving on the *Arisaig* tonight and to ask you whether you would come with me. Remember?'

'Yes, I —' She stood very still as though petrified. 'I — Oh, Jim, I don't know what to say. I can't stay here, I know that. But — Italy! It seems so far. Couldn't we stay somewhere in Cornwall?'

'Don't forget I'm still a deserter,' I said. 'And the police are

225

looking for me. The *Arisaig* will be off Wheal Garth —' I looked at my watch. It was still going. The time was just after three. 'In less than an hour. It's my only hope.' I took her by the shoulders. 'I've got to be on that ship,' I said. 'It's my one way out of the country. I don't want to go back to Italy. But I'd rather do that than serve a sentence for desertion, and possibly get involved with what's happened here. They might hang me.'

'No. They wouldn't do that. You haven't done anything.'

'True. But there's only my word for that. Don't forget, four revenue officers lost their lives. I've got to go, Kitty. Say you'll come. It wouldn't be so bad with you.'

She hesitated. Then she raised her head. Her eyes looked into mine in the gloom. 'You'll not desert me, Jim.'

'Of course not,' I said.

'Promise.'

'I promise.'

'All right. Then I'll come.'

I kissed her gently on the forehead. 'Soon as we can find a ship we'll go to Canada. I can always get work in the mines.'

We went round to the back of the house and entered by the kitchen. Old Mrs Brynd was seated in her usual chair by the fire. She started up as we entered. 'What's happened?' she asked in a quavering voice. 'I know something terrible has happened. What is it? T'edn't no use lyin' to me. I can tell from the looks of 'ee that something's happened.'

'It's all right, Mrs Brynd,' Kitty said.

The old woman sat down in her chair again. 'The Master's come back,' she muttered. 'In a dreadful state, he was.'

'Now, don't you fret,' Kitty said.

'Better get some dry clothes on,' I told Kitty. 'Anything you want to take bundle into an oilskin. We'll have to swim for it, unless there's some place where a boat can come in.'

'Not with the wind in the sou'-west,' she answered. 'I'll do as you say. What about you? I'll get you some of old Mr Manack's clothes.'

'No, I'll get them,' I said.

'All right,' she said. 'It's the first on the left at the top of the stairs.'

I lit a spare lamp and went out into the corridor. A light glowed on the landing above. I started up the stairs, but as I reached the bend I stopped. The old man was standing there, a lamp in his left hand and the little mining pick held in his right.

We stood there looking at each other for a moment. Then I started up the stairs again. He half-raised the pick. The steel of it gleamed in the lamplight. It was a vicious little weapon. His eyes watched me as I came up the stairs. He was trembling and he kept passing his tongue across his lips.

As I came round the bend of the stairs, a shiver seemed to run through him. He gave a little moan like an animal that's been hurt. Then he turned and stumbled down the corridor. I heard his feet on the bare stairboards leading to the attic room as I reached the top of the stairs. I went after him, up the staircase to the room where he had put my mother. He was standing there in the middle of the bare room. Behind him was the iron-barred window. He was still trembling.

I pulled the door to. The key with which Mrs Brynd had opened it for him was still in the lock. I turned it. The hatch was open. He hadn't moved. He just stood there, the lamp in his hand. I went back down the little staircase then.

In his room I found all I wanted. I towelled myself down and changed into dry clothes. I found some oilskins and a sou'wester. I made a bundle of them and went downstairs to his son's office. His desk was almost clear of papers and the safe door was closed. I had expected that. He would have got rid of all dangerous papers and hidden his surplus cash. I was looking for something quite different. I found it in the bottom drawer of the desk under a pile of bills. It was a .38 Service pattern revolver. There were rounds for it in a cardboard box. I loaded the weapon and slipped it inside the oilskins; I wasn't taking any chances with Mulligan.

There was a tap at the door and Kitty entered. She had on

a brown tweed suit and her hair was brushed back and tied with a ribbon. She had a bottle in her hand and a glass. 'I thought you'd need a drink,' she said hesitantly.

'What is it — Scotch?'

She nodded and poured me out half a tumblerful. 'There, drink that up,' she said. 'You need it after all you've done today.'

'I'll say I do.' She gave me the glass and I took a big gulp. I could feel the fiery liquid running down into my stomach. I gasped and drank again. 'What about you?' I asked. 'You need some, too.'

'Yes,' she said. 'Perhaps I do.'

I passed her the tumbler. She took a sip at it and made a wry face. 'Go on,' I said. 'It'll keep you warm.' She nodded and drank again. Her face flushed and she gasped.

I took the glass from her and finished it off. 'We'd better get moving,' I said, looking at my watch. It was a quarter to four.

'What about Mr Manack?'

'I've locked him in upstairs. Come on.'

I picked up a torch that was lying on a table, tested it and then followed her out into the passage. She got a small bundle of things wrapped in oilskins from the kitchen and joined me.

We left the house by the front door and went straight down through the shadowy outlines of the ruined mine workings. As we started down the slope I turned and looked back. Cripples' Ease lay like a dark shadow against the night sky. Only one light burned there. That was in the little room at the top. The bars were clearly visible, and behind them, inside the room, the old man's shadow moved back and forth across the ceiling as he paced the floor.

I went on then down the slope, my face turned to the clean wind that came up from the sea. The ruined buildings seemed remote and primitive. They stood there like decaying tombstones, marking the passage of generations of miners. They were the only indications of the honeycomb of workings running deep down below the cliffs and out under the sea. I shivered and tried to forget about the events of the last few hours. It was like a nightmare, something that only existed in the imagination. But the old engine house, built of great granite slabs, which came to meet us out of the darkness reminded me that it was all real enough, that Manack and Friar and Slim and Dave were not the first men to die like rats beneath the ground we walked on. I was glad to be going. I'm a Cornishman and a miner, but, by God, I tell you I was glad to be leaving the tin coast.

Kitty found a place where we could climb down not far from the adit mouth of Wheal Garth. We found a patch of grass halfway down and sat there, gazing out into the dark vista of the sea. Below us the waves rolled ceaselessly against the cliffs, fringing the base with a line of surf. Beyond was a dark void in which the advancing lines of the Atlantic swell were sensed rather than seen.

We had not long to wait. Just after four a dark shape drew in towards the cliffs. Kitty seized my arm and pointed. It was the *Arisaig* all right. I could dimly see the outline of her schooner rig. I pulled my torch out and flashed in morse: *Send boat — Manack*.

There was no answering signal. I repeated the message. Still no anwering signal, but a moment later a small shape detached itself from the dark bulk of the schooner and came bobbing across the waves towards the cliffs. We scrambled down to a ledge of rock that ran out into the sea. I flashed my torch to direct them. Then we stripped to our underclothes, tied our things up in the oilskins and swam out to meet the boat.

Mulligan was in the stern sheets. 'What the devil's this girl doing here?' he asked as they pulled us aboard. 'Where's Tanner?'

'Dead,' I said. 'So's Manack.'

'You're lying,' he snarled.

Briefly I told him what had happened as we lay there rocking on the long Atlantic swell. 'I don't believe ye,' he said when I'd finished.

'Then row in and take a look at the adit,' I said.

He hesitated. I could see he didn't like the idea of hanging about. Dawn would soon be breaking, and then the *Arisaig* would be in full view from the coastguards' look-out at Cape Cornwall. But he gave the order and the boat's bows turned in towards the cliffs. We had no difficulty in finding the mouth of the adit. Even in the dim light the sea looked a muddy brown, and where the waves beat in against the cliffs an ochre-coloured torrent foamed up from just below the surface.

He ordered the boat to put about then and the seamen pulled out from underneath the cliffs, back towards the *Arisaig*.

'The girl comes with me,' I said. 'Before all this happened Manack had appointed me his representative in Italy. I'll show you his letters later. If you want any more cargoes, you'd better see that we get there safely.'

He grunted, but said nothing.

Kitty was getting into her clothes. She had towelled herself down with an oilskin jacket wrapped round her. I did the same, and when I was dressed I slipped the pistol into my jacket pocket. The dark outline of the schooner showed in the gloom. In a few minutes we were on board and the boat was in its davits.

Orders were given in a subdued voice. The sails ceased to flap and bulked out as they tightened and filled. Kitty had gone for'ard to the bows. I joined her there. Behind us the light of Pendeen Watch outlined the rugged cliffs at regular intervals. But she never looked back. She stared straight ahead, her hair blowing in the wind.

The bows began to talk as they dipped and rose across the waves. I took her hand. It trembled slightly. 'We'll be married in Rome, shall we?' I said.

'Married?' She looked at me in surprise.

'Of course.'

'I — I didn't know.' Her fingers tightened on my hand and her eyes were shining in the darkness. 'Oh, Jim,' she said. 'I'm so glad.'

She turned away then and stared out ahead as the schooner ploughed her way through the water. Far out across the dark sea the Wolf lighthouse winked at us. And beyond, on the edge of the horizon, the Bishop light showed for a moment, pointing the way to a new life.

THE END

Hammond Innes

'The master storyteller' *Daily Express*

Air Bridge
'Hammond Innes achieves a mastery sense of urgency as the story rises to the climax.' *Daily Telegraph*

Campbell's Kingdom
'A fast and expertly-managed story . . . The Rockies, the squalid "ghost towns", the oil-boring – these are memorably presented.' *Sunday Times*

Golden Soak
Embittered and disillusioned with his life, Alec Falls fakes his own death and starts for Australia – and the Golden Soak mine. But he is not the only person interested in the derelict mine. The shadows of the past and the blistering hell of the Australian bush combine in a deadly maze which Falls must unravel if he is to survive at all . . .
'Pace, atmosphere, tension. Evokes Australia as few other books have done.' *Listener*

The Black Tide
The details of maritime fraud, international piracy and the working of Lloyd's insurance are presented with an authority that give *The Black Tide* an uncanny credibility.
'Exciting . . . credible . . . a polished novel.' *Sunday Express*

FONTANA PAPERBACKS

Hammond Innes

The Strode Venturer

Five frightened directors and a ship on a clandestine voyage: this is the story of a disillusioned naval officer caught up in a young man's dream of carving a future for an island people out of a heap of volcanic ash.'

'Hammond Innes at the very top of his form.' *Daily Mirror*
'Excellent . . . his expertise is beyond question.' *Guardian*

The Big Footprints

In the aftermath of a black African war, two men – old friends, old enemies – shadow one another in a running conflict through one of the most inhospitable areas of the Rift Valley. One seeks to save, the other destroy, the last remaining herd of elephant as they trek north.

'The novel is bold, original, colourful and sinewy . . . Mr Innes is a master.' *The Times*

The White South

The great whaling factory ship *Southern Cross* is caught and crushed in the deadly embrace of the Polar ice – 500 men face an agonising death in the frozen wastes of the Antarctic.

'Hammond Innes proves his mastery of suspense.' *TLS*

FONTANA PAPERBACKS

Duncan Kyle

'One of the modern masters of the high adventure
story.' *Daily Telegraph*

Helen MacInnes

'The queen of spy writers.' *Sunday Express*

ABOVE SUSPICION
ASSIGNMENT IN BRITTANY
THE UNCONQUERABLE
HORIZON
FRIENDS AND LOVERS
REST AND BE THANKFUL
NEITHER FIVE NOR THREE
I AND MY TRUE LOVE
PRAY FOR A BRAVE HEART
NORTH FROM ROME
DECISION AT DELPHI
THE VENETIAN AFFAIR
THE DOUBLE IMAGE
THE SALZBURG CONNECTION
MESSAGE FROM MALAGA
THE SNARE OF THE HUNTER
AGENT IN PLACE
PRELUDE TO TERROR
THE HIDDEN TARGET
CLOAK OF DARKNESS
RIDE A PALE HORSE

'Helen MacInnes is totally original. No one creates more realistic, more credible characters than she does.'
Alistair Maclean

'The hallmarks of a MacInnes novel of suspense are as individual and clearly stamped as a Hitchcock thriller.'
New York Times

'Helen MacInnes can hang her cloak and dagger right up there with Eric Ambler and Graham Greene.' *Newsweek*

FONTANA PAPERBACKS

GERALD SEYMOUR

'The finest thriller writer in the world today.'
Jonathan Cox, DAILY TELEGRAPH

HARRY'S GAME
THE GLORY BOYS
KINGFISHER
RED FOX
THE CONTRACT
ARCHANGEL
IN HONOUR BOUND
FIELD OF BLOOD
A SONG IN THE MORNING
AT CLOSE QUARTERS
HOME RUN

'Not since Le Carré has the emergence of an international suspense writer been as stunning as that of Gerald Seymour.'
LOS ANGELES TIMES

FONTANA PAPERBACKS/Collins Harvill

Desmond Bagley

– a master of suspense –

'I've read all Bagley's books and he's marvellous, the best.' *Alistair MacLean*

THE ENEMY
FLYAWAY
THE FREEDOM TRAP
THE GOLDEN KEEL
LANDSLIDE
RUNNING BLIND
THE TIGHTROPE MEN
THE VIVERO LETTER
WYATT'S HURRICANE
BAHAMA CRISIS
WINDFALL
NIGHT OF ERROR
JUGGERNAUT
THE SNOW TIGER
THE SPOILERS

FONTANA PAPERBACKS

Fontana Paperbacks: Fiction

Fontana is a leading paperback publisher of fiction. Below are some recent titles.

- ☐ ULTIMATE PRIZES Susan Howarth £3.99
- ☐ THE CLONING OF JOANNA MAY Fay Weldon £3.50
- ☐ HOME RUN Gerald Seymour £3.99
- ☐ HOT TYPE Kristy Daniels £3.99
- ☐ BLACK RAIN Masuji Ibuse £3.99
- ☐ HOSTAGE TOWER John Denis £2.99
- ☐ PHOTO FINISH Ngaio Marsh £2.99

You can buy Fontana paperbacks at your local bookshop or newsagent. Or you can order them from Fontana Paperbacks, Cash Sales Department, Box 29, Douglas, Isle of Man. Please send a cheque, postal or money order (not currency) worth the purchase price plus 22p per book for postage (maximum postage required is £3.00 for orders within the UK).

NAME (Block letters)_____

ADDRESS_____

_____